BEYOND MEASURE

A DARK BRATVA ROMANCE (RUTHLESS DOMS)

JANE HENRY

Copyright © 2019 by Jane Henry

All rights reserved.

No part of this book may be reproduced in any form or by any electronic or mechanical means, including information storage and retrieval systems, without written permission from the author, except for the use of brief quotations in a book review.

Photography by Wander Aguiar

Cover art by PopKitty Designs

SYNOPSIS

USA Today bestselling author Jane Henry delivers a gritty, impassioned romance of arranged marriage, fearless love, and ultimate triumph over evil.

I'm the girl no one wants.

Scarred beyond repair and locked away, I'm tainted and tarnished.

Unworthy of friendship, love, or hope.

But I was born into Bratva life, and my life is not my own.

I'm ripped from my home and forced to marry a man I've never met, sight unseen.

He's ruthless, possessive, fierce... *My husband.*

Chapter 1

Tomas

I scowl at the computer screen in front of me. As *pakhan*, the weight of everything falls onto my shoulders, and today is one day when I wish I could shrug it off.

A knock comes at my office door.

"Who is it?" I snap. I don't want to see or hear anything right now. I'm pissed off, and I haven't had time to compose myself. As the leader of the Boston Bratva, it's imperative that I maintain composure.

"Nicolai."

"Come in."

Nicolai can withstand my anger and rage. Over the past few months, he's become my most trusted advisor. My friend.

The door swings open and Nicolai enters, bowing his head politely to greet me.

"Brother."

I nod. "Welcome. Have a seat."

When I first met Nicolai, he wore the face of a much older man. Troubled and anguished, he was in the throes of fighting for his woman. The woman who now bears his name and his baby. But I've watched the worry lines around his eyes diminish, his smile become more ready. While every bit as fierce and determined to dutifully fill his role as ever, he's grown softer because of Marissa, more devoted to her.

"You look thrilled," he says, quirking a brow at me. Unlike my other men, who often quake in my presence, having been taught by my father before me that men in authority are to be feared and obeyed, Nicolai is more relaxed. He's earned the title of *brother* more readily than even my most trusted allies.

"Fucking pissed," I tell him, pushing up from my desk and heading to the sideboard. I pour myself a shot of vodka. It's eleven o'clock in the fucking morning, but it doesn't matter. I've been up all night. "Drink?"

He nods silently and takes the proffered shot glass. We raise our drinks and toss them back together. I take in a deep breath and place the glass back on the sideboard before I go back to my desk.

"Want to tell Uncle Nicolai your troubles?" he asks, his eyes twinkling.

I roll my eyes at him.

I made an unconventional decision when I inducted Nicolai into our brotherhood. The son of another *pakhan*, Nicolai came here under an alias, but I knew he had the integrity of a brother I wanted in my order. I offered him dual enrollment in both groups, under both the authority of his father and me, and he readily agreed. We've come to be good friends, and I would trust the man with my life.

"Uncle Nicolai," I snort, shaking my head. None of my other brothers take liberties like Nicolai does, but none are as trustworthy and loyal as him, so he gets away with giving me shit unlike anyone else. "It's fucking Aren Koslov."

Nicolai grimaces. "Fucking Aren Koslov," he mutters in commiseration. "What'd the bastard do now?" He shakes his head. "Give me one good reason to beat his ass and I'll take the next red-eye to San Diego."

He would, too. Nicolai inspires fear in our enemies and respect in our contemporaries. Aren falls into both categories.

"Owed me a fucking mint a month ago, and hasn't paid up," I tell him. I spin my monitor around to show him the number in red. "And you don't need me to tell you we need that money." As my most trusted advisor, Nicolai knows we're right on the cusp of securing the next alliance with the Spanish drug cartel. Our location in Boston, near the wharf and airport, puts us in the perfect position to manage imports, but the buy-in is fucking huge. We have the upfront money, but the payout from San Diego would put us in a moderately better financial position.

Nicolai leans back in his chair, rubbing his hand across his jawline.

"And you have meeting after meeting coming up with politicians, leaders, and the like."

I eye him warily. Where's he going with this?

"It's easy to say you need money. But that isn't what you need, brother."

I roll my eyes. "I suppose you're going to tell me what I need."

"Of course."

"Go on."

"You know what you need more than the money?" he asks. I'm growing impatient. He needs to come out with it already.

I give him a look that says *spill*.

"You need a wife," he says.

A wife?

I roll my eyes and shake my head. "Sometimes I think your father dropped you on your head as a child," I tell him. What bullshit. I look back at the computer screen, but Nicolai presses on.

"Tomas, listen to me," he says, insistent. "Money comes and goes, and you know that. Tomorrow you could seal a deal with the arms trade you've been working, and you know our investments have been paying off in spades. But a good wife is beyond measure, and Aren has a sister."

"You've been married, for what, two fucking days and you're giving me this shit?" I reply, but my mind is already spinning with what he's saying. I never dismiss Nicolai's suggestions without really weighing my options. Aren is one of the youngest brigadiers in America and has a reputation that precedes him everywhere he goes. He commands men under him, and I'm grateful he hasn't risen higher in power.

He grunts at me and narrows his eyes. "I've loved Marissa for a lot longer than we've had rings on our fingers."

"I know it, brother," I tell him. "Just giving you shit. Go on."

"Aren's sister is single, lives with him on their compound. Young. I don't know much about her, and haven't seen a recent picture, but I met her years ago when I first came to America. And she was a beauty then. I imagine she's only grown more beautiful."

Seconds ago, this idea seemed preposterous, but now that I'm beginning to think about it, I'm warming to the idea.

"You think he'd let her go to pay off his debt?"

"With enough persuasion? Hell yeah. And a good leader needs a wife. You've seen it yourself. There's something to be said for having a woman to come home to. The most powerful men in the brotherhood are all married."

He's right. Just last week, I met with Demyan from Moscow and his wife Larissa. He brings her everywhere with him. The two are inseparable. And he's risen to be one of the most powerful men the Bratva has ever known.

"And face it, Tomas. You're not exactly in the position to meet a pretty girl at church."

I huff out a laugh. The men of the Bratva rarely obtain women by traditional means.

I lift my phone and dial Lev.

"Boss?"

"Get me a picture of Aren Kosolov's sister," I tell him. Our resident hacker and computer genius, Lev works quickly and efficiently.

"Give me five minutes," he says.

"Done."

I hang up the phone and turn to Nicolai. "I want to see her first," I tell him.

"Of course."

"How's Marissa?"

He fills me in about home, his voice growing softer as he talks about Marissa, but I'm only half-listening to him. I'm thinking about the way a woman changes a man, and how he's changed because of her.

Do I need a wife?

The better question is, do I want Aren Kosolov's sister to be the one?

My phone buzzes, and Nicolai gestures for me to answer it. A text from Lev with a grainy picture pops up on the screen, followed by a text.

There are no recent pictures. This was from a few years ago, but it should give you a good idea.

Still, it's a full profile picture. I murmur appreciatively. Wavy, unruly chestnut hair pulled back at the nape of her neck, with fetching tendrils curling around her forehead. Haunting hazel colored eyes below dark brows. High cheekbones, her skin flushed pink, and full, pink lips. She's thin and graceful, though if I'm honest, a little too thin for me. The women I bed tend to be sturdier and curvy, able to withstand the way I like to fuck.

I don't want to have this conversation via text. I call him and he answers right away.

"Background?" I ask.

"Never went to college. Under her brother's watchful eye since her father died."

"Lovely," I mutter. He might not give her up easily.

"Temperament?" I ask, aware that I sound like I'm asking about adopting a puppy, but it fucking matters.

"Not sure, but she has no record on file at school or legally. Perfect record. Graduated top of her class in high school." He snorts. "Volunteers in a soup kitchen in San Diego and attends the Orthodox Church on the weekend."

Ah. A good girl. Points in her favor. Sometimes the good girls fall hard, and sometimes they're tougher to break, but they intrigue me.

"Boyfriend?"

"None."

"Name?"

"Caroline."

"Caroline?" I repeat. "That isn't a Russian name."

"Her mother was American."

I nod thoughtfully. Caroline Koslov.

She would take my name.

Caroline Dobrynin.

I drum my fingers on my desk, contemplating. I nod to Nicolai when I instruct Lev. "Get Aren on the phone."

Chapter 2

Caroline

IT'S STILL DARK when I wake, but the black outside my window is already beginning to turn to light. I reach over to shut off the blaring alarm on my phone and it goes skidding to the floor, spinning out.

"Crap," I mutter, rubbing my eyes and sitting up in bed. God, I wish I'd woken sooner. I don't remember my dream, but it was unpleasant, the weight of it still on my chest, my eyes gritty with sleep. Was I crying? I haven't slept well in years, but I rarely remember what I dream. Maybe I don't even dream. Maybe I just want to escape into a new life and new place, away from the domineering ways of my brother and the men who obey his orders.

Yawning, I stumble in the dark, reaching for my

phone, until I finally find it. I take my glasses off the bedside table and slide them on my face, blinking into the dark room. I groan out loud when I look at my phone. The damn thing's shattered. I don't much care about communicating with anyone. No one texts me, and I deleted all social media off my phone a while ago. But I love to read, I keep my books private on an app, and I hate that the stupid thing is broken. I'll have to find a way to fix it.

Aren will give me money if he's feeling generous, but I don't like to take handouts from him, and he won't allow me to get a job. It isn't for safety reasons, though. He doesn't much care about my safety or really anything about me at all. If he did, he never would have allowed—but no, I won't think about that now. I can't.

Aren doesn't want me to share anything about the brotherhood.

I look at the time. It's five thirty-three. I stretch and toss the phone back on my bed, then go to throw some clothes on.

I get up every day before nearly everyone else on the compound except Camila, the resident chef. She's teaching me how to cook and being in the kitchen with her is the highlight of my day.

I throw on a pair of black leggings and a black top, oversized, bulky, and unlikely to draw suspicion. I draw my fingers through my unruly wavy hair and quickly brush my teeth. I don't wear makeup or bother fixing my hair. My clothes are intentionally muted and frumpy. The less the men that I live with notice me, the better. Before, they would sometimes look my way, and occasionally one would even talk to me. But not since what Aren calls "the accident."

I make my mind blank as I go downstairs. I focus instead on the huevos rancheros and quiche we're making today. Camila's specialty lies in Mexican foods, but my brother insists every morning they have both Mexican and American options.

"Buenos días, preciosa," Camila says. She's a middle-aged woman with dark hair graying around the temples, barely five feet tall. She's tying an apron around her ample waist.

"You are literally the *only* person in the world that would call me that," I say with a self-deprecating laugh. She knows as well as I do that I'm not beautiful.

But she only shakes her head and smiles sadly. "Beauty is inside *and* out, Caroline," she says. "Never forget that." I roll my eyes at the cliché but take secret solace in her words. I have never forgotten that, and it's the one thing that I hold onto. I work hard at not letting myself grow bitter or angry. In a family like mine, it's an uphill battle.

The large front door clangs open and shut, and footsteps approach the kitchen. I stare at Camila in surprise. No one ever comes in here this early, and I can't be seen. My brother would lose his mind if he knew I was in here, doing servant's work, and if my brother is here to see me, there's a good chance Andros is with him. And I *despise* Andros.

Voices approach. I cover my mouth with my hand, stifling a groan, when I recognize both Aren and Andros' voices. They're growing closer. I *hate* Andros with a fiery passion and don't want either of them to see me. Camila points wildly to the pantry and silently mouths, *Go.*

I run to the pantry just in time, crouching in the corner. God, I wish there was a door on this stupid thing.

"Good morning, Camila," Aren says, helping himself to a muffin from a plate she's already prepared this morning. "By any chance have you seen Caroline?" Politeness is a dead giveaway that he's about to do something terrible.

"No, sir," Camila lies. I cringe. If he finds out she's lying, he'll punish her, or worse, fire her. She has a family to support. She lied for me. I'll remember that.

"Really?" he says. I freeze at the icy tone of his voice. I know that tone well, and it sends a shiver of fear skating down my spine.

He knows I'm here.

I gasp when Camila screams. Oh, God, oh *God.* He's hurting her.

"Tell me where she is," he growls, and I feel my heartbeat race at the familiar sound of him cocking his gun. I don't even make a conscious decision but scramble out of the pantry on all fours, shocked to see my brother holding Camila by the hair and Andros pointing a gun at her temple.

"Leave her alone!" I scream. "My God, you two are monsters. Leave her *alone!*"

I run to pull him off her, but Andros points the gun at me instead.

"There she is," he says with sickening delight. "I told you she'd come running if we threatened the old lady."

Camila whimpers.

"Let her go," I say through clenched teeth, though my heart pounds in fear when I see Andros' soulless eyes. "You want me, you have me."

Andros snorts. "No one *wants* you, you stupid bitch."

Aren laughs right along with him. I hate these two so much my vision goes temporarily blurry, and even though I *know* they're douchebags, their jeering stings. I know no one wants me. Hearing someone say it is another thing altogether.

I hold my ground and glare at them. "Let her *go.*"

It's obvious both of them are drunk and likely high, their eyes glassy. They haven't even been to bed, I bet. Andros releases Camila and keeps his gun trained on me as Aren tells Camila to go home.

"You're fired," he says. "Pack your bags. You should have known better than to sneak around behind my back." He takes out a pack of cigarettes and lights one right there in the kitchen. "You have fifteen minutes before I'll get you a personal escort. *Go.*"

"Aren, you can't! Don't fire her!" My heart breaks at the sight of tears falling down Camila's cheeks. I go to follow her, but Aren grabs me by the arm and yanks me to him.

"And you will come with me," he says tightly. "Sneaking around my back, Caroline? Did you not think I'd find out?" He throws his cigarette down and stomps it out on the kitchen floor, leaving an angry black mark on the white tile.

I don't say anything. I steel myself for whatever he plans on doing, resigned to the worst, but he doesn't strike me this time or worse, leave me to Andros. Instead, he drags me out of the kitchen and toward his study. Dread gallops across my chest as we walk down the hall to his office, where he conducts most of his most vicious business. His office opens directly to the back of the house via a door in the back. I've seen boxes delivered through that door, men brought in for "private meetings," and even bodies dragged out to be disposed of.

Terrible, wicked things happen behind these doors.

"I just wanted to learn how to cook," I tell him.

"This isn't about that," he snaps, surprising me. Andros opens the door and he shoves me in before they shut and lock the door behind me. Aren takes my wrists and holds them to my sides.

"You'll listen to me, little sister, and listen well," he says. He's so close to me I can see the red rims of his eyes and smell the whiskey on his breath. It pains me to see him like this. He looks so much like my mother with her soft brown hair and dark brown eyes. It would have killed her to see what my brother has become.

"Aren," I plead. "You're hurting me. Please, let me go."

"Shut up," he snaps.

I freeze. Something is wrong. Though he treats me badly, there's a desperation in him I rarely see. A wild look in his eyes that makes fear shiver down my spine.

He shoves me toward Andros. He knows the wicked things Andros has done to me, though he denies it and has punished me for lying. He knows how I freeze in Andros' presence and can't bring myself to speak or move. Andros takes my wrists in his firm grasp and holds me in front of my brother. Aren holds my gaze with unsteady eyes.

"I've made an arrangement," he says furiously, as if I forced his hand in this. "A win-win situation, one might say."

I don't respond, held tightly in Andros' grasp but I'm surprised to see Andros freezes. Waiting. He doesn't know, then?

"This afternoon, you'll be taken to Atlanta, to a

neutral brotherhood. The *pakhan* there will officiate at the ceremony."

Andros is a statue. I'm not sure he's even breathing, but I quickly forget about him because I'm trying to wrap my brain around what Aren has just said.

Wait. *What?*

Officiate what? I shake my head, confused.

"Your future husband will collect you there and take you back with him to Boston. I'm telling you this, so you know, not because you have a say. I want this done swiftly, before your future husband knows what you really look like."

I blink, unable to stop helpless tears forming in my eyes. I can't stop him. I can't control this.

"You arranged… my marriage?" I ask stupidly.

"You did what?" Andros asks, his voice taut with anger. "Are you fucking joking?" His protest doesn't come out of concern for me, though. Of course he doesn't want me away from here. Who else would he torment? And getting away from him is the only silver lining in what Aren is telling me.

"Yes," Aren says, turning away from me with a look of disgust. "I don't want you here anymore anyway. You're a burden to me, and no one will ever have you. The key is to make sure he's committed to you before he actually sees you."

Anger boils up inside me so hard and fast I have to

breathe through my nose, so I don't snap at him and draw out his wrath. Tears blur my vision.

"Aren," I whisper. "Why would you?"

But he won't meet my eyes. He won't talk to me.

"Give her to me," he says, and it seems he surprises Andros. Perhaps Aren doesn't think I lied about his friend after all, about what he did to me, and he doesn't trust him. I stumble toward him and he grabs my arms.

I am frozen in place as that ominous black door swings open and three men I know, three men I thought I *trusted* come in ready to take me.

I look at all of them in shock. I can't run, as they're all much bigger and faster and I'm seriously outnumbered. I look to Peter, the most sympathetic of the bunch. I thought he was my friend.

"Peter," I plead. "I know you're obedient to your brigadier, but how could you?"

"Come, Caroline," he says, more gently than I'd expect, especially given how strong his grip is when he takes me from Aren's hands. "I know you're fighting this, but many in our brotherhood have found that an arrangement has suited them."

"You're a traitor. All of you. Spineless!" I don't even recognize my own voice as it rises in pitch and breaks.

"Caroline," Peter says more sternly. "Behave, or this will be worse for you and you know it." He's warning me so I don't upset my brother and incur his wrath. "Don't make Aren angry."

"Fuck you," I say. "I thought you were my friend." That gets a flicker of remorse from him but doesn't stop the inevitable.

I'm being dragged outside, to a jet that waits. My God, I haven't even had a chance to pack my bags. They're sending me away without a second glance, with nothing but the clothes on my back.

"It might go well for you," Peter repeats, hopefully, as if he wants to alleviate his conscience. "Don't fight this."

Voices rise behind me. Andros and Aren fighting, but I can't think about that now. I can't worry about them. It's hard to form logical thoughts with the fears that swirl in my head like a brewing tornado. I'm being taken away from the only home I've known.

I'm crying freely now. I hate that I've succumbed to this. I hate what they've done to me.

But more than anything, I hate that there's no one I would say good-bye to if I could.

I'm brought onto a private jet, and six full-grown men join us. Peter is not one of them. I know their faces, but not their names. My brother has intentionally chosen the men I know nothing about to escort me to our destination.

Am I that dangerous?

Do I have any way to escape this? I know the Bratva men are fearless and powerful. Even if I did escape, they would find me.

I never expected that I would be subjected to a forced marriage. I honestly don't know what I expected. My brother considers me useless, and he likely thinks he copped one over on the man who has agreed to marry me. I swallow the lump in my throat.

But I was born into Bratva life. I was brought into this world shackled to expectations and a future I couldn't control.

What will my new husband think of me? There isn't an escape from my inevitable future at this point. Even if I ran, they would find me, and then what?

I take in a deep breath and square my shoulders.

My emotions swing like a pendulum, and for a brief moment I try to think positively. I'm a student of literature. I've read about arranged marriage. There is a rich history of arranged marriages turning out well, but my life is no fairy tale. What if the man I marry despises me? Finds me as hideous as the men of our brotherhood? What if he's mean or cruel? I've met men from every walk of life in connection with our brotherhood. He could be anyone.

Old and wizened. I shudder. I can't imagine being touched by an old, unattractive man. Or what if he's young and ruthless? I close my eyes and pinch the bridge of my nose. I've met many just like that, with hair-trigger tempers and a swagger in their step, and I'd almost prefer the old, shriveled man.

What if he's domineering? God, I swear they're *all* like that. Even when obeying their superiors, the lowest men on the totem pole are bred to protect the honor of the brotherhood. They're ruthless, merciless.

I shake my head. I have no idea who he will be or how he'll treat me. There's no use speculating about what could be.

My fate is sealed.

But what if he hates me? What if he turns me out on the street because he despises even looking at me? Will he reject me, like everyone else has? I'm not sure which is worse—the prospect of rejection or ill treatment.

I bite my lip and look out the window. One of the men sits me down and buckles me in.

"I can do that myself," I snap. "Get your hands off of me."

To my surprise, he actually does, giving me space to buckle myself, but a second man behind him growls out an order in clipped Russian.

"We don't take orders from her." The buckle is pried from my fingers, and I'm forced under the restraints like a child. It feels symbolic, having even this small freedom taken.

What would my father think of me now? Would

seeing me under the thumb of my brother make him angry? He's rolling over in his grave at what my brother has done.

My eyes water as I look out the small window.

It doesn't matter. None of it does. The only thing that matters now is my future.

I can fight this, or I can lean into this.

Chapter 3

Tomas

"Do you have confirmation from Aren that he followed through with his promise?" I don't bother modulating my voice. I need an outlet, and Stefan easily bears my temper in stride.

He sits at his desk, nodding. "I do, brother," he says, turning his phone over and showing me a picture. "That's the plane with his sister on it, fifteen minutes away from arriving here." He's dressed in a suit and tie, already prepared to officiate. I myself am wearing my most formal attire. So much could go wrong at this juncture that we'll waste no time.

I look at the picture on his phone and nod, but I say nothing else. I don't trust Aren and won't believe he's followed through on his promise until I see his sister with my very own eyes, until she wears my ring on her finger and takes my surname as her own.

I despise that the bastard will be my brother-in-law, but I'll have as little to do with him as possible. Though all of my contemporaries and associates are ruthless, we all live by a code of conduct we can't deny. But Aren? He's the lowliest of them all. Crass and self-serving, he's a terrible leader who's done nothing to earn the respect of his brothers.

Stefan sits back and eyes me, stroking the salt and pepper stubble on his chin. He's Nicolai's father, so it comes as no surprise that his eyes are the same vivid blue as Nicolai's. He's older, though, and wiser, more serious than Nicolai.

"You don't trust Aren."

"I do not. He agreed too readily." I shake my head and look out the window. "Would you give your sister to a *pakhan*?"

"It would depend," Stefan says reasonably. "I was raised to respect the laws of The Bratva. It might kill me to hand my sister over to another man, but if it was expected, I might. I wouldn't want to, but I would do what is expected for the good of the brotherhood."

"Right," I mutter. I know he's right, but there's something about the agreement with Aren that doesn't sit well with me. Something that troubles me in a raw, intuitive way that I can't quite put my finger on. He agreed too readily. He didn't fight it. He sent her to me as fast as he could, and demanded she be accompanied by half a dozen of his strike force, "for safety purposes."

There was no interview. No questionnaire from him. Not even so much as a background check that I'm aware of. He seemed as if he were relieved to be rid of her, and that unsettles me.

Is she someone he doesn't like? Is she defiant, or problematic in some way? That doesn't bother me so much. I'm confident I can deal with defiance from a woman. I'm the *pakhan,* after all, used to giving orders and being obeyed, and she'll learn her place quickly enough.

Or is there something else about her he doesn't want me to know?

"Can you show me her picture?" I ask.

Stefan shakes his head. "They've not given me access to any of that footage."

I scowl. There's an air of mystery about this I don't like. Would Nicolai have steered me wrong? He made good points about arranging a marriage, but I'm not sure this was the right decision.

I get to my feet and run my hands through my hair. "I have to get back to Boston as soon as possible," I tell Stefan.

"I know," he says, his eyes twinkling as he watches me. "Which is why you've asked me to officiate tonight, correct?"

"Yes," I tell him. "Are we ready?"

Stefan gets to his feet. "Of course. When Marissa heard who we were bringing here, she begged to be allowed time to help prepare Caroline for the ceremony. So your betrothed will be brought to Marissa and Nicolai's apartment, and both Marissa and Nicolai will bear witness as you take your vows. Once everything is official, I've arranged for you to have a private apartment for the evening, dinner, and chilled champagne."

I smile at that. "Thank you."

He shrugs a shoulder. "Think nothing of it. Nice to see you smile, brother."

It's all he says, but he doesn't need to say more. I've heard it my entire life.

Loosen up.

Relax.

I do loosen up, and I'm not always serious, but when I'm on the cusp of making a monumental decision that will not only affect my life but the good of my brotherhood, I don't fucking loosen up.

Stefan claps me on the back. "Another hour, and she'll be yours."

I've treated Nicolai and Stefan well, and in turn, they've become my most trusted allies. My closest friends and confidantes.

"Now while the plane lands and our car prepares to bring your future wife to our compound, let's meet Nicolai and Marissa, shall we?"

"Yes," I say. "I'm ready."

"Let's go then," Stefan says. He sighs as he opens the door to his office. "You know, many people scorn the thought of an arranged married. But in many ways, it removes so many of the complications of relationships."

"Right," I tell him dryly. It also introduces a whole host of further complications. "Easy for a man who isn't going through with this to say."

"I'm serious," he says. "With the blessing of her family, you don't have to worry about them interfering. She's had no previous lover, so there will be no jealousy or baggage. And she's young, still what one might say, in her formative years."

I grunt but don't respond. She's twenty-one years old and has never gone to college. I wonder if her brother is one of the old-fashioned sorts who doesn't believe in higher education for women.

"You don't have to worry about seducing her, or having her fall in love with you," he continues.

At that, I grow serious. Though her duty to me will trounce any romantic notion of love, I can't help but wonder if feelings between us will grow. I've seen arranged marriages in which both became devoted to one another and some that merely fulfilled a duty, though I'll admit I don't much care about her feelings toward me as much as I do her obedience and loyalty.

We step outside and head to a little walkway that

takes us to a separate apartment. Almost like a series of in-law apartments, the Atlanta Bratva's quarters are unique from others I've visited. Small, private residences all lie within a gated community, though the main estate, large and sprawling, is where most of the men conduct their business.

Why the hell did I let Nicolai talk me into this?

"What if she's hideous?"

He looks at me curiously. "I thought you looked at her before you agreed to this?"

I shake my head. "It was an old picture, taken years ago," I tell him.

"And she was beautiful then?"

"She looked it."

Stefan shrugs. "It's unlikely she's grown *less* attractive."

"It isn't unlikely. It's really fucking likely. And what if she's a nag?"

He quirks a brow at me. "You'll have to teach her not to be."

"And if she's willful and defiant?"

Stefan's eyes twinkle, and a corner of his lips quirks up.

"Do you mean to tell me that you, *pakhan* of one of the most powerful brotherhoods in all of America, don't know how to handle a spoiled little girl?"

I can't help but smile at that. "I think I can handle it."

He nods. "You can, and you will."

I'm not really worried, but somehow feel that asking Stefan these questions is a sort of rite of passage, like seeking the advice of a father before taking vows. It helps to voice my fears and hear his calm, steady response. And I like Stefan. He has a paternal air about him others don't. My own father would have sneered at me and decked me for asking anything at all, for committing the unforgivable crime of displaying weakness.

When we arrive at Nicolai and Marissa's door, we pause at the sound of raised voices behind it. Stefan looks at me hesitantly before he knocks, and the voices cease. A minute later, Nicolai comes to the door, his face flushed and blue eyes sparking.

"Welcome," he says tightly, gesturing for us to come in. Marissa stands inside the doorway to their kitchen wearing a little black dress, her arms crossed on her chest, glaring. She's heavy with child, one of the youngest women married into the brotherhood, but she holds herself erect and gives me a look that would rival the ferocity of a much older woman.

"Marissa," I say in greeting, as if she's just welcomed me in politely and offered me a cup of tea.

"Tomas," she says through gritted teeth.

"My wife and I have a difference of opinion when it comes to witnessing your marriage," Nicolai explains curtly, shutting the door behind him.

"It isn't right," Marissa says, ignoring the fierce look Nicolai shoots at her.

I point silently to my chest, asking him if I can interfere. I wouldn't normally butt in at all, but Marissa and I are friends. Nicolai leans against the arm of a sofa in the middle of the living room and nods, giving me permission to speak to her.

"Be specific, Marissa," I tell her. "What exactly do you object to?"

"Arranging a marriage," she says, her eyes pleading with me. "Get to *know* her, Tomas. Let her get to know you. Don't just steal her and—and—" she looks at Stefan and flushes madly. "Make her *yours* without even the courtesy of knowing her!" She doesn't want to mention me fucking my new wife in front of her father-in-law. I, however, have no such qualms.

"You don't want me to rape her. Do you really not know me better than that by now?" Her eyes widen, and her mouth drops open.

"But there are—aren't there rules governing the timeframe for…" she looks to Stefan again, still not wanting to speak frankly about sex and arrangements in front of her father-in-law.

"Consummating the marriage?" I ask her, barely checking the desire to laugh. "Yes, of course. If need be, I'll take my time. Traditional Bratva regulations expect an arranged marriage between two brotherhoods to be consummated within three days." What I don't tell her is I don't give a fuck about traditional regulations, and I'll take my damn time. But I'm not saying that out loud.

"Three days?" she says. "That's not long at all! You don't even know her!"

"It's long enough," I tell her. "You underestimate me, Marissa." I won't abuse my new wife, but I will have my way.

She opens her mouth to speak, but then looks at Nicolai, frowns, and closes her mouth.

"Do you know me to be a fair man?" I ask her.

"Well, yes," she begins, "But you're… you're *stern*," she says, still flushing pink. "*Very* stern. You command men in your group with an iron fist. What if you scare her?"

I shrug. "What if I do?" I hope I do. I'd rather be feared than disrespected or disobeyed.

"It isn't right that a newlywed woman fear her husband!"

"According to whom?" My tone sharpens, my patience waning. "It's perfectly reasonable in the eyes of the Bratva. And anyway, let me ask you a question," I continue. I need to remind her of her own experience, her own role in this. "Is having a stern husband a bad thing? You ought to know." Nicolai is no pushover. Thirteen years her senior, he was her bodyguard and protector, and though he adores her with a fiery passion, I've seen him take her in hand with my own eyes. And it works for them.

"I—well, I wouldn't know any other way," she reluctantly admits, which earns a chuckle from Nicolai. She shoots him a look of hurt, as if he's betrayed something between them, but he ignores her and shakes his head, walking over to her.

"I have to admit, your concern for her is admirable, my love," he says, his tone softer now. "But I trust Tomas, and he will be a good husband to whomever he marries." He lowers his voice and gives her a serious look. "And now that's enough questioning Tomas. He is marrying Caroline Koslov whether you approve or not, but we owe him this, Marissa. Lest you forget, it is because of Tomas that you and I are together."

I don't speak, allowing Nicolai to persuade her in his own way. Looking from me to Nicolai, she finally nods. She inhales, then lets her breath out slowly. "Alright," she says. "I'll be witness." Nicolai takes her arm and leads her into the living room.

Stefan's phone rings.

"Yes? Bring her to Nicolai's," he says. They're here. The tension in the room visibly heightens when Stefan hangs up his phone and shoves it in his pocket. He turns to me. "She's arrived, and they're on their way." He furrows his brow.

"What is it?" I ask. "You look perplexed."

"They said it's their tradition to veil a bride before marriage, and they will not lift the veil until you've said your vows."

I give him a curious look. "Fair enough."

Stefan shakes his head. "It concerns me," he says. "Is there something they're hiding?"

"Like she's ugly?" Marissa asks, giving me a look that dares me to question my future wife's looks. "Maybe there's more to a relationship than looks anyway."

"That's *enough*," Nicolai says to her, giving her a pointed look.

"I agree, Marissa," I say to her. "She was pretty enough when—"

But a knock comes at the door and we all fall silent. Nicolai opens it. I can't see beyond him, but when he steps aside, I see a small, veiled woman flanked on all sides by men. She wears clothes so dark and baggy; I can't see her figure at all. Her hands are clasped below the veil, her head is bowed. She might as well be wearing a paper bag over her entire body for all I can observe of her.

"Come in," Nicolai says.

I try to see my future bride's face, but though the veil is sheer, I see nothing. The thick, clumsy veil and dark, muted clothing make for an almost macabre appearance. I frown at the group that enters.

What game are they playing?

"The bride has requested she see her female witness before the ceremony," one of the men announces.

I nod. "Of course," I agree, even though my heart hammers in my chest like a jackknife, and I want to get this over with as soon as possible. She isn't getting the elaborate wedding with a gown and party afforded a traditional wife of Russia, so I suppose a few minutes to fix her makeup or whatever it is she wants is reasonable. Marissa eagerly takes my betrothed by the arm and leads her to the bedroom. They shut the door behind them, and we all stand in silence.

At first there's no sound at all, but a few seconds later, I hear Marissa's familiar voice and the softer, higher pitched voice of my future wife. I can't hear what either of them say. They talk for long minutes, and I tap my foot impatiently as I wait. What is she asking her? What is she helping her do? What are they saying about *me*? I give them ten minutes before my patience is gone.

I stalk to the door and rap on it. "That's enough," I say through the closed door. "Marissa, bring her out here."

Silence, a few more whispered words, then the door opens, and the two women return to the room. Marissa won't meet me eyes. My impatience and apprehension grow.

"Take your bride's hand," Stefan says. "And join me by the fireplace."

I do. Her hand is smaller than mine, freezing cold, and clammy. On instinct, I take her cold hand in both of mine to warm her, but I don't say anything to alleviate her fear. I need to read her first, to assess her temperament. If she's contrary or willful, she'll learn to fear and respect me.

The ceremony is brief, utilitarian, and within minutes, it's time to say our vows. I say mine in Russian, pleased she does the same. Her voice is clear and musical, like church bells, and it stirs something in me to hear her vow to love, honor, and obey, words that now are merely rote with little meaning, but vows I'll hold her to. Most of them, anyway. The love is optional. Honor and obedience are not. I slide the ring Stefan gives me on her tiny finger.

I've mentally prepared myself for the unveiling. I don't anticipate her to be a raving beauty and have already decided I have a higher purpose. Stefan nods to me to remove her veil, and the poor thing actually whimpers a little. She trembles so badly I have to steady her arm before I even lift the veil.

I grasp the edge of the veil, inhale deeply, and lift it, getting my first real glimpse of the woman I've made vows to.

Her head is bowed, her eyes cast down, and tears stream down her cheeks. Why? I'm not sure. Tears don't move me, but I will find out the reason she cries.

I take her chin in my hand and tip her head

upwards. I notice two things at once: she has the largest, most beautiful pale green eyes I've ever seen, framed in thick black lashes and brimming with tears, but furious. And second, down the side of her face, from cheek to jaw, runs an angry, vivid scar. A knife wound.

I don't think about my reaction but respond instinctively. Cupping her face in my hand, I draw my thumb from the top of the scar to the bottom. My hands shake in anger. I ignore the way she flinches and pulls away. I grab the small of her back to hold her in place, not allowing her to pull away from me. Heat rises in my chest when I vow then and there that I will make whoever did this to her pay, that anyone who would mar a woman's face deserves a swift, merciless death. It could be any one of them. He could be standing in front of us now.

In my anger, to prove she's mine before the witnesses before us, I lean down and kiss my wife to seal our vows. It's a quick, nearly chaste kiss, hard and fast. She nearly stumbles, and when I pull away from her those pretty green eyes shutter, her jaw tightens, and she turns away from me.

Stefan looks from her to me in surprise but maintains composure.

"Thank you for officiating," I tell him, my back to the men who escorted her here. I grasp her elbow, so she doesn't run, and hold Stefan's eyes. He's staring at her scar with undisguised surprise, but quickly schools his features. Still, I want her alone. *Now*.

"Have your men escort our visitors to the exit," I tell him. "Their job here is done."

I want those men gone as far away from her as possible.

Stefan's kind eyes grow hard, his jaw firming, before he turns to Nicolai and gives him instructions in Russian. One of the men protests, but I don't even bother to look his way, trusting Nicolai and Stefan will make them leave.

Marissa stands to my right, wringing her hands. I ignore everyone but Stefan. Once the others have vacated, I nod to him. "Show us to our room?"

Chapter 4

Caroline

HE HATES ME ALREADY, and we only just met. This was exactly what I feared and exactly what happened. I'll never forgive Aren for putting me through this, for forcing my hand. I don't know where I am or who I just married, or what's in store for me from one minute to the next.

The men who escorted me leave, and this man—my *husband*—holds my arm in a grip so tight it hurts. The first time I truly looked into his eyes, I saw what I feared: anger and repulsion. Though it doesn't surprise me, I can't help the way it stings like tearing open a wound all over again.

I insisted I speak with the woman bearing witness to our vows, and they granted me that privilege. She seems nice enough, though our interaction was brief. She expected I wanted her to help fix my hair or do my makeup, but I don't care about things like that. I knew it might be the only access I had to another woman who knew him, and I wanted her to tell me what my new husband was like. So I could prepare.

"My name's Marissa," she said. I lifted my veil so we could see each other, and she quickly schooled her surprise when she saw my scar.

"Caroline," I responded. "I don't need your help to prepare me for this farce of a ceremony," I said bitterly. "We both know why I'm here. I want you to tell me what you know about my future husband."

Her brows shot up in surprise, but she quickly recovered, nodding. "A fair question," she said, then she hesitated, biting her lip. "Your future husband is a good man," she finally said. "He was good to both me and my husband. He will treat you well, but you'd be wise not to defy him. He can be exacting and stern."

I flinched at those words. I'm very familiar with punishment at the hands of angry men, and I hate that it's the first warning she gives me. What will he expect of me? What does she mean by exacting and stern?

And what does she mean by *good?* A bowl of cereal for breakfast is a good breakfast. "Good" is the lamest adjective in the English language that tells me nothing at all about what I need to know.

As if on cue, shortly after we had our brief, hushed conversation, he shouted for us to come back.

Great. Way to make a *good* impression.

And his reaction when he lifted the veil... I'll never forget it. He looked as if he'd just won a prize and found it to be rotten, his lip curled in disgust and whole body taut with anger. I don't know why he cupped my face. Maybe to still his hand that wanted to reject me, when he no longer could. Maybe to pretend to show affection for me in front of my brother's men. His touch felt unlike anything I've felt before, and I couldn't figure it out at first. It wasn't tender, but possessive.

We don't even know one another, and he already grabs me and tosses me around like I'm a piece of property.

And hell, I guess I am now.

Property.

His to do with as he will. There is no escape from Bratva life if one is born into it. Both marriage and birth seal the inevitable fate.

I haven't really even looked at him, I was so worried about the vows and his reaction to me. But now that we're making our way to "our room," as he called it, I sneak a surreptitious glance toward him.

He's a large man, bulky and strong, and even though he wears a suit, beneath the formal attire I can tell he's muscled and powerful. This doesn't surprise me. All men in The Bratva are expected to be. Though I see no visible tattoos, I know the ways of the Bratva. He'll be marked with their signature ink along his back and arms. I don't know his role, but if he's of higher rank, he'll bear more ink than the rest.

His hair is a dark brown, on the longer side on top, and he sports a scruffy but well-trimmed beard. The eyes that looked at me seemed so dark they were nearly black, probing and intense, but now that he's closer I can see flecks of gold. If he didn't look so angry, he would be a handsome man, but I have to admit his bulk scares me a little. I'm sturdy but short, and he's so much bigger than I am he moves me around as if I'm a cardboard cut-out, and not a living breathing *human being*. Grabbing my hand, he tugs me along, and I have no choice but to trot to keep up with his large, powerful strides.

The veil tumbles to the side, its falling a symbol of sorts. I can no longer hide. It slides to the ground and gets crushed beneath his heavy footsteps as he drags me to the furthest end of the property, to a small apartment with lights blazing. He yanks open the door with his left hand, still holding me in his right, then to my shock, bends and lifts me up and right over the threshold, placing me clumsily to my feet so quickly he nearly tosses me through the door. I stumble, but he grabs my elbow to right me, then slams the door behind him.

By now, his fit of temper because he was given marred goods has me in a fury of my own. I can't help who I am. I can't help how I look. And if I'm to be married to this monster, he can have some damn decency.

"Hardly carrying me over the threshold!" I spit out at him, quickly scurrying around the kitchen table to put distance between us. I look quickly around for something to defend myself if he's going to hurt me. Now that I'm his property, I'm fully prepared for him to rape me. There are rules governing consummation. I begin to tremble.

This isn't *my* fault. I didn't agree to this. I didn't scar my face, and I didn't promise him anything, so he has no right to direct his anger at me. His eyes darken as he prowls closer to me, and I fear the worst. I know that look. He's going to hurt me, I know it, but there's something my new husband will learn about me. I won't stand and take it.

Glancing wildly about the room, I see a set of kitchen knives on the counter. I sprint, and grab the largest one by the handle, spinning around to face him. "Do not fucking touch me again."

He freezes and puts his hands up in the universal gesture of surrender.

"Caroline," he says in his deep, angry voice. Unlike the other men of the Bratva, his accent is less noticeable, though still there. He barks out a command that makes me jump and nearly drop the knife. *"Put that down."*

I blink and stare at him, my hand trembling. What will he do if I put it down? What will he do if I *don't*? Oh, God, this was so stupid.

"No," I tell him, shaking so hard the knife vibrates in my hand. "I don't trust you. I don't want you to hurt me. I did nothing to deserve your anger, and you will not touch me!"

At that, he looks at me in surprise and anchors his large hands on his hips. "Is that what you think?"

I blink. "What?"

"That I'm angry with you?"

"You're glaring at me. What am I supposed to think, that you're enamored with my radiant beauty? Look at me. I'm no fool."

He fixes me with a look that would make the most powerful men of the brotherhood quake. "All you've done to earn my anger is wield a knife at me. Before then, my anger was not directed at you."

I grip the blade, unsure of how I would even use this thing if I had to. I suppose I'd slash at him and try to hit an artery or something. Hell, I don't even really know where those are. *Stupid.* Unfortunately, the sight of blood also makes me want to vomit, so this was a very poorly executed decision.

"Oh, really?" I ask incredulously. "Then why have you been glaring at me?"

His lips purse but he doesn't respond. "Put the knife down," he repeats.

"Not until you answer me," I counter.

He takes a step toward me and I hold the knife higher.

"We might as well make this clear from the beginning," he says, almost thoughtfully. "You will not raise your hand to me, ever. You will respect me as your husband, and you will do what I say. I do not respond to ultimatums." His voice sharpens to steel. "Now put that knife down before you hurt yourself."

Clearly, he's the domineering sort. Shocking.

I still hold the knife, but now I'm not exactly sure what I'm going to do. I don't want to hurt him, but I don't want to do what he says either. If I obey, what will he do in retaliation? I look to the door, then the window. There's no escape. If I run, and he has any authority here at all, he could have a legion of men at his beck and call, ready to catch me and return me to him. I don't know what awaits me if I obey him now, but whatever it is will only worsen if I run.

This was a stupid, reckless decision, and I have a feeling I will regret pulling a knife on my new husband. Damn. I already do.

Foolishly, I continue to talk. "And what will you do to me if I put this down?"

A muscle ticks in his jaw. "I will lessen the punishment you've already earned for pulling a knife on me."

I swallow hard. *Damn.* But not a surprise.

"And if I don't?"

His eyes darken and his brows draw together. "I will

take that knife from you before I whip you soundly, cuff you, and put you to bed."

My pulse spikes. He isn't lying.

This is the man I'm married to?

The knife clatters to the floor, and I swear I see him smile when he bends to pick it up. Do I amuse him? There is nothing at all funny about this situation. He bends and lifts the knife, rises with a sigh, and places it on the counter behind him.

"Now come here," he says, his implacable gaze on mine as he quirks a finger at me. Aw, hell. I know I'm in trouble, and I have no idea what to expect. I'm shaking before I reach him. I've botched up our wedding night so badly I want to cry. There's nothing at all romantic about this, but I could have at least kept the peace.

Maybe.

"It was self-defense," I say as I walk toward him taking tiny steps. I bite my lip, unsure what to do next or if the humor I see in his eyes is something I can trust.

"Self-defense?" he repeats. "And what exactly were you defending yourself against?"

"Your anger, obviously," I say. "Big, burly men like you who are angry often hurt people." A shadow crosses his features, but I'm telling him the truth. "And it was… precautionary. Reactionary, even. I wasn't actually going to *hurt* you."

"And isn't that the problem?" he says. I'm close enough to him now that he grabs my arm and yanks me to him. I look up at him, and swallow hard. I can't speak. "You could have hurt yourself sooner than you'd have hurt me," he continues. "I don't believe you could even stand the sight of blood."

"I can!" I lie.

"Really?" he asks. To my surprise, he reaches a hand in his pocket and removes a switch blade. He spins it around and gives me the handle. "Show me."

"What? No! You can't—I—"

"Cut me then," he says, pushing the blade into my palm. "Prove it." My imagination quickly conjures up the image of his skin slicing open and vivid red blood splashing onto the floor. My stomach rolls with nausea, and I shake my head.

"I can't," I admit in defeat, my voice shaking. "I hate the sight of blood and would likely vomit all over this pretty tiled floor."

He purses his lips, folds the knife, and places it back in his pocket, then does something that shocks me. He glides his hand to the small of my back and draws me to him, and when I'm pressed up to his warm, strong body, he holds my chin between his fingers to capture my gaze. He doesn't scold or lecture but looks at me for the first time tonight with kindness in his eyes.

"My initial anger was not directed at you," he says,

his voice softer now, his tone kind. I remember the words Marissa told me.

He's a good man.

In that moment, with the kitchen lighting illuminating his features and his eyes gentling before me, I almost believe it. Almost. But men are chameleons, morphing into what they think you want to see, and I don't trust them. The ones who feign kindness are the worst of the lot, because they lure you in, making you vulnerable before they bite.

"You saw my scar and reacted," I say, my voice hard, but my throat is tight and my voice shakes, so I can't say anything more. I swallow hard. I don't want to cry again. It hurts to cry, and I don't want to hurt anymore. Not tonight.

"I did," he says honestly, nodding, before he releases my chin and gently draws his index finger down the length of my scar. I shudder. No one has ever touched me there, and it disturbs me how easily he does.

"My anger was directed at whoever gave you this scar. Not at *you.*"

Oh.

Oh.

That's… very different.

I swallow hard. "I—I'm sorry, then," I tell him. "I had it in my head that you were angry at me for being ugly, and I—"

His eyes cloud again with anger and he puts a finger to my lips to silence me.

This time, I obey.

"I don't ever want to hear you say that again," he says. "Never, *ever* again. Do you understand me?"

I nod mutely.

He brushes my crazy hair off my forehead and tips my face up to his again with a finger under my chin. "And you must never raise your hand to me again. This is the only warning I'll give you. Threatening me in any way will earn you swift and severe punishment. Is that clear as well?"

I nod again, my heart hammering so hard and fast I can't speak.

"Good," he says shortly. "Then we will put this behind us after I've punished you."

Panic sweeps through me. I don't know what to think or do around this man, and that terrifies me.

How will he punish me? I've been punished in so many ways my imagination runs ragged trying to understand what he's doing, when I realize he's pulling out one of the kitchen chairs.

What will he do?

My answer comes the next second when he gives me a sharp tug and places me belly-down over his knees.

I screw my eyes tight and can't help but throw an

arm up in protest, but without flinching he merely takes my wrist and pins it to my lower back. I freeze when he pats my ass with his huge palm.

I begin to panic. Even though I'm over his lap for clearly what will be my punishment, this feels intimate and borderline sexual. For a girl like me, that's terrifying.

"This will be brief and serve as a reminder only," he says, seemingly oblivious to my distress. "Because I know now why you acted as you did, and I don't wish to mar our wedding night with the memory of a harsh punishment." With that, he yanks down my leggings, and I want to *die.* The only reason I'm over his knees like this is so he can spank me, and I'm utterly humiliated. I whimper but don't move out of his grasp.

"Let me go!" I protest. "Please! I won't do it again."

"You're damn right you won't. Repeat after me. 'I will not raise my hand to my husband.'"

My voice is strangled and tight when I repeat, "I will not raise my hand to my husband."

Whack.

His massive palm cracks against my ass. It hurts worse than I expect, and I gasp in shock, frozen in pain before he speaks again.

"Repeat. *I will do as I'm told."*

I take in a deep breath then repeat, "I will do as I'm told."

Whack.

Another harsh slap has me whimpering and squirming. I'm shocked at how much this spanking hurts, but grit my teeth, determined to take the punishment I've earned. I have no choice, and I don't want to incur further punishment.

His voice lowers, even more serious than before. "Say, 'I will never call myself ugly again.'"

I blink in surprise, but I'm too afraid not to obey. My vision blurs and my throat tightens, but I manage to get the words out. "I will never call myself ugly again." With one massive hand wrapped around my waist, he brings down his palm and gives me the hardest spank he's given me yet. I gasp out loud and dry sob, caught up in so many emotions I don't even know where to begin to sort them.

Then it's over. My punishment was three hard slaps, humiliating but not cruel. He's chosen degradation over pain with this reminder, and it's worked. I want to crawl under a blanket and pull it over my head. I want to lock myself in a closet and huddle in the corner and cry myself to sleep. But I can't. I have to face the man I'll spend the rest of my life with, knowing I belong to him and knowing he has the power to do whatever he wants with me. So when he rights me, I can't look at him. Instead, I instinctively bury my face on his chest, so I don't need to make eye contact with him. Too late I realize that my self-preservation brings me intimately closer to him.

He doesn't respond at first, as if surprised by my reaction, his arms hanging by his sides. I feel him draw in a breath, but then he doesn't speak. I bring my hands to my face and curl up on his lap, miserable and chastened and hurt. I don't want his comfort or consolation, I just have nowhere else to hide. To my chagrin, tears splash on my lap.

After a moment, he loosely brings his arms around me to hold me. I tense. "Look at me," he says, his voice sharp.

Right now, sitting on his knee, my body still aching from the swift but firm punishment, I couldn't disobey him if I wanted to. I'm too raw, too vulnerable, and the tone of his voice sends my pulse spiking. That quickly, he removed my defenses and reduced me to tears. I don't like that he has that power over me, but I can't control my reaction. I don't want to look at him, but the tone of his voice leaves no choice.

With great reluctance, I remove my hands from my face and look at him. I'm shaking from head to foot, my whole body taken with tremors. I'm consumed with so many emotions, I don't know where to begin. I don't know how to process what's happened or how to sort through everything I've felt.

"That can't happen again, Caroline," he says. "Do you understand?"

I nod, and swallow hard.

"Good." His voice hardens and he removes his arms

from me. He's done with this. "Now, I'll not have my wife walking around dressed in clothes like these." He plucks me off his lap and stands me in front of him. "Remove them."

I blink. Of *course* this is what he'll do next, and I hate it. The vulnerability vanishes, and in its place, anger rushes in like a stampede. Powerful, destructive, and all-consuming.

I close my eyes and grit my teeth, resigned to my fate. By Bratva law, he has to consummate our marriage. But this isn't my first rodeo.

He won't be the first man who's taken me against my will. I could resist him and fight him and face whatever punishment he gives me. I have no doubt this is what awaits me if I defy him.

Or, I could surprise him and do what he says.

But he'll get no affection from me. No tenderness. He might as well fuck an ironing board for all the reaction I'll give him. I know how to shut myself off from the physical, to take myself mentally to a place beyond the present. And every time I do, the wall I build up around my heart gets thicker, stronger, a veritable fortress against any and all emotion that even hints at intimacy.

"Fine," I tell him, lifting my chin and meeting his eyes. He doesn't blink or look away but narrows his eyes. I suppose he's prepared to punish me again if he needs to, but he won't have to. I'm not going to disobey his majesty.

My hands travel to my bulky clothes as I hold his gaze. I hope he *doesn't* like what he sees. It's easier for me to hate him if I see repulsion in his eyes rather than lust. And he's stuck with me.

I used to be thin and lithe, but that was before my innocence was taken. I've let my body grow curvy and full.

The truth is, he's wed to a woman scarred inside and out. He chose me, so he'll deal with what he's got. Forever. And he may have punished me for pulling a knife on him, but he's married no submissive wallflower.

"Of course you want me naked," I tell him. "Isn't that what they all want?"

"I wouldn't know," he says, his eyes narrowed on me. "I've never been married before. You?"

I huff out an angry breath. "Well, no."

"Then how do you presume to know what all husbands want from their wives?"

I look at him in surprise. Is he joking? But no, there isn't an ounce of humor in his eyes, and he holds his body erect.

"If you didn't want to have a ready-made fuck toy, then why did you want me?"

"Ready-made fuck toy," he mutters to himself. "Have to admit, I like the sound of that." Then he sobers and shakes his head, and his tone grows curious. "Do you know my role in the Bratva, Caroline?"

"Of course not," I snap. "I know nothing about any of this. I was taken from my home, forced to wear a veil, and told I had no choice but to marry you. I..." I swallow hard and my voice tightens with the realization that hits me. "I don't even know your name."

"Tomas."

"Tomas," I repeat. "And you'll... expect me to call you by name?"

He shrugs a shoulder. "Sometimes. Though sometimes I'll demand *sir*."

I nearly snort out loud. Also, not a surprise.

I've taken vows to this man. I've kissed him and gone over his lap for a spanking. I'm about to strip, and I just found out his name. It's ludicrous. Completely backwards. But then again, this is Bratva life. I'm only a pawn in this, and I know it. I always have been.

"You know I am Bratva, Caroline," he says thoughtfully. "But did you know I am *pakhan?*"

Shit. I had no idea he was the king of a group, at the absolute pinnacle of leadership. I've seen over the years how the *pakhan* gets whatever he wants, how he's king of his domain.

And I'm his wife.

"A leader in my position does well to have a wife," he says. "Your brother owed me a favor."

That's what I've become? A *favor*.

"Lovely," I mutter, and at that, I can tell I've pushed him too far. His eyes narrow and his spine stiffens. My mouth goes suddenly dry.

"This conversation is over. We'll talk later. Now, your only job is to do as I say. Go to the bedroom." He points to the bedroom. "And *strip*."

Chapter 5

Tomas

I WATCH MY WIFE UNDRESS, trying to remain aloof and detached. I don't want her to know how she affects me. I've already demonstrated more tenderness than I wished to show this early. Those under the authority of another obey for two reasons: love or fear. Since we don't love one another and may never, fear is the only option. If I show this woman too much leniency, she won't learn to fear me.

And she *must* learn to fear me.

She stands in front of me, clearly a diamond in the rough. I saw the picture of her when she was younger, and I'm no fool. Though she's unkept and rather haggard in appearance, with wild, frizzy, untamed hair, thick, ugly glasses perched on her thin nose, her bare face pale and freckled, I can already see there's more to her than meets the eye.

But it isn't until she begins to peel off her layers that I truly see what I couldn't at first. Underneath the hideous clothing she wears, she's absolutely exquisite. I swallow and shift uncomfortably, already hard from taking her over my lap, but now it's impossible to ignore.

I have three days to consummate this marriage. I want to do it fucking *now*.

First, she pulls off the cumbersome leggings. I haven't seen anything so ugly in years, and vow once they're off her, these scratchy fabrics will never touch her skin again. Full, delectable thighs meet my eyes, and I can see the very edge of crisp white panties beneath the hem of her black top.

"All of them," I snap out, ready for her to obey. This woman will be the death of me in her training, but if all goes well, it won't break her. It won't break *us*.

Glaring at me, she clenches her jaw and yanks the gruesome black top over her head, slamming it to the ground. Her crazy hair hangs about in her wild, untamed waves, her pale complexion faintly tainted with light pink cheeks. She stands in front of me now wearing a plain white cotton bra and matching panties. She'd look about twelve years old if not for the curves that fill her undergarments.

And *fuck*, those curves. Jesus *Christ*, those curves.

I don't care about her mouth or her history or her

attitude. If this woman is to be mine—and she already is by law—I will worship every inch of this magnificent body.

Her graceful neck slopes downward to sturdy shoulders, flexed when she anchors her hands on her hips. Every goddamn inch of her is curves and valleys and dimpled, creamy skin that I long to taste, touch, and master. Her breasts nearly spill out of her too-small bra, and I long to weigh them in my hands and lick those nipples until she keens with pleasure and need. From her full breasts to her voluptuous thighs, she's a fucking masterpiece.

"Jesus Christ, woman," I say, my voice husky and low. "I owe you thanks for covering a body like that." She's a fucking pin-up.

To my shock, her eyes grow wide for a fraction of a second before they shutter.

"You jerk," she says through gritted teeth. "You wanted me, and now you have me. If you wanted someone thin and gorgeous, you should have chosen better." She turns on her heel to march off from me, and I'm so shocked at her reaction that at first, I don't respond. Then I realize she's stalking away. I will not have that.

I grab her arm and yank her to me.

"What the hell are you talking about?" I ask her, truly confused and ready to spank the truth out of her that quickly.

She tries to pull her arm away but can't and finally sighs and submits to my grasp on her arm.

"You said you're glad I covered my body," she states. "Would you prefer I put my clothing back on, then, if my body offends you so?"

I stare at her, bewildered, before it finally dawns on me how she took my statement. She thought *I* thought a woman like her ought to be ashamed of her body. Jesus, I've got my work cut out for me.

"Sit," I order, pointing to the edge of the bed. She will not disobey me. She will not stomp away in petulance. She will sit and listen to me or face the consequences of her disobedience. With a glare, she flounces on the bed, making her full breasts bounce. I swallow hard and think about spanking her again, of strewing her over my lap and slamming my palm against her ass again. And again. And again.

"You—" she begins, but I've had enough.

I hold up my palm and fix her with a stern glare. "Be quiet," I snap. I wait to ensure she complies. I'm fully prepared to punish her swiftly if she doesn't. But she only sighs and stares at me in resignation. Good. At least she's learned a modicum of fear.

"You listen to me and do not interrupt me, woman."

After a second, she nods, slouched over on the bed.

"Sit up straight."

With a clenched jaw, she obeys.

"I said I was grateful you covered your body," I tell

her. "Not because I think a body like yours is in *any way* repugnant to me, but quite the opposite. I don't know the men of your Bratva, but I'd prefer they didn't have the privilege of seeing you as I do."

I can tell by the way she stares that she doesn't believe me.

I walk to her and gesture for her to stand. She does so, though reluctantly.

"I don't know what you're talking about," she says.

"You're no fool, Caroline," I say, reaching behind her to unclasp her bra. I told her to take off her clothes, and I meant all of them. Her hand flies up to try and trap my wrist, but I quickly deflect her and continue. "There's a reason you've dressed the way you have, and I'll make it my mission to find out why."

"Oh?" she tosses back angrily. "Will you, then?"

I nimbly unclasp her bra and her beautiful, rounded breasts swing free. I swallow hard and gather one full breast in my palm, letting my thumb gently graze her nipple. "I will," I say, my voice husky. I turn her around and switch positions, sitting on the bed and positioning her in front of me. Bending, I take the edge of her panties and draw them down. I can feel the heat of her skin where I spanked her, and when the panties come down her thighs, the sweet feminine scent of her arousal makes me nearly mad with lust.

Now she stands in front of me stark naked, wearing

nothing but a scowl and the faint pink of my handprint where I spanked her.

"Are you aroused by your spanking, Caroline?" I ask, enjoying the way her pale cheeks color.

"No!" she says, pulling away from me, but I quickly grab her arms and yank her closer.

"We'll see about that."

I will not ask permission from her, but I will not take advantage. Does she enjoy being under my authority in some way? Does being turned over my lap excite her? I aim to find out.

"Part your legs," I command, pushing her thighs apart with the back of my hand.

She obeys, and the scent of her feminine musk grows stronger. I gently brush the tip of my finger at the very apex of her thighs.

"Do you like when I take control?" I ask. "Did you like being over my lap for a spanking?"

She shakes her head wildly, her lips parted.

"No, of course not. Are you kidding?"

But one swipe of my finger at her core says otherwise. "Really?" I ask with disbelief. "Are you sure a little part of you isn't fascinated with the idea of bending to my whip? Of receiving measured pain at my hand?"

"No," she says, but her eyes close, and she releases a moan.

"And yet, the thought arouses you," I probe.

"No," she pants, shaking her head, as I work her pussy.

I freeze. "No?"

"No-no. Yes!" she amends, wantonly pushing her hips against my hand for more pressure.

"Tell me what arouses you," I say, before I flick her clit. She whimpers.

"I don't know," she says. It's a fair response. "It hurt when you spanked me." And then she opens her eyes fully and glares at me. "And I fucking hate sex."

I note the antagonism with interest. There's a story there. I make it my mission to find out what it is and to change it.

"Good," I say, withdrawing my hand and bringing my wet fingers to her mouth. As much as I want to lay her down and eat her out until she comes on my face with absolute abandon, the timing isn't right. I have three days to make her mine, and she will learn her place in that time. I won't let her come until she's earned it.

"Suck," I order.

Grimacing, she obeys. The wet feel of her tongue on my fingers makes my dick twitch and my stomach tighten. Jesus, I can't wait to fuck her.

In time.

"That's a good girl," I tell her. I release her, giving her one more longing look. Her body is utter perfection. "Our plane leaves in the morning. You need some sleep and so do I. Unfortunately, I don't trust you, so you'll have to sleep with these on."

I pull a pair of cuffs out of my pocket and lead her to the bedpost to cuff her. Her eyes widen. She likely expected I'd fuck her tonight.

"If it's an emergency, let me know. If not, you're not to bother me, and if you do so prematurely, I'll be forced to punish you." She won't sleep well with her arms secured above her head, but given that she's mine now, and I don't want her near anyone until she proves I can trust her, she'll have plenty of time to rest.

"Where are you going to sleep?" she asks. I nod to the bed beside her.

"You're my wife," I say, aware that my tone is sarcastic and biting. "I'll sleep beside you. But don't worry. I won't touch you."

"You…" she begins, then she thinks better of what she was going to say and clamps her mouth shut.

"Me what?" I ask. "Say it." I begin to undress, slipping out of my coat jacket and hanging it over a chair.

"You say you're not repulsed by me, but you have no interest in consummating our marriage? That makes no logical sense to me."

I like that she's ruled by logic, and I'll keep that in

mind. At the same time, it's my duty to train her to obey me, so she'll only get the bare minimum.

"You're wrong in assuming I don't want to consummate our marriage. I do. Very much so." I unbutton my trousers and push them down my legs. "And that should be obvious to you."

Her eyes travel to the large erection tented in my boxers and real fear crosses her face. She swallows hard.

"But not tonight?" she whispers.

I shake my head.

"Not tonight."

She breathes a sigh of relief and seems almost relaxed in her cuffs. I don't understand this woman but will. I pull off my t-shirt and climb into bed with her. Shyly, she looks me over, lingering on the ink that paints my neck, arms, and back.

"Someday, will you tell me what those mean?" she asks, so innocently, she doesn't sound like the woman of just a few minutes ago.

"Maybe someday," I tell her. "Now no more talking. Sleep."

I wish our wedding night could've ended differently than this, but I'm no romantic. The only reason I do is because I'd have liked to fuck her well and good before we went to sleep, to calm the blood pounding in my veins. To remind her that she belongs to *me*.

I roll over with my back to her. I like the warm feel of her skin against mine. I can almost hear her thinking, as she lies there in the dark and I wonder what she turns over in her mind.

Still, sleep comes swiftly in the end.

When I wake the next morning, she's already stirring beside me, her arms still in cuffs, staring up at the ceiling. I wonder if she's slept at all.

"*Dobroye utro,*" I say. *Good morning.*

She purses her lips and give me a sidelong glance but doesn't respond.

Casually, I reach over to one of her bare breasts and take her nipple between my fingers. She tenses when I squeeze and narrows her eyes. I'm not trying to arouse her. I'm reminding her of what happens when she doesn't behave.

"The proper way to respond to your husband is to say *good morning,* or *dobroye utro,*" I tell her. I hold onto the tender bud. "Go on, now."

"Good morning," she says through gritted teeth, her tone dripping with sarcasm. "Looks like fine weather we're having, doesn't it?"

I look out the window for the first time. It's dark and rainy, and thunder booms in the air.

I shrug. "It's lovely. Are you hungry?" I ask. Her eyes flit to where I still have hold of her nipple.

"Starving. Are you going to let me go or not?"

"Are you going to watch your mouth or not?"

She sighs, briefly closes her eyes, then nods. "Yes."

I release her nipple and watch as it turns a pretty shade of deep pink. With the very tip of my finger, I circle the outer edge and push myself up on my elbow.

"Your breasts are gorgeous," I tell her huskily. "I'd like to taste them for breakfast."

"Charming," she says, which earns her another punishing tweak. Gasping, she tenses. I release her nipple and bend my mouth to her other breast, lazily drawing my tongue along the pretty pink peak. Holding her gaze with mine, I draw her nipple into my mouth and suck hard.

Her back arches but her hands stay in place, still cuffed to the headboard. The way her eyes flutter shut I can tell she likes my ministrations. Gently, I knead one nipple while I lap and suckle the other, until a little moan of pleasure escapes her pretty lips. I release her nipple and drop a kiss to the damp, hardened skin, before I draw my mouth lower and kiss the fullest part of her bare breast.

"Fucking beautiful," I tell her, planting kisses all along her chest. Cuffed, she can't stop me, but I have a feeling that it's only an excuse for her to enjoy this, because she gently parts her knees without prompting and whimpers when I stop.

Pushing myself up to her neck, I kiss her there, inhaling her sweet scent, faintly honeyed and floral.

Christ, she's got me so damn aroused. As *pakhan*, I have women whenever I want them and readily, but they've been willing. Eager, even. This one is not only more beautiful than the slender women I've taken, with her full curves and valleys I could sink into with pleasure. She poses a challenge to me. Maybe it's because she's hard to get. Maybe it's because she's a fucking goddess. Maybe it's because she's *my wife* and deep within I know I own every inch of her.

I want to fuck this woman more than I've ever wanted to fuck anyone before. But I can be patient, and I will.

"You can't mean that," she says softly It makes me pause.

"Mean what?"

"That you find me beautiful."

I'm taken aback by her response. I can tell she's sincere. I shake my head. We need to clear this up.

"There's one thing you need to know about me, Caroline. I never say anything I don't mean. I don't mince words, and I don't sugarcoat the truth."

How could she not think she's beautiful?

But she says nothing else as I make my way up the column of her neck to her lips. Bracing my hand against one side of her face, I cup her jaw and lower my mouth to hers.

She tastes delicious, sweet, and seductive, like the

most delectable wine. Pungent and sweet, fruity and intoxicating. I take one sip and can't stop, can't pull away from her. She moans beneath me as I kiss her deeply, even as her body tenses. I wait until she arches into me, wanting more, before I pull away.

When I do, she opens her eyes and glares at me.

"I'm not sure I like the way you're looking at me," I tell her, pushing out of bed and getting to my feet. "There's defiance laced in every part of your body."

"Oh?" she throws back. "I suppose you'll whip that out of me or something?"

She has no fucking idea.

I head to the bathroom and look over my shoulder at her, thinking before I respond.

"I have many methods, Caroline. And time will tell which works best. If I were you, I wouldn't test me unless a part of you *wants* to be punished by me." I open the door to the bathroom. "Then by all means, do it. Defy me and see where that lands you."

I use the bathroom quickly, listening hard to the other side of the door, but there's no movement or sound. When I come back in the room, a little bit of the fiery temper has faded from her gaze, and she licks her lips. I'd give anything to know what's going on in that mind of hers. The woman runs deep, a veritable chasm of thoughts and emotions and intellect I'm eager to explore.

"May I please use the bathroom?" she asks politely.

I nod. "You may." She watches as I retrieve the key, slip it in, and free her wrists. "Be quick about it. We need to go eat breakfast."

She gets out on the side of the bed away from me, walks around in a large loop to avoid coming close, walks to the bathroom and shuts the door hard. Almost a slam, though not quite. She's skirting the edge of defiance on purpose.

I shake my head to myself and stifle a chuckle. She's so predictable it's almost amusing. I dress before I open the dresser drawer and find some clothes for her. Nicolai told me Marissa would outfit her, and she's done a good job. I choose a soft blue cotton dress and undergarments and lay them on the bed and wait for her. When she comes out of the bathroom I point silently to the clothes. I watch as she tugs them on and doesn't question my choice. So there are areas where she chooses to draw the line. I note this well.

When she's done, I gesture for her to have a seat. Nicolai said we had a choice to either eat with the brotherhood or eat privately, and I'm not sure I trust her well enough to bring her around the others.

"You may sit at the table until I tell you to get up," I tell her. I wait until she sits obediently and places her hands in her lap before I check my messages.

Lev: Complications in San Diego. Call when you can.

I huff out an angry breath. Of *course* there are complications in San Diego. Why did I think my marriage to Caroline would actually go off without a hitch?

Caroline taps her foot and bites her lip while I text Lev back. *I'll call you after I eat breakfast.* My stomach rumbles with hunger, and my irritation grows. I need to eat something before I bite someone's head off, and the closest person to me is the woman I've married.

I look at her in silence, and she meets my steady gaze. I call her wife, and yet we're as unalike as two people could be, as well as total strangers. At least I think so. The truth is, I don't know anything about her.

Well, that's easy enough to remedy. But not until I've put some damn food in me.

"Are you always angry?" she asks.

I look at her in surprise, because the question actually gives me pause. Her question doesn't anger me. It's honest, and not necessarily disrespectful. I'll have questions for her, too.

"No," I tell her. "Though as *pakhan*, much responsibility falls on my shoulders. I don't like when I give an instruction and it isn't obeyed. I expect those who are under my authority to do what they're told."

"Clearly," she mutters.

"Clearly," I repeat. "When that doesn't happen, I do get angry. But that isn't a constant."

"Good to know," she mutters, pursing her lips and looking away.

"When we get back to Boston, you'll have duties as wife to the *pakhan*. To begin, you'll see someone who will help prepare you for the day," I tell her. "As my wife, you must be presentable at all times."

She purses her lips but doesn't say anything.

"My men are trained to obey, and each of them demands obedience from his partner. They will expect that you have learned to obey me. Do you understand that?"

"Yeah," she says, but a sharp look makes her amend herself. "Yes, of course."

Perhaps we'll join them for breakfast after all. It will be what they call an "educational opportunity."

"So we begin today," I tell her, rising to my feet. "Take my hand and join me for breakfast."

We go to the door and she actually giggles to herself.

"What?" I ask her. "Something amusing?"

But she shakes her head and won't tell me, trying to sober, but the corners of her lips tug upward.

"Caroline," I prod. "Tell me."

"Fine," she says with a sigh. "You're just like the beast," she says. *"Join me for dinner, rawr."*

The beast? Who the fuck is the beast? Her comparison annoys me, even if I am secretly pleased that she's amused.

"Did the beast whip his pretty little wife's ass?" I ask pleasantly, and she quickly sobers then sighs.

"That I don't know," she mutters.

We walk in silence to the dining room, her little hand tucked into mine. When we arrive, Marissa and Nicolai are sitting at a small, circular table nearby. He nods, and Marissa stands to greet us.

Caroline flushes when Marissa gives her a quick hug and a probing look, as if to see if I've abused my new wife. Nicolai clears his throat and pulls Marissa's hand to make her sit.

The waitstaff brings us bacon, eggs, and toast. I allow Caroline to take her own place, and she quietly eats.

"Hungry?" I ask curiously as she polishes her plate off.

"Starving," she says, leaning back in her chair with a sigh. "And that was delicious."

"Did they not feed you well in your home?" I ask, finishing my own breakfast.

The question brings a fire to her eyes once more. "Clearly, I'm not underfed."

Oh, no, we won't go there.

"I only meant were you hungry before you came?" My tone is hard, commanding, reminding her not to get snappy with me and I hate when she makes deprecating remarks about her body.

She merely shrugs. "It wasn't that," she says. "But I preferred being in the kitchen than out of it. And there were people I didn't want to see, so I—" Then it's like someone flicks a switch. Her eyes shudder and her lips clamp shut. I look at her in surprise. What caused such a drastic response from her? "I preferred being in the kitchen," she repeats.

I nod, lift my hand, and order more food. "Do you?" I ask. "Do you know how to cook?"

She snorts out loud. "Know how to cook? Yes, certainly, though my brother hated if I spent time in the kitchen. Still, I learned from the best." For the very first time, her eyes light up and she clasps her hands beneath her chin. "I was passionate about it," she explains. She doesn't need to tell me. I can tell just from the light in her eyes.

"I see," I tell her with a nod. "Perhaps you can work with our chefs back in Boston."

She's holding the crust of a piece of toast when she freezes, the food halfway to her mouth. She swallows hard.

"You'd let me do that?"

Some choose to train with a stick, others with a carrot. I choose both.

"If you learn to behave, there are many things I'd allow you to do."

If she knows she can pursue what she calls her "passion," perhaps training her will go easier on the both of us with one contingency: she needs to prove she'll do as I say.

Marissa watches us keenly from where she sits, pretending she isn't listening to every word we say, so it comes as no surprise that when we rise, she leans over to talk to Nicolai and says something. He's staring at his phone frowning and nods absentmindedly for her to go. I watch her curiously as I take Caroline's hand and lead her out of the dining room. I'd bet money that she's up to no good.

Nicolai stands and gestures for me to wait. "I'll see you off," he says. "I need to take a call. You good, brother?"

I nod. He kisses Marissa on the cheek then leaves abruptly. Marissa follows behind us. She has something to say to me.

"Go ahead of me," I tell Caroline. She nods and does what I say. Marissa immediately pounces when Caroline is several paces ahead.

"You have to woo her, you know," she says, giving me a piercing look. Honest to God, Nicolai needs to keep a better handle on his wife. If she were mine…

"I don't need your advice, Marissa," I tell her. "Mind your own fucking business."

"This *is* my business," she says, then to my shock, she grabs my arm to stop me. "Let me ask you a question, Tomas."

I will have to talk to Nicolai. She oversteps.

"Go on," I spit out, not even bothering to attempt to hide my anger.

"Would you prefer to be wedded to a woman who adores the ground you walk on? Who does what you ask without question, because she's eager to please you? Or would you prefer to be married to a cold, detached woman who only does what you say out of fear of punishment?"

"It doesn't matter to me," I tell her honestly. "All I care about is that she obeys me."

Her eyes cloud and she purses her lips. "That isn't true, and you know it. If you'd only take the time to really *win* her, to really get to know who she is and how she ticks, you may find that she is far easier to get along with than if you force her hand."

"I don't remember asking you," I tell her, pulling away. "Now no more of this or I'll call Nicolai."

"Just think about it!" she yells down the hall as I march toward my wife. "Please, just think about it."

And dammit, I can't help but do just that.

Goddamn Marissa.

Chapter 6

Caroline

I HAVE no idea what Marissa said to him, but his eyes are narrow and that stern brow of his is drawn when he takes my arm, firmer than before. "I've ordered our bags taken to the car," he says. "We've got a ride to the airport."

"Yes. What was she saying to you?"

His lips thin and his jaw firms, and a cloud passes over his features. "None of your business."

"Alrighty then," I mutter. This guy is a barrel of laughs. I've had the briefest moments of fleeting thoughts that I might actually learn to fall for him one day... a *little*. He's hot as hell, and maybe will make a devoted husband. And hell, the way he commands my body with the faintest touch or wisp of seduction.

But just as soon as the idea comes to me, I dismiss it.

There's no way I'll fall for a man like him. He's a veritable caveman like my brother, and I *despise* my brother almost as much as Andros.

I barely even see where we're going until I realize we're exiting, and a car idles at the curb waiting for us.

"Tomas!" One of the men who was in the dining room earlier stands nearby, his phone up to his ear. He shuts it off and gestures for Tomas to join him.

"Stay here," he orders. And then he's gone, though not far.

I wonder what Boston will be like. I've always wanted to visit but I've never been allowed to leave our home in San Diego. I wonder how much Tomas will allow me to explore.

I sigh and close my eyes, leaning against the car, as Tomas speaks to his friend, willing myself to be anywhere but here. I hate being out of control like this and at the mercy of another. It grates against everything I stand for. I start when I hear footsteps approach, and step instinctively closer to the door of the car when I see it isn't Tomas but one of my brother's men.

I know instinctively that Tomas considers me his, now, and will not take kindly to anyone speaking to me. But he's deep in conversation with his friend, his back to us, and doesn't notice. "Get away," I say.

"There you are," he says, ignoring me. I don't even know this one's name. A newer recruit, he works under Andros, but that's all I know about him. He's thin and lithe with oily blond hair and a scraggly beard, his green eyes both hungry and beady. I wonder what he's doing here. I don't know all the ways of the Bratva, how the others should treat a man of a leader, but I know he shouldn't be here. He's bold as hell coming anywhere near me.

"Andros wants a picture," he says.

"Tell him to go to hell. I'm married now." It's the first time since I took my vows that I actually feel almost pleased to say this.

But the man pulls out a phone and flicks it on, then raises it. The son of a bitch isn't giving anything to Andros. On instinct I flip him off. Instantly, he turns livid, his eyes narrowed in anger and he launches at me, his fist raised. I cringe and scream blocking my face, prepared for the attack.

"You stupid bitch," he growls. "Think you have the right to—"

But he doesn't get any further when he's lifted straight in the air and away from me. I gasp when he howls and flails, until I see Tomas' furious face. In a second, the body of my assailant flies into the air in an arc before he lands in a sickening thump on the ground. Tomas steps over to him and kicks him viciously. I wince when he places his boot on the man's neck.

"Tell me what he did, Caroline," Tomas says evenly

before he drags the guy up off the ground. He holds him by the back of the shirt, dangling like a piece of clothing hung on a line. This time it's an easy matter to do what my husband says.

"He demanded a picture for my brother's friend," I say, my voice shaking but determined. "When I told him no and flipped him off, he tried to hit me."

Tomas grows deadly quiet, the only indication he's breathing at all his flared nostrils. I haven't known him for long but already know that the stillness means danger for the man on the ground. In the background, Nicolai stands with narrowed eyes, a weapon drawn, and a few paces away, I see the man who officiated at our ceremony watching as well. Tomas takes a deep breath in then lets it out and pulls his gun from his pocket. He eyes on the man on the ground.

They speak in Russian. Tomas yanks the man's phone out of his pocket and tosses it to me. I catch it mid-air.

"Call your brother on video chat," he orders. My hands shaking, I obey. Aren picks up on the second ring, glaring into the camera.

"Caroline? What the fuck? You stupid bitch—"

It's like their pet name for me. I clench the phone so hard my knuckles whiten. When Tomas' furious gaze lands on me, he signals for me to train the camera on him.

"I'll tell you what the fuck," Tomas says furiously. "I

married your sister yesterday. And one of your men tried to attack her today. Why he thought it wise to come within a mile of her makes no sense, but I thought you'd want to heed my warning." He cocks his gun and bends, pointing it at the back of the man's head. The guy he's got pinned starts crying like a baby, and it sickens me. He knows with one pull of a trigger, he's dead. "If any of your men ever come within a mile of her, I'll kill them. Do you understand me?"

My heart begins to beat more rapidly. He won't allow any of them near me. That includes Andros.

And if I'm honest, I *want* Andros to disobey, if only to give Tomas a reason to make good on his promise.

"Jesus, I'm sorry," he says. "I have no idea what he was doing or why he was anywhere near her."

"I do," I bite out. Tomas looks to me, his hand on the gun shaking with rage.

"Andros sent him," I say to Aren. Aren's eyes narrow on me, but he doesn't respond, well aware my bear of a husband stands just paces away.

Then my brother is apologizing, bending over backwards to tell Tomas he had nothing to do with it. This is a side of him I've never seen, and I'm a little in awe that he cows so easily to Tomas. Clearly, there's much at stake here. He gave me to Tomas for a reason, and he doesn't want to incur Tomas' wrath.

"Would you like me to do you a favor, then?" Tomas asks. "I'm happy to pull this trigger."

The man on the ground whimpers, his eyes shut, and he begs for mercy.

"No?" Tomas shakes his head. "That's a shame. But I'll honor that as long as you make it clear to your men that your sister belongs to *me*. Also?" He turns the full force of his glare to my brother. "You ever call your sister a stupid bitch again, I'll personally fly to San Diego and you'll deal with *me*. You'll treat my wife with respect or suffer the consequences."

He gestures for me to hand him the phone, puts his gun away, then lifts the guy on the ground up by the shirt. He may not have shot him, but this is far from over. Tomas rears back and hits the man so hard in the jaw I can hear bone snap. Then knees the man so harshly I wince and begin to cry as he unleashes the full punishing power of his fists. I can't look. It's brutal and savage and terrifying. I scream and cover my mouth with my hands when strong arms pull me away, turning me from the brutal scene. Nicolai pulls me away, shielding me from the beating. He brings me over to the waiting car, but I can hear Tomas from where I am.

"I hope you never forget my face. I hope you fucking know who you crossed today."

Opening the door, Nicolai shoves me in and locks the door. I cover my face with my hands, my emotions tight and unchecked.

He's vicious. Savage, even. But hell, I need a savage

in my court, and Christ is he ever. The way he told my brother to respect me…

I roll down the window with shaking hands, needing to see what happens next. Nicolai's on the phone, issuing sharp commands, and within a minute, several large SUV's pull up to where we stand. To my shock, Tomas comes to me, yanks open the door, and pulls me out. His fists are covered in blood when he grabs my arm, fingerprint splotches of blood painting my pale skin. I yield to him, allowing him to drag me around and yank me to his chest.

Somehow, I intuitively know he needs this. He needs *me*. He captures my mouth in a hard kiss, his blood-stained fingers slipping on my chin as he grips me so hard, he'll leave marks. He's holding my face to his with one hand while his second hand is raised with his phone.

I blink when he releases me. He took a selfie?

Then a second later, I understand why. He nods to Nicolai.

"Sending you a picture of me and my wife. Make sure you release that to every fucking Bratva in America and beyond. Tell them that the woman who was Caroline Koslov no longer bears her brother's name." He pauses, and there's a note of raw pride in his voice when he continues. "She is now Caroline Dobrynin. *My wife.*"

Chapter 7

Tomas

I SWEAR I don't even see straight as we drive to the airport, my vision still blurred with rage. I'm thankful we have a driver, because I wouldn't trust myself to drive right now. I'm shaking, still. I regret that I didn't put a bullet in that man's head. If given the chance again, I won't hesitate.

It takes me a minute to realize that she's unfastened her belt and come around to sit beside me.

"Put your seatbelt on," I order. "It's dangerous to drive without one."

She holds my gaze for a moment before she obeys with trembling hands and looks away. Caroline is no submissive, but I think she's a little shell-shocked. I gentle my voice.

"Caroline, look at me."

She brings her large eyes to mine, wide and fearful, as a tear rolls down her cheek. "This is a brutal world," she says in a whisper. "And I will never get used to it."

I run my thumb along her tears and drag the wet to the splash of blood on her chin, using the salty water to clean her. I press a button on the door. "Do you have anything at all I can use to clean up?" I ask the driver.

"Certainly, sir." Through the opening between the back and front seat, he lowers the divider and hands me a small package of wipes. He'd probably have a sewing kit, breath mints, and a safety pin if I asked him.

"Thank you," I tell him, hitting the privacy screen button so we're alone again. But before I can open the package, she reaches over and takes it from me, tears open the top, and yanks out a few damp wipes. Taking my bloodied hand in both of hers, she wipes the red off of me. I watch, mesmerized, as the white towelette becomes stained in pink.

"This is a brutal world," I agree, using the very words she did. "And I don't ever want you to get used to it."

She looks up in surprise, then looks away again, finishing cleaning one hand before she takes the second in both of hers. I like the feel of my rough hands in her softer, gentler ones. I can't remember anyone holding my hands like this, and it seems fitting the first person to do so is the woman I've taken as wife.

"What do you mean?" she asks, as she rubs a clean wipe along my skin, wiping away the traces of the brutal beating I just administered.

I'd fucking do it again.

"If you grow used to violence, you become complacent," I tell her. "I fight hard to let the violence sharpen me, not dull me." I sigh. "Believe it or not, Caroline, I'm not typically a violent man."

To my surprise she actually giggles at that, and it's the prettiest little sound I've ever heard. It cuts through the tension, and I feel the lines around my mouth softening a bit.

"You don't believe me?"

"No," she says again. "You're the beast, remember?" Her eyes come to mine, so beautiful and momentarily trusting. "You have fits of rage like he does, but deep inside I wonder if you're as tender as he is."

I roll my eyes. "Fairy tales," I mutter. "I have no time for that, and I'm not sure I like being called a *beast*."

But she's still holding my hand and gets my attention with a firm tug. I look back to her. She's grown serious now, her luminous eyes wide and sincere. "Fairy tales are the dreams we grew up with," she says. "And though real life isn't a fairy tale, there are parallels we can all draw from."

I'm tempted to roll my eyes again, but she's so sincere I can't bring myself to do it. "Fair enough," I mutter, which makes her laugh again. I'm not sure what she finds so amusing, but I enjoy her laughter. It loosens something in me. "It will be rare for you to see me enact violence as I did today," I tell her. "I have men who work as my strike force. And if I do have to punish someone personally, I'll do my best to keep you apart from it." Then my stomach tightens. "Unless someone threatens your safety again."

I don't realize I've clenched my hand into a fist until she winces, her fingers trapped in my grasp. I release her so quickly her hand falls to my lap. I take the wipes from her and remove one before I dab her chin, then clean her off in silence. She sits still, allowing me.

"Or unless *I'm* the person you're punishing," she says, casting me a look through lowered lashes that's at once fetching and coy. My cock tightens, my pulse throbbing at the thought of her earning a real punishment. Though I want her obedience, a part of me hopes she gives me reason to administer punishment. Pleasure and pain, dominance and submission, the need to control and master fuels me. Deeply erotic. Intoxicating. Dangerous, if not consumed in moderation.

I swallow hard, needing to both change the subject and find answers to what troubles me. "Tell me, Caroline," I say, making sure there's both command and sympathy in my voice. I want her obedience and even her fear but finding the answers to the questions I have are crucial. If I push too hard, she'll hide from me.

I wait until I've captured her gaze and she drops my hand. We're sitting so close in the small, intimate interior of the car that our knees brush.

"Yes?" she asks. Her chin quivers. She knows I'm going to ask her things she doesn't want to answer.

"What's your brother like?"

Her startled blink tells me she didn't expect me to start there, but I need to know who he is and what fuels him.

Her frank expression tells me she hides nothing when she replies. "My brother," she says with a bitter note in her tone. "Is a complete and utter asshole."

I'm not surprised, but it isn't enough of an answer.

"Tell me more." Though he's below me by quite a bit in rank in the Bratva, his rank within his own brotherhood gives him power and prestige. His position is something I need to be wary of.

"He is the type that preys on the innocent," she says. "A bully, as it were. When he was a child, he found a cruel man who lived nearby that bred his dogs and sold the puppies for profit. My brother's favorite pastime was taking the pups that didn't sell and drowning them to earn pocket money."

I listen without comment, allowing her to continue. "He will do anything and everything to earn more power in the brotherhood, even if it means selling out his own brothers." She laughs mirthlessly. "Or sister."

I nod. "Did he treat you poorly?"

Holding my eyes, she nods. "He did." But she says nothing more.

I note this with calculating precision. He's given me no reason to get on a plane and hunt him down, not, at least, according to protocol. When he mistreated her, she didn't belong to me. That said, I'll find a reason to seek retribution for what he's done.

"Why did one of your brother's men wish to take a picture of you?"

At first, she doesn't answer, worrying her lip as she gazes out the tinted window, muted houses and buildings flitting past us as we drive on.

"For Andros," she whispers. At the paper-thin skin at her temple, a tiny light blue vein throbs. Her voice shakes, but she continues despite her evident pain in discussing this with me. "Andros will not like that I'm gone. My brother didn't tell him until the last minute, and he made sure Andros was not one of the men who brought me here."

"Who is Andros?"

Her answer is swift and vehement. "The devil incarnate." The tone of her voice is chilling and harsh, her eyes narrowed in utter hatred.

I need more than that. I'll find out who Andros is, as well. Anyone that causes that type of response in her… But I plod on carefully, so she doesn't retreat.

"I've met some evil men in my line of work," I tell her, keeping my tone casual. "In fact, I'd say most of us had a bit of the devil in us. Some more so than others." I stare at my clean hands that were covered in another man's blood only minutes ago. If she knew what I've done to get where I am, the steps I've taken within the Bratva to rise to power…

"Not like him," she says, her tone frigid. "I've met many of you. You live by a code of conduct. And yes, some of you do wicked things." She sighs, looking out the window. "The truth is, most of you do. I know this." Shaking her head, she crosses her arms on her chest and pulls inward. "But I've never met a man with soulless eyes until I met him."

He hurt her. The wounds he inflicted may be hidden, but she bears the scars of something terrible and cruel.

I'll find out what he did if it kills me. I start with the most obvious question, though I know before I ask her that she won't tell me.

"What did he do to you?"

Predictably, she pinches her lips together, rubbing her hands up and down her arms as if she's freezing cold. She won't say, and I suspect it's because she doesn't trust me. Not yet. She's just seen me beat a man and threaten to end his life. Why would she?

I'll find out what he did to her, if it takes me a year to earn her trust and respect. Even if I have to hire someone to investigate. I'll find out what he did, and he will pay.

"Caroline."

Though I know she won't tell me more, it's still unacceptable not to answer me when I speak to her. She looks to me, her eyes still shuttered after speaking of Andros.

"When I ask you a question, I expect an answer," I chide. "It's imperative that you obey me and respond when I speak to you. This time, I won't insist, but in the future I will."

At my challenge, her gaze narrows on me and her lips pinch tighter together. I'll have her answer me.

"Are you a virgin?"

A beat passes before she responds. I watch as she swallows hard. "You didn't want to know that before you took me? Didn't you want someone pure and untainted?"

"Answer the question." She will learn to obey me and answer my questions.

"No," she says, and at first, I think she's defying me. But no, she's answering my question.

"You're not a virgin?"

She snorts derisively. "Do you find it surprising that a woman who looks like me isn't a virgin? That someone would actually want to put his—"

"*Enough.*" I can't wait to get home to my own room where my tools lie at my disposal. One good round with a rattan cane ought to curb that tongue of hers. I wait until she's closed her mouth and sits silently before I continue. "Now that I have your undivided attention, this is as good a time as any to talk about your duties to me as my wife."

"Oh? Do go on," she says, her voice dripping in sarcasm. "When you're through, can we discuss your duties to me as my husband?"

Yes, she will *definitely* be giving me reason to punish her. I can't help but smile at her when I squeeze her knee. "I'm *well* aware of my duties to you as your husband."

A faint color creeps up her neck and tints her cheeks, and she swallows hard. I love making her flush like that.

"To begin, you'll stay in my bedroom," I tell her, and when her brow draws together, confused, I explain, "In the past, some *pakhans* have given their wives permission to wander freely, but for me that will be imperative."

"Right. So… always? I'm not allowed to leave the room?"

"You will," I tell her. "I'll give you freedom if you earn it. But what I mean is you will not have a room apart from me."

"Fair," she says, but I imagine she looks a little relieved. "In fact, I'd prefer that." I don't ask her why, but it pleases me she acquiesces to this readily. Some of my other demands will be harder for her to swallow.

"You'll be expected to obey me. I'll demand obedience, respect, and honesty from you."

"Of course." Though she verbally agrees, her body language gives me a different response, her rigid spine and fiery eyes promising me that earning her obedience and respect will be a difficult task.

"You'll accompany me to social obligations, both within our brotherhood and with extended brotherhoods."

Her lips part and her eyes widen a little, but she swallows and nods. I'm a little surprised by her response. "Do you... do you have many social obligations?" she asks.

"As *pakhan*, I do." I continue to list her duties. "I'll expect you to bear my children—"

"No."

I didn't expect such a defiant and immediate response. She explains herself promptly. "I will not bring children into Bratva life," she says. "Never."

Though I dislike the defiance in her voice, I can't help but admire her tenacity. The woman's will is made of iron.

"Caroline, married couples within the Bratva bear children," I explain to her. "We will need an heir to take on my role when it's time."

"*No.*"

We will see about that. I will do what I have to. Impregnating my wife is crucial but doing so against her will puts everything else at risk. Plus, I hate the very thought. I want to come home after a hard day of work to a wife that's eager for my return, not plotting my demise.

The window between us and our driver rolls down. "Sir, we've arrived at the airport."

"We will speak more of this later," I say, as we cruise to a stop.

"We will *not*."

We're about to exit the vehicle. My men wait for us and will attend us on our journey home, and when we arrive more of my men will greet us. She *will not* speak to me this way.

I reach for her jaw and grasp it in my hand, noting the way her eyes widen when I yank her gaze to mine. "That's enough," I tell her. "No more defiance from you. No more backtalk. If you speak out of turn again, I'll remove your privilege of speaking."

Her eyes are molten embers. I can feel her jaw clench as she glares at me.

"Fine."

I shake my head, and she growls a little. I hold her more firmly.

"Yes, sir," she manages through clenched teeth.

"Good girl," I tell her with sarcasm. She's not a good girl at all but a very, very naughty one.

The door to our vehicle opens and our bodyguards and escorts wait outside. I put my arm out for her to take, which she does without comment. I lead her to the where our private plane waits, the entryway by the gate surrounded by my men, armed.

"That's the plane we're taking?" she says when we arrive. The plane stands right outside this window, right near the loading dock.

"It is," I tell her. "Private, and the swiftest in our fleet."

"Excellent."

The woman needs a good, hard spanking over my lap then a good, hard fucking to tame her. To start, anyway. It's a shame we won't have room or privacy enough on the way home, though I'll be sure we do after we arrive.

"Are you a nervous flier?"

"I haven't flown enough to say," she explains. "Though my last trip I was nervous before I got on, so yeah, I probably am."

What the hell did they do to her before they brought her to me? Still, I know she was afraid of coming at all. Now it looks like my wife is nervous.

We board, and I have her sit right beside me. This is a first-class flight, only two and a half hours long, so there's plenty of room for both of us, as well as private TV's, music, and in-flight food and drink. I'm curious what she'll choose as entertainment. I want to know everything about her.

"Do you need something to help you for the flight?"

She shakes her head, but she's already white knuckling the seat.

The attendant brings us a menu. I order Caroline a glass of champagne and orange juice.

"What if I don't want that?" she says, her lips pulled into an almost-pout.

I shrug. "You could fight me if you'd like. But it'll help you relax for the flight. And if I were you, I'd save my fight for something bigger. A little drink can help loosen you up."

The pout loosens a little. When the drinks arrive, I pour the champagne and orange juice in one glass for me and another for her.

"Cheers. To our honeymoon."

"Cheers," she says, clinking the glass with chagrin and a sigh. She says nothing about our honeymoon. We both know we aren't the traditional couple, and we won't follow the usual methods or customs.

She may not like her circumstances or me, and I've already accepted that. But given what she's come from, I hope I can offer her something at least a little better.

I have two more days to consummate this marriage.

When she finishes her drink, I pour her a second.

"Drink." Wordlessly, she holds my eyes and obeys. "This is delicious," she says. "Do you drink often?"

I shrug. Social drinking is a way of life for me and my brothers, though I hold my liquor well. "My father was a mean drunk and I vowed I would never follow in those footsteps. You?"

"I never drink," she says, while she upends her glass and polishes off her second. "I'm too much of a control freak." She finishes her drink and places it on the tray in front of her, then leans and head back and closes her eyes. "But for now, I'd like to rest."

I wait until she falls asleep, her head tipped to the side. She's never had alcohol. She was mistreated at the hands of her brother, and her brother's friend.

What does she secretly long for? Fantasize about? What is it that her heart longs for?

I make it my mission to find out.

Chapter 8

Caroline

"CAROLINE." I'm in my bed, covered in blankets, and Andros has broken into my room. I've fastened bolts and locks but no matter what I do, he finds a way to me. This time, I will fight him. He will not take advantage of me. Not now. Not ever again. Under my pillow I've hidden a knife. If I can only take it out, when he pulls back the covers, I will plunge it between his ribcage and twist it until he bleeds out to his death. I reach for the knife, but I can't find it. My fingers search fruitlessly for the cold metal blade but find nothing.

"Caroline." The voice is more insistent now, and I'm being shaken. I don't wake yet, because I'm still in a panic, trying to find the knife.

"Caroline."

I blink awake, staring into Tomas' dark brown, concerned eyes.

"We've just landed," he says. "We're here."

My head feels as if it's been stuffed with cotton, the taste of the drink he plied me with now sour in my mouth. I forgot that a plane ride to Boston would take fewer than three hours. I stretch, ignoring the way my heart still pounds in my chest. I don't remember what I dreamt about, but it's left a sad weight on my chest that only worsens when I remember where I am and where we're going.

I'm married to a fierce beast of a man who expects obedience and submission from me. I know no one in his brotherhood and don't even know anything about Boston. I'm tired, my body still on West Coast time and not yet used to the three-hour time difference. Everything is new to me, but considering where I've come from, that isn't a bad thing.

I have so many questions for him, but it's time to exit the plane. He takes me by the hand and leads me down the small ladder that leads to the runway. It's a little chilly and rainy, and I shiver. A full dozen men stand at attention as if we're royalty and they're prepared to do his bidding.

Hell, maybe we are. I don't know anything about this group at all. I know that Tomas is *pakhan*, and with that bears the weight of responsibility and prestige. Does he command the respect of fellow leaders? The way his men look to him is a far cry from the way my brother's men did. They look to Tomas with respect and deference, their eyes on me curious but detached. I saw what he did to the man in Atlanta. They likely know to keep their distance from me.

Good. I prefer it that way.

Tomas is shaking hands, and they're clapping him on the back, congratulating him in Russian.

"Sir, we've prepared a banquet tonight," one of the men says. "To celebrate your marriage."

"Excellent," Tomas says. "Thank you."

The man goes on to list the political officials who will be in attendance, as well as the prominent local businessmen. I cringe inwardly but don't respond. I *hate* the idea of being paraded around in front of a crowd of beautiful, wealthy, and influential people. *Hate it*.

But when I remember the litany of duties I have as his wife, I sigh. I have no choice. Not this time.

And even if I did... *would* I choose another road? Tomas is fiercely protective. Though the beating he gave the man in Atlanta terrified me, the very memory making my stomach clench in fear, I like knowing he will not let anyone harm me. It feels nice to be cherished by someone, even if the only reason he treasures me is because he's proprietary. Because I belong to him.

He doesn't care about you.

I can't help but admonish myself. Though I've been mistreated, that doesn't mean that I can fall for him. That I can let my silly hopes and weak desires influence my behavior around him at all.

A car waits for us, and I wearily step to the door when one of his men opens it for me. "Welcome to Boston," he says with a smile.

"Thank you."

The windows here are also tinted, but this interior is larger than the last car we were in. Tomas joins me and we leave the airport.

"How many men do you command?" I ask him.

He shrugs. "Somewhere in the neighborhood of four dozen total, though some live in areas outside our immediate vicinity."

Four dozen? He has nearly fifty men under his authority?

Wow. My brother had ten, and some obeyed in surly reluctance.

"Are you obedient to anyone?" I ask. I'm only superficially aware of the laws of Bratva hierarchy.

He smiles. "Only to the laws of the brotherhood."

The laws of the brotherhood. Like, say, *consummate your marriage to your new wife?*

Our drive takes about half an hour through traffic. The entire time, Tomas frowns at his phone, his fingers flying over the small screen. I assume he's doing work of some sort. Finally, we pull off the highway, and park in a huge parking lot filled with powerful, shiny trucks, SUVs and more lucrative sports cars. This brotherhood has money. Tomas leads us out.

He takes our bags and leads me to a large brick building that looks almost like an apartment building. It's well-kept and maintained outside, neatly trimmed green bushes flanking the entrance, and stone steps leading to the main door. A wreath graces its center, with oranges and golds.

It isn't until then that I really look around us. I couldn't see much from the airport and even less through the tinted windows of our ride, but now my eyes widen in surprise and I breathe out, "*Wow.*"

It's… like nothing I've seen before. The trees around us are afire with golden, burnt orange, and crimson leaves. We've arrived during peak foliage in New England, the magnificent vibrant colors more beautiful than I could've imagined. We don't see a change in seasons like this in San Diego.

"Welcome home, Mrs. Dobrynin," Tomas says with a smile. He's proud, but I'm not sure if he's proud of his home or me. Both? "Have you ever visited New England in fall?"

"Never," I breathe. "It's stunning."

He chuckles. Something in me thrills at the sound, so rare it's precious. I like making him smile.

"I'm honored to witness your first visit." Opening the door to the large building, he gestures for me to go in ahead of him. I do, still turning to look around us at everything I missed before the large, solid door shuts.

"How long does it last?" I ask him.

"Weeks," he says. "It's a stage, a process if you will. What begins as minor coloring as the leaves die off morphs into full, beautiful foliage. But the beauty is a sign of dying. The leaves need to die off before new ones grow."

I mull over his words quietly, the romantic in me wondering if it's a sort of metaphor. Does everything die in beauty before welcoming new growth and opportunity?

"How many weeks do we have left?" I ask him.

He shrugs. "All depends on the weather."

"My guess is three." A soft female voice comes from behind me. I start, then swivel around to look at who spoke. She's a pale blonde woman wearing a simple dress. When I turn to look at her, she flushes madly, as if embarrassed that she captured my attention. She looks as if she wants the earth to swallow her hole, which amuses me considering she volunteered this information. Do *I* intimidate her? Or does she always flush so easily?

"Yvonne," Tomas says in greeting. She bows her head when he speaks to her and doesn't meet his eyes.

"I spoke out of turn, sir," she whispers. "I'm sorry."

"You're fine," he says. "You're allowed to speak." His permission startles me. What sort of command does he hold that others wonder if they're allowed to speak?

"Yvonne, meet my wife Caroline. Caroline, Yvonne." I feel a bit shy myself after the introduction.

She shakes my hand, her own cold and clammy.

"Pleased to meet you," I say.

"Yvonne, where is Yakov?"

"He said he'd be waiting for you in your office, sir."

Tomas nods and looks to me. "Yvonne, will you show Caroline to our room? A few things have happened that I need to catch up on with Yakov."

"Yes, of course."

Yvonne comes to me and gestures for me to follow her. It surprises me how hard it is for me to leave Tomas. I know nothing of where we are or who I'll meet within these walls, and my past experience makes me hesitant to be without the man who protects me. Reluctantly, I go down a hall while Tomas walks in the opposite direction.

"Who is Yakov?" I ask her.

"My husband," she says quietly, a small smile playing on her lips.

We walk in silence, and I'm pleased to note she seems happy to be married to him.

"And your husband…" I think for a moment. Tomas says he's under no one's authority, which means her husband must be under Tomas' authority. "He answers to Tomas?"

She nods eagerly, her eyes wide and brilliant. "We all do," she says, then adds as an afterthought. "Even you."

I don't respond, mulling this over.

"How long have you been married?" I ask.

"Not long. Only several weeks."

There are so many things I want to ask her. Surely Tomas wouldn't have allowed me to be alone with her if I wasn't to speak of my situation?

"Do you know how I came to be here?" I ask her curiously.

"Yes. You were given to Tomas by your brother." She doesn't even flinch. This is nothing out of the ordinary to her.

She leads me up a flight of stairs. The wooden floorboards are shiny and polished but creak a little when we step on them. This is an old house, but well kept. The ceilings are so high I couldn't reach them on a ladder, and the staircase we're ascending goes up four more flights. I wonder how many of his brotherhood live here. And just when I wonder why he didn't guard me more heavily, and I'm flirting with the idea that he actually might trust me a little, I see the two armed men following only several paces behind us. He wouldn't need to protect me within the walls of the brotherhood commands. It only stands to reason, then, that they're here to make sure I don't leave.

My belly drops to my toes and I don't hear what Yvonne is saying at first. I'm too busy taking in the large, magnificent paintings on the walls, magnificent leaders painted in bold brush strokes, many wearing uniforms and bearing arms. I look to Yvonne. "Your husband likes to surround himself with those he looks up to. The greats, he calls them."

I nod. It's interesting to note. I recognize none of them.

When we reach the landing on the second floor, she takes a right and leads me down a long hallway. There's a small table on this floor with a vase overflowing with bright yellow and golden flowers, the fragrance vibrant and intoxicating. I remember the home I came from, my little room that was no more than a closet, the stark white walls and utilitarian black and gray tiled floors. I wonder if the furnishings of a home speak to the character of its occupants. But sometimes I think too much. I hope too much. And I've learned doing so is very, very dangerous.

"This is the door to Tomas' quarters," Yvonne says, looking down at the floor as she bites her lip. "He told me to come here with you, but I'm not sure if he kept it locked." Gingerly, she tries the knob, giving a startled little gasp when the door swings open. She's so easily frightened, I wonder at her history.

Gesturing for me to go in ahead of her, she waits patiently. I step inside, and feel my jaw drop in surprise. I didn't expect a place like this.

For starters, it's huge, the large open floor plan opening to a sitting room, an office, several bedrooms and a kitchen off to one side as well. I step inside and look around at everything in silence. I've never seen anything like this.

The entryway is crafted in golds and creams, with a circular marble floor that gleams from the light of the overhead chandelier. There's a large round mirror with a golden frame on the wall and below it, a matching table and framed landscape prints. Beyond the sitting room is a formal dining room and kitchen area, also decorated in cream and gold. I stare at the chandelier above the dining room table, little crystals dangling and catching the light. I want to explore every inch of this gorgeous home, every fine detail and luxury.

"Tomas has outfitted this place well," she says with a smile. "And before you came, he asked me for my advice."

"Your advice?" I ask. What sort of advice would a man like Tomas need?

"Yes," she says in her soft voice, and her pale face flushes pink again. "He asked me to help pick out some clothes for you, new bedding, and things like that. I hope you like them."

I walk around the apartment in a sort of haze, taking in the luxury detail. "Oh, I'm sure I will," I tell her. "I've never had anything like this."

"I understand," she says. "Me neither."

She leaps a foot when someone knocks at the door. "Are you expecting someone?" she asks. I shake my head no. Walking over to the peephole, she looks out. "Oh, that's Eliott and his team," she says, opening the door. "You'll like him."

Unlocking the door, she opens it to welcome a very attractive young man who has spiky black hair and small round spectacles magnifying bright blue eyes. He wears a hot pink t-shirt and designer black jeans, and behind him he brings several men carrying so many things I can't keep track.

"Oooohhhh," he says stepping into the large entryway. "Oh, my love, I cannot wait to get my hands on you."

He has a thick French accent and is immediately all up in my space. I blink in surprise. Tomas sanctioned this?

"Caroline, Eliott is a stylist Tomas has hired to take care of you," she says. "It's time for me to take my leave. Enjoy, and I'll likely see you this evening for dinner." She's gone, and I'm left with this team of people I've never met. I stand dumbly in front of them.

"I'm...Caroline," I say awkwardly, giving them a small smile.

"Of course you are," Eliott says. He's got a heavy French accent, his hand anchored on his hips, he wags his finger in front of me. "And you are so beautiful, it comes as no wonder Tomas chose you."

I blink. Is he looking at the wrong girl? I must look bewildered because he throws his head back and laughs.

"Oh, darling," he says, drawing the words out as if they're sticky and sweet like caramel, "little do you know what Eliott will do for you. We have disposable contacts so you can lose the glasses and stop shielding those beautiful eyes from the world." He reaches for my hair. I flinch but he ignores me, gathering the insane, untamed waves between his fingers and twirling them. It feels immediately intimate and so shocking, I cringe. Would Tomas approve?

And how can I be so concerned about what he thinks already?

Eliott continues, unaware of my inner turmoil. "This hair needs a good cut and some highlights to bolster the body, but it's thick and full and lustrous." He makes a sound of approval. "What woman wouldn't kill for hair like this."

"Are you high?" I ask him, completely baffled by his admiration. "This is frizz ball hair to the nth degree. It's hideous."

"Oh, hush," he says, playfully smacking my arm. "Sacrilege." He snaps his gum and winks at me. "You wait to see what Eliott does for you." He claps his hands over his head. "Come, team. Let us beautify the new bride."

Chapter 9

Tomas

I DON'T like being apart from her. Though I trust the men I've sent to guard her and I trust Yvonne, and I even trust Eliott and his team of men who should be with her now, after what happened in Atlanta, I want her where I can see her. Where I can touch her. Where I can throw my body over her to protect her if any harm comes her way. But I am *pakhan,* and I have business to attend to.

Yakov is in my office, one knee crossed over the other when I enter.

"Yakov," I greet.

"Sir, how are you?" he asks. He wants to know how everything went. I fill him in about the wedding, briefly touch on Caroline, then tell him about the incident before we left.

"Bastard," he says. "I hate Aren Koslov. I'm glad you took his sister. Arranged marriage aside, you probably rescued her."

I don't tell him that I agree with this suspicion.

"I'm not sure I trust her yet, though," I tell him. "I'm keeping her under a watchful eye. She's willful and disobedient, among other things."

Yakov smirks. "Aren't they all?"

I roll my eyes at him, but he only laughs. Yakov was commanded by me to take a wife from a virgin auction. He purchased Yvonne but has treated her with kindness and it shows. She's dedicated to him, and clearly submissive. He's throwing down the gauntlet. Men in our brotherhood don't play by the rules.

"She'll learn to obey you," he says, sobering. Given what we do and where we rank, she'll have no choice. A glint of humor lights his eyes. "And if you're lucky, she'll enjoy it."

He fills me in on what's happened in my absence and who to expect at this evening's dinner. I check in on a few of our transactions and instruct him to clear Aren's debt.

"Tomas, you know the rule, though, right?"

I nod. "Yeah. Consummate the marriage. Believe me, I know."

Yakov nods but doesn't pry. A prideful man like him would know that I don't want to take my new wife by force. I'll want her willing participation, though a little struggle is welcome. Anyone could take a woman by force. It takes a much stronger man to seduce her. I'm too proud, and I want her begging.

After going over everything I need to know, he leaves. I make the necessary phone calls for tonight. Lev, my brigadier, has made sure that food is prepared, the caterers coming this evening. He shows me pictures of the wedding cake he's gotten me, and the reception hall decorated with pearly white balloons and flowers. It feels almost normal, that we're celebrating our wedding reception this evening, and that I haven't taken her against her will and brought her here in payment for her brother's debt.

I spend over an hour going over details with Lev, answering calls and issuing commands for the security for tonight's event. After Aren's henchman threatened my girl, I'm not too thrilled that I'll be taking her into a crowded setting. I want her alone. I want her to myself.

I want to *own* her.

I wonder if she's afraid, and if so, what it is she fears most. Is she curious? Hopeful? Will she ask Yvonne how she came to be here, and what will she think of me when she does? But as a woman raised in Bratva life, I assume she will not be a stranger to our ways.

Several hours later, I'm ready to go to her and prepare for tonight, and when I reach my door, either side still flanked by guards, I hear voices talking within.

"Eliott and his team are almost finished," one of the guards says. I nod and open the door. When I step in, a hush falls over the apartment.

I've taken women here before but none with any permanence. No one has even so much as spent the night in my bed. Now, not only do I have a woman with me, that woman is my wife. This is all new to me, and I'm not sure how much freedom to give her. The protection I've ordered is for her safety as well as supervision. She could run, though I wonder where she'd go. From what little I've gathered; I doubt she'd want to return to her home in San Diego.

"Is that you, Tomas?" Eliott's voice, prettied up in his thick French accent, comes from the master suite's bathroom.

"It is." I kick my shoes off at the entrance, marveling at the way the housecleaners have prepared this place. There's a decided feminine touch that wasn't there before with flowers and even dainty throw pillows in my living room.

I like it.

It feels good to be home, and I feel a bit of the tension leaving me as I walk across the thick carpet toward the bedroom. I can pick out Caroline's voice talking to Eliott's team. I've only known her for a short time but already know the sweet but certain lilt. She's speaking in hushed tones, though, so I can't make out the words.

"We are not ready yet, sir!" Eliott says. "Out!"

But no one tells me to leave my own room. I open the door and enter.

Eliott sighs. "Of *course* he doesn't listen to me." I give him a warning look, but soon get distracted by the sight in front of me. "I told you she's not ready yet!" Eliott says, lifting his hands to shield her from me. "If you'd only give me a few minutes—"

"Put your hands down."

Eliott isn't Bratva but knows to obey. With a mournful sigh, he obeys and steps to the side. Caroline turns to me.

I can't help but stare unabashedly at the woman who sits in front of me. Gone are the cumbersome glasses, nothing shielding me now from her wide, beautiful eyes accented with thick lashes and arched brows. I don't even notice her scar I'm so enamored with everything else about her.

Her freckled complexion looks somehow softer, smoother, and though the freckles are still there, her face looks radiant. She *glows,* her cheeks faintly flushed, her delicate creamy skin begging to be touched. A light pink gloss adorns her full, pouty lips. I need to kiss those lips. Own them. Make them mine.

Her hair that was once wild and untamed now frames her face in silky sheets, so full and beautiful it affects her whole appearance. She clutches the tie to the robe she wears as if to shield herself from me. It won't work.

"What do you think?" Eliott says proudly, as I walk slowly toward her, my arms outstretched. I want to gather her in my arms, but an irrational part of me fears that if I do, she'll vanish like a ghost, as if this stunning woman in front of me is only a mirage.

"What do I think?" I repeat. "I think you and your team needs to leave this room." Her eyes widen and she takes an involuntary step back.

"Sir, I haven't even *dressed* her yet," he says, shaking his head, and I know if I was anyone other than the *pakhan*, he would slap my hand and send me out of here until he was done.

"It's precisely because you haven't dressed her yet that you need to leave," I tell him. "*Now.*"

He actually has the nerve to chuckle, gathering up his team and rustling out to the door.

"See you tonight," he says. I overhear him whisper to his assistant in a stage whisper, "I predict we will soon see little Bratva boys and girls in this house. You watch."

The door shuts. They're gone.

She stands in front of me, eyeing me with a good deal of trepidation. Capturing her lips between her teeth, she looks shyly my way.

"They did a good job," she whispers. "I—" She

freezes, and I wonder if she remembers my admonition not to make self-deprecating remarks. She was about to. "It's sort of miraculous," she finally mutters, like she can't even believe it. I'll let that pass.

"Come here."

I quirk a finger at her. Though taken with her beauty, I haven't forgotten my primary duty, to train her in obedience so we can fill our roles, so we can lead this group of men with the clear understanding of who we are and what our duties are. Holding my gaze, she comes to me, and it isn't until she's within arm's reach of me that I realize she's trembling.

When she reaches me, I take her hand and tug her closer. She gives a little squeal and trots quickly to me.

"Tomas," she whispers, fear written in her wide eyes. "I don't... please—"

But I ignore her. Whatever it is she fears, she'll face it and I will lead her. We don't have the luxury of a lengthy courtship or weeks to get to know one another. Tonight, our hall will be filled to capacity with the most powerful leaders in America. My men will come in droves, expecting to see me arrive with my wife on my arm. An obedient, beautiful, submissive wife.

I reach one hand to her thick, gorgeous hair, running my fingertips through it from scalp to tip. The first time I do it she tenses, but the second time she begins to relax. By the third, she's leaning into me, her eyes closed. The faintest scent of honey and violets lingers, carefree and feminine. It stirs something within me.

She's ignorant to how beautiful she is. I'm losing myself to her already, and she doesn't even know.

I kiss her forehead, marveling at the silky feel of her skin at my lips. Dragging my hand along her shoulder, I draw it down, grasping her lower back and pulling her to me. She grasps my shoulders, anchoring onto me as I make my way down from her forehead to the apple of her cheek, the tip of her nose, the delicate chin, her graceful neck. But I don't kiss her lips.

I release her just enough so that I can grasp the sash to her robe.

"Tomas," she breathes.

"Caroline. What do you have under that robe?"

"Undergarments," she says on a shaky whisper. One tug, and the tie comes undone.

"Show me."

With her head bowed, she shrugs out of the robe and lets it fall to the floor. She stands in front of me now wearing nothing but a push-up bra and the thinnest pair of panties. I feel as if I've just unwrapped a gift of immense worth, and I'm not worthy.

"Did they leave you clothes to change into?" I ask, looking around the room. Logically, I know they had to but a part of me wishes they didn't. I want to keep her in my room forever with nothing but this robe between us. And I could if I wanted to.

She swallows hard and points to a gown hung on a hook at the back of the bathroom door. It's pale blue and edged in delicate lace and silver, almost old-fashioned yet low-cut enough to be modern.

"I'll dress you myself," I tell her. "But first you will spend some time with me."

I can see her pulse at her neck, and when I take her wrist between my fingers, I can feel the way her heartbeat thunders.

"You're afraid."

"Of course." She swallows hard.

"What are you afraid of?"

A pause before she responds.

"You."

My cock tightens, the need to claim her hard and fast all consuming. I want to show her where fear can take us while at the same time giving her more to fear. She doesn't know what I have stored in this room, the tools in my closet and in the table beside the bed. The instruments of torture and pleasure I'll use to command her body to orgasm over, and over, and over again.

"When do we have to go?" she asks, lifting her fingers to her neck, an automatic move of self-protection. "I should maybe get ready, you know. It looks hard getting into that dress and my hair will have to be done again. And makeup. Maybe everything. You should maybe even call Eliott back."

It's cute how she's trying to distract me, as if mentioning a commitment will somehow make me forget I have a beautiful woman who is *all mine* standing in front of me. As if I don't command the time we arrive tonight. I could call everything off with one word. I answer to no one.

"Should we?" I ask. I close the distance between us with one step and bend at the knee, lifting her straight up in my arms and to my chest. She squeals like a little girl as I step toward the bed, her arms encircling my neck on instinct. "We have plenty of time, Caroline. *Plenty.*"

The bed is the largest one I could find, custom made. King-sized and four-poser, the headboard is sturdy and outfitted with solid rings to suit my purposes. I look briefly at the new bedding Yvonne purchased, pinks and ivory, just before I lay my wife down. I approve.

"What are you going to do with me?"

"Anything I want."

"Charming," she mutters.

I roll her over and slam my palm against her full backside. Though she gasps, she closes her mouth obediently.

"Tonight I want you on your best behavior. No backtalk or sarcasm, *detka.*"

"I'm not a brat!"

I chuckle. "Baby, brat. *This* time, I meant baby. The term can vary depending on your behavior." I tweak her nose. "You sure there isn't a brat in there?"

The way her brows draw together and she *hmphs* out loud, I suspect there's more *brat* in there than I first realized.

"Now close your eyes and no more talking," I tell her. "We're home now, and I'll only warn you once. In my closet hang my whips and tools, and I won't hesitate to punish you if I need to." A low throbbing stretches across my chest at the thought, and I swear she swallows, aware of the sexual tension between us.

Her lower lip sticks out and her brows draw together. "You're dying to punish me, aren't you?"

She knows. She fucking knows.

My dick presses up against her side, a steel rod that throbs with unadulterated need at her taunting. "You have no idea."

"That seems rather disordered. Deviant even. If I—"

I take her mouth with mine to silence her. It almost amuses me she calls me deviant.

She has no fucking clue.

I've long since given up any flirtation with normalcy. I like control. I like pain. I fuck hard, often, and without regret, and when I do, I want my woman beneath me, submissive, and begging.

Her delicate lips meld with mine, sweet and decadent like strawberries and cream. Gently, I explore the fullness of her lips with my tongue before I take her lower lip between my teeth and bite down. She bucks and gasps then moans when I reach for her back and unfasten her bra, still holding my mouth over hers.

I palm her full breasts and work my fingers over her nipples.

"You like that, *detka?*" I ask. "Do you, baby?" She can't answer pinned beneath me. When I take her mouth again, she moans into my mouth, filling me with her essence. She wants this so damn bad she doesn't even bother trying to resist me.

I work her nipples until she squirms and moans, then drive one of my fingers between her legs, pushing them apart. I release her mouth and kiss her jaw, her neck, the sweet valley between her breasts until I reach the fullness of her breast and her peaked nipple, fluttering whispers of adoration to this beautiful goddess of a woman.

"Prosit."

Beg.

She shakes her head, biting her lip to keep from crying out. I crash my palm on the fullest part of her thigh which makes her cringe and whimper, but she still shakes her head.

I will have her obey me if we need to travel the road of deep pain and contrition before I have her where I want her. I will have her deferring to me.

"No?" I ask, pulling away just long enough to fix her with a stern glare. She winces as if I struck her, then shakes her head again.

"Never," she whispers. "I won't *beg* you."

There's the girl I was after. There's the feisty one I wanted.

I shake my head with mock regret. "Baby, if you don't learn to beg, you'll never learn the pleasure that could be yours." I *tsk* under my breath. "And I'll also be forced to punish you."

I'm pushing off the bed when she protests, her voice shrill and nervous. "Punish me! Like I'm a prisoner or a child. I'm neither, Tomas. I'm *your wife*. And need I remind you that you're only setting me up so that you have a reason to punish me!"

"I am well aware of who you are, Caroline." I push off the bed and take a step toward the little bedside table, to my tools. "However, I'm not exactly sure you yet know who *I* am." I point my finger to her. "Stay in that bed until I come back to you or your ass feels my whip." I don't address her accusation. I won't deny it. I'm so eager to punish her my mouth is dry at the prospect.

And I mean every word. I'm fully prepared to strap her if I need to.

She watches me with curious, angry eyes, lying so

still I wonder if she's breathing. Removing a pair of handcuffs from the drawer beside the bed, I go back to her and quickly fasten her wrists. "Here we go again," she mutters. "Just like last night."

I ignore her protest. If she won't cooperate, I'll have to force her, and the prospect excites me. "No, not quite. This won't be like last night. Last night, you were given the opportunity to sleep when cuffed. This time, the restraints will hold you still for punishment." Her eyes flicker with fear, and she doesn't move when I open the door of the closet and look at the tools I have at my disposal. Tonight, will be a reminder and a warning. Foreplay. There will likely come a time when she needs more intensity, but tonight I'll choose the lesser implement. With a smile, I remove a feather-tipped riding crop. The tamest of the lot. I don't want her marked and wincing before our reception tonight, but a good taste of a lash will keep her tongue in check. Plus, the alternating sensation will keep her on her toes.

Her eyes follow the solid black in my hand, from the feather tip to the little square strip of leather at the bottom.

"How original," she quips. "A riding crop?"

"You know what this is?" I ask her, dragging it from her shoulder down her side, the leather traveling over her skin leaving goosebumps in its wake.

"A crop," she says. "Thought we established that."

"A crop designed for impact and sensation play," I tell her. I quickly unfasten the cuffs, lift her up, and place her chest-down on the bed. Positioning her hands on the headboard, I cuff her to the rings I have there. The bed bounces a little with the force, and I step back to admire how gorgeous she is. Her beautiful breasts swing free, her ass barely covered by thin panties and pushed prominently in the air, the quick movement making her full hair bounce in fragrant raves. Over her shoulder she shoots me a look that dares me to let the crop fly.

Swish. The leather strikes her, making a small splotch of faint pink bloom against her pale skin and eliciting the most beautiful little cry. I lash her again and again, each flick a little harder than the last. At first, she actually growls at me, cursing under her breath but unable to get away. She whimpers, squirming, when the crop lands with more intensity. When I've painted her a fetching shade of pink, I flip the wand around and tickle her abused flesh with the feather.

"Ohh!" she gasps in protest, squirming, likely surprised by the different sensation. I take the delicate feather-tipped crop and trace it up her back and to her neck, tickling her just there, before I flip the crop again and give her another sharp spank.

"Beg."

"*No.*"

I continue the same torturous teasing, alternating flicks of the crop and tickling feathers until she's moaning, her hips rising, and I know that if I touch her secret folds she'll be sopping.

Another swishing swing of the crop, "Beg me."

"*No.*"

I'm growing impatient.

"It's unfortunate you've chosen to be so stubborn," I say. "You'll need something more serious, then?"

Clenching her jaw, she refuses to give in.

I shake my head and cluck my tongue, walk to the bedside table and open it again. She watches every move. I take out a leather flogger and tap it against my palm. Tame, but would work if we had more time. I place it back in the drawer and take out a stout cane. Too harsh. Then I eye a lightweight but sturdy wooden paddle. I nod to myself. That will do well.

"You're crazy," she says with a scowl, staring at the solid wood. "Insane!"

"And you're stubborn as fuck," I say with admiration. "I like it."

Without another word, I place my hand on her lower back and slam the wood against her full ass cheeks.

"Ow!" she screams and bucks, but I've got her tightly secured. I do want to subdue her, but I also want to take her to a place where pain and pleasure blend. I don't strike her again yet but rather run my hand along her heated skin, massaging. She freezes, unsure of what I'm doing next. I drag my fingers along her inner thighs, so silky and warm to the touch.

"Beg."

This time there's a slight pause, and her refusal is tamer when she whispers, "*No.*"

I shake my head with mock regret. I'm not at all disappointed I need to continue to punish her. I hold her in place with my hand on the small of her back and bring the paddle down a second time, but lower so it catches the edge of her upper thighs.

"I will not have a disobedient wife," I scold. "You will do as I say and learn your place."

Smack.

A third swat with the paddle has her whimpering. Again, I stroke her inner thighs, but this time I go higher, just to the very edge of her sweet spot. Leaning down, I brace myself on the bed and blow out a breath, letting the warm air ghost over her skin. She shivers and ever so slightly parts her knees. With slow, deliberate moves, I graze her clit, just enough to arouse but not enough to really stimulate.

"Pl—" she freezes when she realizes she almost did what I asked. Again, I tease her, one gentle stroke of my fingers touching her most sensitive parts before I draw back.

"Beg."

She doesn't obey, but she doesn't defy me, either. I

lift the paddle and push it between her thighs, parting them, drunk on the scent of her arousal, the way she's fully at my mercy. I glide the paddle to her clit and gently push, making her moan so beautifully my cock aches with the need to fuck her.

"Caroline," I say sternly. A warning.

I move the paddle from side to side, working her clit with the hard edge. She's grinding on the pressure, her breathing labored, her fists clenching the sheets white-knuckled. I remove the paddle and graze it along her reddened backside, lift it back, and slam it again, but this time not quite as hard. She doesn't even flinch but moans when I spank her with firm, deliberate, sensual strokes.

"Beg." The command is sharp, demanding, and she bites her lip in response, her eyes closed so tightly I know she's warring within herself. I don't care how long this takes. I don't care how long I torture and punish her. The longer it goes, the harder I get.

Another tap of the paddle.

"Beg."

Smack.

"Me."

She won't.

Chapter 10

Caroline

I WILL NOT BEG.

I. Will. *Not.*

I don't care if he keeps me on the very edge of arousal or if he beats me with that goddamn frat paddle all night long, he will not make me cave.

"You are my husband," I hiss, as if somehow reminding him of this will get him to stop assaulting me. Husbands aren't supposed to treat their wives poorly. *Doesn't he get that?*

"I'm well aware of who I am," he says to me, and I swear the bastard chuckles. "But I think perhaps you've forgotten who *I* am."

I open my mouth to respond when I feel something wet and sensual slip between my legs and I clamp my mouth shut. There's nothing he won't stop at, apparently, because the next thing I know there's something… *vibrating* in me. Oh my *God.* He's stuck some kind of sex toy in me.

"Beg," he reminds me as the toy hums, sending bolts of electricity shooting through my limbs, my clit pulsing.

"My God," I say without even realizing I've spoken.

"Not him," he quips. "Beg *me. Your husband.* The man you took your vows to. The one who *owns* you."

As he speaks, he expertly teases me, making me grind against his hand. I've never felt anything like this before. The pain he inflicted somehow heightened my senses, making me even more aroused than ever when he teases and tortures me.

Another stroke, then another, and I'm right on the edge of coming, so close I can *taste* it, rainbow color already exploding behind my closed eyes, I can taste the sweet, delectable taste of bliss right there on the very edge.

But I won't cave. There is no way I will let this man own me the way he says he will. I won't be the little fuck toy he wants. I won't obey his every whim as if he's majesty of this castle, no matter who else bows to him under his authority and command. I won't.

He can't have me that easily.

If I don't beg him, he won't let me come and *I need to.*

Then he stops. He *stops.*

Noooo.

"Tomas," I whisper. My voice shaking. I'm so close to begging I'm ashamed.

Stroke. Pleasure. Vibration. Pulsing, throbbing, coursing through me, ready to explode and I want this, I need this. I want to come so badly my mouth is dry, I can't even breathe or swallow or blink.

"You know what I've told you to do," he says, before he punctuates his words with another stroke of the paddle. And *damn him.*

It feels good. The solid smack sends pleasure right to my clit. He's done this on purpose, manipulated me, and I hate him for it.

I clamp my lips together. I'm more stubborn than he thinks.

Smack.

I gasp.

Smack.

I'm moaning.

Smack.

I think another stroke of his paddle and I'm going to come. I didn't know I was the kind of girl who got aroused like this, but he's a master of pleasurable pain. He knows exactly how to dance between pleasure and pain so that both are irrevocably intertwined.

One more gentle stroke of his fingers, then another, and he stops, resting his hand on my inner thigh.

"Please," I say before I can stop the word. As soon as I do, I wish I could take it back, grab it out of the air between us where it hangs and shove it away out of sight. I'm ashamed of myself that I caved like that. I didn't mean to.

"Good girl," he says approvingly, and then he does the unthinkable. He moves to the side and stares down at me, unbuttons his pants, and removes his cock. No. He wouldn't. He couldn't!

But he fucking *does,* stands right beside me and strokes himself. I'm impossibly more aroused watching his thick cock in his palm, the way he throws his head back in ecstasy before he climaxes, hot come splashing on my back. Oh my God. He *didn't*.

"You'll keep this in mind tonight at the reception," he says casually, placing his cock back in his pants and turning away from me.

"Wait! I did what you said!" I protest. The stupid thing he put in me still vibrates, and I could almost come just from that alone, but I'm too in my head to get to the point of release.

"You did. Good girl. I don't need to spank you anymore for now." He slides open the drawer beside the bed and replaces the paddle, then walks to the large bathroom on the other side of the room. I close my eyes, trying to mentally take myself to a place far away from here, but my only focus is the bundle of nerves between my thighs, the vibration that ricochets through my body, his come on my back.

When he returns he has a towel and washcloth. Quickly, efficiently, he cleans me off.

"No shower," he says. "I want the traces of me to scent you tonight, to fill your pores and your memory of how you belong to no one but me." Weaving his fingers through my hair, he yanks my head back. "Do you understand me?"

"Yes," I say through clenched teeth. I hate him. How could I have ever even entertained the thought that this asshole was anything more than a sadistic monster bent on his own pleasure? He didn't defend me because he cares about me. He only did so because he got bent over someone touching what was *his*.

I curse him out so viciously in my mind, I swear he can read me just from looking.

You fucking bastard.

You selfish prick.

You're a motherfucking asshole.

I never swear out loud, but hell, this situation seems to warrant it. It so does.

"Up you go, little brat," he says.

"I thought you meant baby?" I say, but he shakes his head with a chuckle.

"That was before you looked at me with those beautiful, murderous eyes. Now there's only the brat about you, my *detka*."

"Could that have anything to do with the fact that you just manhandled me, brought me to the edge of climax, jerked yourself all over me, and beat me?"

"A spanking isn't the same as a *beating,* sweetheart," he says with sickening condescension. "I gave the bastard who tried to take advantage of you a beating. What *you* got was a reminder of my authority and a taste of how pain can become pleasure."

"Pleasure? You call that pleasure? You left me hanging, with no pleasure in sight, while you—"

But he's had enough. His eyes harden, and he grips my hair one more time.

"That's enough of this," he says, giving me a little tug. "My patience is growing thin. Behave yourself. If you do, this evening I'll make good on my promise to pleasure you."

He drops me and my face falls to the pillow before he takes my wrists and unfastens the cuffs. "Up you go," he says, and I want to literally punch him in the throat for treating me like this. I've never been aroused and left hanging, and I fucking hate it. It's like some sadistic game for him or something.

Was it in my head before, imagining that he had any tenderness in him at all?

"I'll call Eliott," he says. Of course. I'm a mess now

thanks to him and he won't have me tattered and unkempt before his associates. I can't help but grumble under my breath, barely stifling the desire to smack him with my newly freed hands or cuss him out, but I'm a quick learner.

I sit on the edge of the bed fuming, when he stands right in front of me and chucks a finger under my chin. "Look at me, Caroline."

I look into his deep brown eyes and see something that surprises me: compassion.

But he isn't trying to get my attention or control me. This time, he's actually looking at the scar on my chin in the light of the bedside table.

"Who did this to you?"

I swallow, weighing my options. "If I tell you, what will you do?"

He doesn't hesitate. "Punish them."

"Is that what you do to anyone who doesn't do what you wish?"

Meeting my gaze, he nods. "Yes."

"Is there no one more powerful than you?" Is he that arrogant? I have sense enough not to ask the second question aloud.

"Of course there are," he says. "But even the mighty can fall."

Does he consider himself one of the "mighty" ones? Is he capable, then, of falling?

My chin still in his hand, I watch as his eyes wander back to my scar.

"Do you consider yourself infallible?" I ask him.

Still focusing on my scar, he shakes his head. "No man is infallible, Caroline." His eyes wander to my hair. "And I changed my mind. We won't need Eliott. I'm capable of helping you get ready myself."

I look at his thick fingers and imagine they're clumsy. And hell if I know how to put on makeup or fix my hair. The traditional Russian women fix themselves up to perfection and I pale in comparison. But if I'm to be paraded around in front of all of the visitors he has coming, I want to look my best.

"Are you sure about that?" I ask.

With a chuckle, he drops my chin and grabs my elbow, lifting me to my feet and doesn't answer. He leads me to the bathroom by the hand, and it feels intimate, holding his hand, somehow even more intimate than what he did to me sexually.

I hate that he manipulated me that way. After what I've been through, the abuse at Andros' hands, I hate sex. I don't want to like it. Damn Tomas for making me want more.

Damn him.

But when he leads me to the bathroom, I begin to quiet a little. He's preparing to take me to present to his brotherhood. To local politicians and wealthy leaders. When I'm ready, it will be time.

My stomach clenches with fear and nausea. He instructs me to stand in front of him and releases my hand, oblivious to my worry.

"This is a beautiful dress," he murmurs. "Fitting for the woman who will wear it."

"Why do you keep saying that?" I whisper. "Is it, like, your duty or something? Are you trying to seduce me?"

He gathers my undergarments, and when he returns, he gives me a curious look. "Seduce you. Of course I'm trying to seduce you." He takes the panties and tosses them into a basket in the corner of the large bathroom. "You won't be needing those. The bra I'll allow." He hands it to me to put on.

"You're not even going to deny it?" I ask while I fasten the strap. Then it dawns on me he just said no panties. "And what do you mean no *panties?* What if I... I don't know, need them?"

"Why would you need them?" he asks, but his back is to me while he's getting the dress off the hanger, so I'm not sure if the tightness in his voice means he's amused or impatient.

"To keep me... clean or something. It feels terribly indecent."

"I don't want you decent," he says, as if that's explanation enough. My eyes roll heavenward, and I'm grateful he's occupied taking the dress off the hanger, because he probably wouldn't be cool with me rolling my eyes at him.

When he turns to me, I can't help but admire how pretty it is. The pale blue gown with silver and lace accents dips into a low vee in the front, and I wonder if it will even cover my… ample assets. A filmy overlay gives the gown an almost ethereal appearance, as if I'm wearing something made of fairy dust. I don't know how much this is worth, but I know I've never even touched anything worth what this is in my life. How did they know it would fit me?

He bends with the dress in hand. "Hold onto my shoulders." With a sigh, I comply, stepping into the dress and allowing him to dress me. In silence, he gently spins me around so he can zip me up and fasten the little buttons in the very back.

"Turn around, now," he says. I do, not looking at him. My bust looks good, I guess. It sure feels ample and… bare. But the sleeves don't hide my arms, I still have a rounded belly under which there are curves upon curves. But when he takes me to the full-length mirror in the corner of the massive bathroom, I stare.

I don't recognize the girl staring back at me. Beneath the makeup I'm wearing, I can still see the scar. This *is* me. Scars don't just magically vanish. But I'm not this beautiful. What magic did he work? I turn around in wonder, alarmed at how some preening and this dress have impacted my overall appearance so quickly.

Standing behind me, he takes hold of my waist, his hands spanning either side.

"You are beautiful," he says with emphasis, as if he's already predicted my response and knows how uncomfortable this makes me. I prefer being hidden and unobtrusive. I hate the idea of attracting anyone's attention, because God forbid, they think I'm worthy of attention.

I shake my head. "I don't like this," I tell him. "Not at all. Please don't make me go." I turn away from the mirror, unable to look at myself for another minute. But his grip on my waist tightens when I try to pull away.

"You have no choice in this."

"Why not?" I say, my emotions rising. I swallow hard and stare at the floor. I don't want to look at myself again.

"I've already explained to you," he says tightly. "You're expected to show yourself to others as my wife. And because I asked."

To my surprise, his hand comes to my chin and he yanks my face back up, making me look back at the mirror. He grips my chin in his fingers. "You are beautiful. Say it."

I clench my jaw. His grip on my face tightens.

"Caroline." There's warning in his voice I've already learned to heed.

"I'm beautiful," I lie.

He holds my gaze in the mirror, his full of determination and bossiness and mine full of anger and denial. He actually smiles.

"Keep that fire," he says. "It colors your cheeks and I quite like it."

I open my mouth to protest, when I realize his command to stay feisty makes my response complicated. Has he tricked me? If I snap at him or act like the little brat he calls me, I'll be giving him exactly what he wants. I open my mouth to protest, even though I'm not sure what I'll actually say, when he turns me to face him. Holding my gaze with challenge in his eyes, he lifts my face, bends down, and captures my mouth with his, not bothering to even ask permission with the brush of lips but plundering me with firm, purposeful lashes of his tongue against mine. My knees buckle and I move involuntarily closer to him, my arms grasping his neck for purchase before I swoon, and *I will not swoon.*

With his lips on mine, I can believe for a minute that he has the potential of being so much more than the man I'm shackled to for life. In my mind, I tell myself to resist this, not to allow him to seduce me and master my thoughts and actions so skillfully. But I can't help it. Damn it, I'm only human and his kiss tricks me into believing there's a hint of passion in all this.

As he kisses me, he yanks the skirt of the dress up, gathering the filmy layers in his fist and reaching underneath them to stroke me before he takes out the vibrator. I shudder, then pull closer to him and part my legs, welcoming the pressure and teasing, but he only ghosts a touch before he removes his hand.

"Good girl. I'll give you good reason not to wear those."

I'm panting and disheveled, but he quickly rights me and hands me a lip gloss.

"Fix yourself," he says. I blink, startled by his cold tone. "And then we leave."

Chapter 11

Tomas

As we prepare to go downstairs, a strange sort of pride comes over me. I didn't earn this woman or even fight for her, and I have no real claim on her yet, but none of that matters. She wears my ring and bears my name. She belongs to *me*. I hate even leaving her for the brief time I need to connect with my men. Though I trust my brothers with my life, I want Caroline within arm's reach. I tell myself it's so I can keep an eye on her, but there's more to it than that. I want to shield her from anyone and anything that could threaten her.

It surprises me that I feel this level of intensity, this need to protect her as deeply as I do. When her brother's man attacked her back in Atlanta, that was an obvious reaction. She belongs to me, and as such, he had no right to come anywhere near my woman. But why do I feel the way I do now so intensely? As if I need to tuck her against me and shield her from the eyes of the others?

When we step into the hall, I place my hand on her lower back and draw her close to me.

"Why do you keep doing that?" she hisses.

"Doing what?" Her angry tone and hissed voice give me pause.

"Touching me there." I look down at my hand as if my body has moved of its own accord.

"On your lower back?"

"*Yes,*" she hisses. "It's so… intimate."

Her reaction amuses me. "Sweetheart, I've done a lot more intimate things than *that*," I say. I don't know why she finds the lower back touch that much more offensive, but I'll note it. Her cheeks flush a bit at the reminder of what "intimate things" I've done to her.

"It's like you want to make it clear to all of them that you own me or something."

I don't hesitate with my response. "I do."

She stops walking and eyes me curiously. "You do what?"

"Own you."

Those beautiful eyes narrow to slits. "You cannot own another human being."

I snort. "How naïve of you."

"It's illegal!"

"Your point?"

"You're sadistic. You know that?"

"I'm well aware."

She breathes out an exasperated breath but can't seem to form any words beyond a strangled, "*Argh!*"

"Easy, darling," I tell her, allowing my voice to drip with condescension. "You don't want to burst a blood vessel. And remember, Caroline. Your behavior determines a punishment or reward. Choose carefully."

We've arrived on the main floor and she suddenly becomes much more subdued than she was before, bowing her head and pulling closer to me. I like this. Without her even realizing it, I've become her refuge when all else fails.

Sweet girl, I think. Beneath her barbed exterior, I suspect she's a lot more innocent than she lets on. And inside, I bet she's far more vulnerable than she cares to admit.

Her breathing grows ragged, and she closes her eyes. Christ, she's gorgeous, so pretty I can hardly believe she finds herself unattractive. She has a scar, yes, but it's rather unremarkable, and I've stopped really seeing scars long ago. For many within my brotherhood, violence that leaves marks is a way of life. For many, it serves as more of a distinction than blemish. She'd likely deny it, but there's an innocence about her that can't be refuted.

"Tomas."

Yakov and Yvonne stand just a few paces away, entering the main room from a hallway ahead of us. Yakov wears a navy-blue suit. I haven't seen him this dressed up since he got here. I appreciate the show of respect. Yvonne wears a soft pink dress, her hair pinned atop her head, silver earrings dangling from her ears. When she first got here, she was intimidated, so much so she could hardly speak. It's taken some time, but she's finally grown a bit more accustomed to our methods and our brotherhood. The men of my brotherhood like their women soft, feminine, yielding. Yvonne epitomizes a wife of Bratva leadership. Caroline will learn to do so as well.

"Yakov," I respond, taking his hand with a firm shake. I nod toward Caroline. "Meet my bride." I can't hide the note of pride in my voice. It pleases me to walk into this room with her on my arm.

Yakov reaches out a hand to shake hers, and she reaches a shaky hand out to greet him. Stepping toward him, she gets flustered and catches her toe on thin air, trips, and nearly goes sprawling. Yakov reaches out to catch her just seconds after I do, and I pull her against me.

"Are you okay?" he asks. I have to school myself, so I don't deck him for coming anywhere near her. I'd kill him if he treated her badly but treating her kindly is almost just as bad. Apparently, I can't hide my gut reaction, because Yvonne looks at me with wide, terrified eyes. She quickly grabs Yakov's arm as if to remind me that she's his.

"You look beautiful, Caroline," she says in her soft-pitched voice. "Like a princess."

Caroline turns away and nods, visibly uncomfortable from the praise. "Thank you," she says. "I'm not sure what they did, but I—" she looks at me and closes her mouth, contemplating, before she continues. "Thank you."

Yakov steps aside so that we can enter ahead of them. The anteroom to the ballroom is filled with guests just arriving, and a hush goes over the crowd when we enter. I want to leave this room. Just like before, I want to pick her up and whisk her away, away from the eyes of men who do wicked things. Away from the eyes of women who help them. To my private suite where no one can touch us.

"Tomas," Yakov says in my ear to my left. "Did you invite her brother to join us?"

"Of course not," I say tightly, smiling at our guests despite wanting to punch someone. What the hell is he asking me this for? "Why?"

"Just asking," he responds, then moves to the side before I can ask him any questions. He isn't *just asking*. For Christ's sake, you don't plant an idea like this and leave. Is her brother here? I'll fucking kill him for showing his face. But Yakov is already gone, and that quickly, people fill in his place. Well-wishers and the like swarm around us so heavily, I feel her tense beside me, her breathing heavy and labored. I will not do this again with her.

Why the *fuck* did Yakov ask me that?

I need to anchor Caroline to me, so we don't get separated. I look to my guards and snap my fingers, and instantly they part the crowds. Caroline breathes more easily as we finally enter the main room, but only for a second. I beckon one of the guards over. "Get Yakov back here."

"Yes, sir."

Cheers erupt all around us. Our guests are on their feet, clapping to welcome us, the sound of the applause deafening. So many people have arrived, I don't recognize them all. I snap my fingers to Lev, who's standing to the side watching us all.

"I want a detailed list of how many guests we have," I tell him. "This is far more than I was expecting."

"I think we had more show up than we planned for," he says apologetically. "I'm sorry, sir."

Who the hell was in charge of this? Heads will fucking *roll* for the haphazard way this has been put together. I don't like the way she looks at me, pale and trembling. It takes me a second to realize she's too still. She isn't breathing.

"Breathe," I whisper in her ear, and she gasps for breath, clutching my arm. She moves so easily from one feeling to the next, but her anxiety gives me pause. I don't think she's as defiant as she initially appeared. Her disobedience masks something else. Something hidden. It will be my job to unearth the reason for her anxiety, and I suspect her scar is my first clue.

A waiter offers me champagne. I take two flutes from the tray and hand one to Caroline. She downs it in one big gulp, then hands me the empty flute. I feel a corner of my lips quirk up. I order a second and hand it to her. "Drink."

She drinks champagne while music plays and guests mingle. I allow it because the flutes are small, and I reason it will help her relax. I lead us to our seats, a small table at the far end of the room adorned with a large vase of red roses.

"Sit." She sort of wobbles when she takes her seat, but she obeys.

"Good girl," I praise. "Just follow my lead."

"You make it sound so easy," she says through pursed lips. She sways a little.

Is she more of a lightweight than I expected?

"Then don't follow my lead. Disobey and earn a punishment."

Her eyes narrow.

I shrug. "You know what's on the table."

"Looks like a bottle of wine," she quips, pretending I'm speaking literally. I suddenly realize that she's slurring her words. Is she that sensitive that three small flutes of champagne have her tipsy?

I smirk, open the bottle, and pour her a small glass.

"My dear sir," she says through thick lips. "If I didn't know any better, I would think you're trying to get me *drunk*."

Drunk, no. Relaxed and in good humor? Yes.

"Just be sure you drink a glass of water in between each glass of champagne," I tell her.

"Then looks like I need a six-pack of water," she mutters.

"Are you serious? You drank that much already? Did you take more when I wasn't looking?"

She bites her lip and puts her fingers out, counting clumsily. "Maybe," she mutters. "I can't *exactly* remember." She frowns. "I never drink much. I promise. I just didn't know it would taste that good and help me feel so nice. Did I drink too much?"

I reach for her wine glass, because it's time I cut her off, but someone comes to say hello, and after we've spoken, I see her polishing off yet another drink.

"Caroline!" I say in surprise.

She tips her head to the side, like a little curious puppy. Her hair falls in her eyes. So fetching and innocent. "What? You have your angry face on."

I grunt. She'll end up earning good spanking if she doesn't stop.

"You shouldn't have had so much to drink. You'll give yourself a hangover."

"What I'll do is give myself *courage,*" she says. "Courage, said the lion!" She pitches off in a sing-song voice, "If I were king of the forr-ressst…"

I blink in surprise. She's quoting something but I don't know what.

Excellent. My new wife is accidentally drunk. I should have been more careful.

At that moment, Lev comes over to us. Caroline greets everyone readily. She's damn near sociable. Lev whispers something in my ear about a rumor involving a party crasher. He says someone assumed it was her brother, or someone in his group, but there are more guests than we've accounted for.

The local governor is here, and other major power players. I don't want to cause a scene, but this concerns me.

"I don't fucking care what you need to do. Find out," I tell him. We get the guest list and I look it over, but everything looks kosher, and there are too many people mingling for us to track down who's here unexpectedly.

"What is it, husband?" she asks in her tipsy voice. "You seem… pler-plexed. No. *Perplexed.*"

I have to admit, I like the tipsy Caroline. She smiles more easily, cracks jokes, and isn't anywhere near as self-conscious as before.

"I'm not happy with my wife, because she's had too

much to drink," I tell her, raising a stern brown in her direction.

"Oh," she says with mock repentance. "Will that earn me…" she drops her voice and bites her lip before she continues, her finger delicately tracing her collarbone. *"A spanking?"*

I swallow hard. "It does," I tell her sternly. "A *bad* girl spanking. The kind that *hurts."*

Sticking her lower lip out in mock repentance, she looks at me from beneath lowered lashes. "Over your knee, sir?"

Jesus, I like drunk Caroline. My dick's already hard at the thought.

"Over my lap." I brush her hair off her forehead and bring my mouth to her ear. "I'll strip you first. Then your ass feels my palm tonight."

She fairly purrs in my ear. I have absolutely no control over my wife, but I'm enjoying this, because she forces my hand. She gives me reason to exert my dominance over her and coquettishly bows to meet my demands.

"Let's go," she whispers in my ear. "I've been a very bad little girl who needs to be punished." It surprises me that she's flirting from this angle, but I'm not going to miss my opportunity.

Lev nods to me and gives me a thumbs up. He's done a head count, and all is well. No one's come here who shouldn't. We're safe.

"Back to the room," I growl. Now that we've talked about what will happen, I need to have her alone. The clock is ticking on my need to consummate our marriage, and the more intimate we grow, the easier that will be.

"The groom has to cut the cake!" Someone shouts out. I squint at the crowd but don't see who it is. I wave them off, but Caroline takes me by the hand.

"I've always wanted to do this!" she says. "And *oh*, Tomas, it's *chocolate*."

"Is that good?" I'm not a cake eater.

"I *love* chocolate. Oh my God, I need some."

I definitely need to get Caroline drunk more often.

They're playing some kind of crazy song as we approach the table, and Caroline's laughing her head off. I shake my head and make her wait while I cut a large wedge of cake, then hand her the knife to do the same. She cuts a large slice and swipes her finger through the chocolate center.

"Mmm," she says. "Oh God this is the best."

"Would you like a whole piece?" I ask.

She nods eagerly, so I hold the cake in front of her until she opens her mouth, then I shove a large portion in. She giggles, her mouth spraying crumbs everywhere, before she swallows the rest of the large slice. Laughing out loud, she picks up the piece she cut for me and shoves it in my mouth. Crumbs scatter and icing smears my upper lip, but it's worth it to see her eyes light up and hear that musical giggle. The crowd laughs at our antics, but when I turn to take Caroline with me back to our table, or preferably *my room*, I see Lev raise his hand and signal to me. I look up at him. Four fingers are raised in the air, his thumb tucked beneath them.

It's our sign for danger.

Fuck.

He's telling me she's in danger but doesn't want to risk rousing suspicion from the crowd.

It's then that I realize my guards are on the move, and several have weapons drawn. Lev reaches me first.

"Get her back to your room," he says, "Go!"

A few people around us notice the tension and whispers begin hushing through the crowd. When he reaches me he comes straight to me. "One of our guards is missing," he says.

"Impossible. We've just counted them not a minute ago."

"Very possible," he says. "Think about it. But we don't want to be overheard." He looks at me and shakes his head.

"Who?"

"Ilya."

I don't know each man by name, but I know Ilya is young and fairly new to the brotherhood.

I'm not going to fuck around with this. He's right, I need to get her out of here, though I hate leaving my men unprotected.

"Time to go," I tell her, taking her hand and leading her to the exit. Immediately, a dozen uniformed guards flank my side, but it doesn't bring me the security it once did. If one of our guards may have been killed, one of them could be an infiltrator.

I march her quickly to my room, my gun already drawn. I'm prepared. Whoever it is, I'm ready to defend my wife. I'm ready to fucking kill.

Is she the reason they're even here?

I imagine I hear someone in the hall, and I swivel around with my gun drawn. Caroline shrieks and sobers when she sees me holding my gun, prepared to fight.

"You do what I tell you," I say.

"You've mentioned that once or twice," she quips. "It's kind of like your motto."

"I'll give you motto," I mutter, tugging her into the bedroom. "Go sit on the bed."

"Oh, wow, this is *weird*," she says, walking toward the bed but wobbling around the room as if we're at sea.

"It's what happens when you drink too much," I tell her.

"Right," she says, before she faceplants on the bed.

"That's better," she mumbles into the blanket, still face down. "Am I getting my spanking now?"

I'll give her a spanking alright. She might regret taking this so lightly.

Kneeling on the bed beside her, I unfasten the buttons on her beautiful dress. She shivers when I lift her out of the dress, one arm at a time.

"Cold?" I ask her, my mind elsewhere, on what is happening with my men.

"No," she says. "You're sexy."

I place my gun on the bedside table, and she doesn't even flinch this time but opens her arms. Welcoming me.

"Come here, husband," she whispers. "Was I a good girl tonight?"

I shake my head. "No, *detka*. You were very, very naughty."

"Oh, right," she says with a pout. "And I earned a spanking?" Biting her lip, she's absolutely adorable.

"Yes," I say, my voice husky. "Now lie over my lap."

She captures her lip between her teeth and sashays over to me, holding my gaze the whole time.

I sit on the edge of the bed and pat my lap.

"Naughty little girl," I say, dragging this out. I like watching the way her eyes go half-lidded and she moans when I run my hand over the fullest curve of her ass. "Such a naughty little girl."

Without warning, I slam my palm against her full, beautiful backside. She gasps and moans, and I'm already hard as a rock. I give her a second smack, then a third, before I start fingering her between strokes.

"Oh, God," she moans, squirming over my knee. "Does alcohol turn you on?"

"It can," I say, slapping the underside of her curvy ass.

"You've earned this," I tell her. "Haven't you?"

"I think so," she groans. With slow, deliberate strokes of my palm, I take her just to the edge of climax, until she's panting and squirming over my knee. I part her legs and gently stroke her swollen, slick folds.

"You need to come, don't you, sweetheart?"

"Mmmmm," she moans, pushing herself on my hand.

"On the bed," I tell her, lifting her off my knee and placing her on her back. "Stroke yourself," I order. Her eyes are half-lidded when she parts her knees and gingerly places her fingers on her pussy. She bites her lip but doesn't look away. I watch her stroke harder and faster, until she's right on the cusp of release.

"Stop," I order.

She freezes, whimpering, and meets my eyes. I climb on the bed and part her knees, inhaling the seductive scent of her arousal, before I lower my face to her bare pussy and lazily drag my tongue between her folds.

"Oh my God," she moans, squirming beneath the onslaught of my tongue, but just as she's on the cusp, I pull away.

"Jesus, Tomas," she whispers. "Oh, God, that's so *good*. Why did you stop?"

I hold her gaze before I order. *"Beg."*

Swallowing, she nods. I'm an asshole for taking advantage of her. She's on the verge of climax and plastered, but it's broken down walls that nothing else would. But the look she gives me is completely sober.

"Please."

I look at her in surprise. I wasn't expecting this. I thought she'd fight me.

I don't want to make her ask twice. I need to do this. I need to do this now.

I roll on a condom while I brace myself above her and my conscious plagues me. She'll be sober in the morning, and I don't want her anger and regret.

I line the head of my cock at her entrance and hold her eyes with mine.

"Are you sure?"

Taking in a deep breath, she nods. "I'm sure."

"Hands above your head," I command quietly, holding her gaze as she moves to obey.

"Yes, sir." She knows I need this now, her submission empowering me to claim her the way I need to.

"Good girl. Keep them there," I order. "Do not move them."

She only nods, swallowing and licking her lips. If eyes are a window to the soul, hers are a veritable well of passion I want to explore and study, until I know the meaning of the very tempo of her heart.

"You said you've done this before," I say. I want to know everything. I need to know.

"Please don't talk of that now," she begs, her flirty eyes so serious something in me hurts for her. My natural instinct to protect rises.

"I won't," I promise, because she needs to know she can trust me. But I'll also give her honesty, so I amend, "For now."

I bend down to her and take her mouth with mine, tasting the sweet, tangy champagne, while I trap her wrists with my left hand and keep them pinned above her head. I move my mouth above hers, swallowing her gasp as I glide into her. Her whole body tenses beneath me and she whimpers, but I push through. I'm not hurting her. She feels so damn tight and perfect wrapped around me I need to hold myself back.

"Relax," I tell her.

"I'm scared," she whispers.

"Don't be. I won't hurt you." Not this way, anyway, not when she's lying beneath me, vulnerable and trembling.

She shakes her head, still pinned beneath me, her eyes filling with tears. "Do you promise?"

I nod once. "I promise."

And it's all she needs. Sighing, she sinks into this, melting into my touch, welcoming the rocking of my hips and the friction I build with firm, steady strokes.

"Mmm," she groans, her eyes fluttering, hips swaying, breath growing ragged and eager. My own pleasure is building to a crescendo, and when she throws her head back in utter bliss, her sweet moans of pleasure echoing in the room, I chase my own bliss right behind her.

It's finished.

She's mine.

For one brief moment, I rest my forehead on hers. Our breath mingles, our bodies clasped in a lovers' irrevocable bond. She's my wife, now, fully.

Too soon, I roll over off of her and pull her onto my chest. The room is still save our steady breath, and I run my hand through her hair once, twice, three times. It's soft, silky, fragrant, this moment so intimate I want to savor it. I'm not a sentimental man, but I know this moment is sacred.

It isn't until I realize my chest is wet that I notice she's crying.

"Caroline!" I say in surprise. "What is it? Are you okay?"

Christ, I hurt her. Did she lie to me? Was she a virgin?

She's trying hard to keep back her tears, but she can't seem to help it.

I wrap my arms around her and don't say anything for a minute, but it kills me not to demand the truth. My patience quickly evaporates, though. I have to know. "Did I hurt you?"

She shakes her head and cries harder.

"I hate it," she says. This woman is an enigma.

I take in a deep breath to give me much-needed patience.

"Tell me," I press. "What do you hate? You need to give me the truth."

She surprises me by doing just that, as if being wholly bared to me makes it easier to be honest.

"My brother's friend," she whispers. "The one who sent someone to take a picture? I hate sex because of him. Hate it. He… took advantage of me."

My grip on her tightens. I'll kill him. Slowly, painfully kill him, and not until he suffers first.

"How? Say it."

She cries harder but pushes on.

"Rape. Repeatedly. There was nowhere for me to escape. I told my brother and he said I was a liar, and when Andros found out I told my brother, he cut me."

I sit up in bed, taking her with me. I feel my whole body tense and chill at once.

"I'll fucking kill him."

She breathes out, "Would you really?" It shouldn't surprise me that there's both awe and hope in her voice. "You hardly even know me, though," she muses, but when her tear-filled eyes meet mine once more, her gaze pierces my soul. "I want him dead. I want to go to bed at night knowing that he can't find me again. That he won't do again what he's done before." Closing her eyes, she breathes in and out before repeating, "Would you really, Tomas?"

"Of course, I would. No one hurts my wife."

"I wasn't your wife when he hurt me."

"Irrelevant. He'll suffer for what he's done, but I'll need more details." I'll need to know *everything*.

"Tomas... you do know that you'll start a war between brotherhoods?"

"I do."

My blood pounds furiously in my veins, searing and destructive, annihilating reason and logic. I will murder the motherfucking bastard who hurt my wife.

Rape.

Repeatedly.

"Any bastard who would do that deserves to be on the frontline in a Bratva war," I tell her. "And your brother is a douchebag for not murdering him with his own hands. Both deserve to die. They both will."

"He will," she says quietly. "We all do eventually." Her voice fades to a whisper, contemplative and thoughtful, and I tighten my grip around her.

I'll assemble my men. I will have the truth.

And I will end them.

Chapter 12

Caroline

I WAKE the next day before Tomas, my entire body wracked with pain.

I remember the night before when I reach a hand to my head. It feels like someone's pounding it against a wall, over, and over, and over again.

Great.

I can hear him breathing heavily beside me, and one of his massive arms is strewn crazily about my lower back. Though I'm awake, I close my eyes and rest in this moment. This bed is massive and luxurious, soft but firm, the sheets like satin. And I'm tired. I yawn and take inventory of my body.

My head isn't the only thing that hurts. My butt aches from being spanked, but there's more. Even though Tomas is a dominant, chest-beating alpha male, who *does* expect nothing short of full obedience, I've learned in this short timeframe that he can also make being dominated sexy as hell. How? I have no idea. But I have some vague notion of handcuffs and spanking as being sexy to some people. Am I one of those people? I didn't think so, until Tomas showed me otherwise. And if I'm honest, I'm eager for him to show me more.

My association with sex is anything but pleasurable. I *want* to view it differently. I want to learn to enjoy what should be pleasurable.

My core is mildly sore, and I feel dampness between my legs. I'm lying here naked, next to a man I hardly know, and for a moment, I panic. Why am I wet between my legs? Did I start my period? Oh, God, that would be terrible. But a quick inspection shows me it's only… him. I swallow.

He used a condom, but those aren't foolproof...

Shit.

My period is due in a few days, so I *think* I can't get pregnant now anyway. But still. This is something we need to discuss.

But it isn't until I open my eyes and bright sunlight blinds me that I groan out loud.

"What is it, sweetheart? Are you alright?" Tomas' voice is low and husky, and it does something to my heart, but I push it away. I can't let myself go all female and flirty now, because I'm gonna *die*.

"My head," I groan. I lie flat on my back and don't

move, my eyes closed tightly. If I lie still enough, I don't feel like I'll vomit.

"Ahh," he says as the truth dawns on him. "We have an expression in Russia. 'What is good for a Russian in the evening is bad for him in the morning.'" With my eyes shut tight, I don't see him, but his voice is near, and I can feel the warmth of his body drawing closer to me.

"Is that, like, your mother's saying or something?" I ask with a sigh.

"Not my mother's," he responds. "But it is an old Russian proverb. You had too much to drink last night. I shouldn't have allowed it. I won't again."

"Stop talking," I moan. "It hurts to listen. Oh, God, I think I'm going to throw up." I sit up in bed and the room swirls around me, but he holds me to him.

"Breathe in through your nose," he says. I obey. "Now out through your mouth." Thankfully, the nausea passes. "Lie back down and don't open your eyes," he says. "I'll get something that will help." He steps into the other room.

He picks up his phone and calls someone who answers immediately. I can't hear what he orders, and he comes back soon after making the call. I moan, not moving so I don't cause nausea to spike again. Damn.

Someone comes to the door, and I hear hushed whispers. I groan when the door clicks shut. Then he's sitting beside me on the bed. Reaching out, he strokes his hand across my forehead. It feels nice.

"Sit up slowly, Caroline," he says. "No quick movements."

My head hurts so badly I can't think, so it's actually nice to have someone take charge. I do what he says, my eyes still closed.

"Open your mouth."

Okay now *that* I won't do unless I can see why. I tentatively open one eye. He's holding a bottle of water to my mouth. I take a small sip, but he shakes his head sternly. "More."

"It makes me want to throw up," I say, not bothering to tone the petulant tone of my voice.

"*More,*" he orders. He's sitting up wearing nothing but a pair of boxers, his tattoos swirled around his neck and arms like galaxies in the night sky.

I obey.

"Good girl," he says approvingly. "Now medicine."

He hands me white, oval-shaped tablets I assume are pain relievers. I swallow them down.

Nodding with approval, he instructs, "Now eat."

The strong smell of vinegar assaults my senses, and my stomach rolls with nausea before I see what he's holding. Is it some sort of weird Russian food? Even though I was raised in the Bratva, our food choices were decidedly American.

"Oh God no," I say, squeezing my eyes shut and clamping my mouth closed. Is he out of his damn mind?

But his voice hardens, and the glare he gives me dares me to defy. "You will do what I say and eat this. *Now*."

I close my mouth and glare at him, shaking my head firmly from side to side.

His gaze grows ferocious and he actually literally *growls*. "You'll do what I say or earn a sound spanking."

"Tomas," I whine, my voice unfamiliar to my own ears. I'm not a whiner, but I feel like I want to curl up and die. "If you make me eat that I'm gonna *hurl*. And I will absolutely die if I throw up all over my new husband. Just *ew*."

"And if you don't eat it, you'll land belly-down over your new husband's lap, get your pretty little bottom paddled, and then still might throw up. Seems like an easy choice to me."

I grit my teeth. "I'm not going to do it."

He huffs out an angry breath, shakes his head, and places the tray down on the bed before he reaches for me. It isn't until I'm halfway over his lap, hair swinging wildly about my face and hands flailing, that I realize he does indeed intend to make good on his promise. And this is *not* the time for a spanking, thank you very much.

"Stop! Okay, okay, I'll eat whatever smelly thing you have."

"It's a pickled cucumber," he says, placing me back on my back in bed. I breathe out a sigh of relief. *God.* I married a man with a heavy hand, and I'd do well to remember that.

"You mean a pickle? We call them pickles in America," I retort with a grumpy huff. "And I can literally think of nothing I'd like to eat less right now."

His eyes narrow in warning.

"Caroline." He lifts it to my mouth, before his tone softens. "It's an old-fashioned Russian remedy. Just trust me."

I don't want a spanking, and I don't want a pickle, but my choices here are pretty dismal. With a sigh, I open my mouth a fraction of an inch. Shaking his head, he slides the pickle between my lips.

It's tart and sweet, and nausea clenches my stomach, but as soon as I chew and swallow, the nausea abates a little. I give him a curious look. What magic is this?

"See? Eat the whole thing." I want to smack the smug look off his face, but I know I'd regret that choice. And I'm too focused on helping the nausea abate. I swallow my pride and eagerly eat it, grateful that I'm no longer nauseous. He follows the pickle with a hot cup of tea and more water, then lays me back down in the bed. "Lay here for a few minutes and let the food settle. I'll draw a bath and help you into it."

A bath? Weird.

"Is that part of the Russian remedy, too?"

"It is."

I lay on my side watching him walk toward the bathroom, all tats and muscles and glorious alpha male, and even though I'm uncomfortable and my head hurts so bad I want to cry, it makes me wonder. Is my new arrangement so bad? His fierce protection is something I didn't even know I wanted until I had it. Once again, I think of my choices.

I could fight this or lean in.

Lean in.

Embrace his fierce loyalty and learn to be the wife he wants me to be.

Could I?

"Come, little *detka*," he says, walking back over to me. "Let's get you your bath." I sit up, but he reaches for me first, drawing me to his chest and holding me like a baby. I love this. Oh, it feels nice to be carried by him as he steps toward the bathroom. I let my head fall to his shoulder, my arms strewn about his neck. The nausea is at bay, but my head still pounds.

"Oh, God, the lights," I groan when we reach the bathroom. He flicks them off so that the only light in the room filters through large windows, daylight illuminating the large tub filled with water and bubbles.

I close my eyes because even the soft natural light makes my head hurt, but soon he's lowering me into the tub.

"Hold onto the edge," he says, just before he submerges me in the warm, soothing depths. It feels *divine.* I'm enveloped in fragrant clouds, warm and soothing. The nausea is better, and the pounding of my head is beginning to lessen.

"That's a girl," he says. I'm surprised by the tenderness he shows, this brass, powerful man who commands an army. "You're being a very good girl." To my surprise, he strips out of his boxers and steps into the tub with me.

"Come here," he says. Sitting beside me, he draws me between his legs. My head falls to his shoulder. God, this feels so good, the warmth of the tub, his strong body behind me, holding me to him. "Let's wash your hair."

I let him, leaning my head back while he runs warm water over my scalp, massages shampoo into my hair, then rinses it all off with a handheld shower head. I'm shocked at how good it feels being taken care of like this. Though I remember how my mother cared for me, I was so young when she died that I remember very little beyond what she looked like, my memory refreshed by the pictures I still own at home. And of my family members, she's the only one who could have possibly had a nurturing bone in her body.

When my hair is washed and the water begins to cool, he pulls the drain and stands me up, before draping a thick, plush towel around me.

"That's my girl," he says approvingly. "I like that you let me take care of you."

I like it, too, though I won't admit it. I lift my chin high. "You didn't give me much choice."

He smiles with a twinkle in his eye. "But I did. You could have complied in action alone, but you didn't. You complied with your spirit as well. And that makes all the difference."

He needs to take care of me. I'll remember that as well. It's in his nature to protect and provide. Though a part of me resists this, my mind warring with my desire to be taken care of and my inner desire to be strong and powerful, there are times like this when it makes sense to allow someone to care for me. Especially if that someone is my husband.

He lays me back down in bed and covers me with a blanket. "Rest, Caroline. I'll be back in a while to check on you."

I don't need to be told twice. I nod, turning over and closing my eyes. A little more sleep sounds delicious. But as I lay there and hear him going about the room, I can't help but open my eyes and watch him as he lays out clean clothes and shoes. Every once in a while, he looks my way, and each time I pretend I'm sleeping. On his way to the bathroom he walks up to me and gives me a playful slap on the ass.

"Sleep," he orders.

I listen to the lulling sound of the water in the bathroom and don't think I've actually relaxed enough to drop off, when I hear his shower shut off. I open one eye. My stomach feels a little less queasy, and my head is a little less pained than before. A few moments later, Tomas emerges, still damp from the shower, a towel tucked around his waist sturdy, powerful waist.

"Did you sleep?" he asks, fixing me with a stern gaze as if he wants to be sure I obeyed.

I yawn wildly. "I think so."

It's good enough for him. He nods and walks to where he has his clothes hung up beside a chair. I quietly roll to my back and watch him dress.

First, the towel falls to the floor. I swallow hard at the sight before me, and I feel my pulse begin to quicken. This man is a fucking god, from the deep, wide barrel of his chest to the muscled planes and valleys dotted with dark hair. The tattoos complement each other, each one telling a story. He seems oblivious to the way I shameless stare at him, efficiently pulling on trousers, a t-shirt, then sliding into a stark white Oxford shirt.

Wow, he looks fucking amazing.

I swallow hard, observing his cufflinks and the attention to detail. He taps cologne onto the palm of his hand from a bedside table, and the masculine scent pervades my senses.

"Where are you going?" I whisper. "You're so dressed up."

"Just a meeting with my men," he says, reaching for a leather belt and threading it around his waist.

"Oh," I whisper. And then a strange question comes to me. "Are there going to be any women there?"

He smiles. "No. We have no women in the Bratva. There are a few married to my men, but no women will attend one of my meetings."

As he buckles his belt, my breasts swell, a satisfying tingle rising between my legs. Wow. Again? What bewitchment is this, that I'm getting aroused just by looking at him? What has he done to me?

"Why do you ask, Caroline?"

"Because you look nice," I tell him pointedly. "And you're my husband. And I'm not super cool with some other chick ogling you."

His eyes widen as he finishes buckling the belt, placing the tail end of it in the loops around his waist. "Are you jealous, wife?"

"Maybe," I say thoughtfully. *Am* I?

But just last night he told me he would kill the men who hurt me. The prospect scares me, so I haven't thought much more about it since then. I'm not sure how I feel about that.

I shouldn't want him to hurt my brother.

But I do.

Jesus, *I do.*

I shouldn't want him to hurt Andros. Good people don't hurt each other.

But if he does, I know that I'll worship the ground he walks on.

Worship it.

And I'm not sure what that says about me. It scares me a little to think about how much the promise of revenge excites me. I swallow hard.

This isn't right. But what part about this is? We live by a code of conduct outside the norm.

He's running his fingers through his hair, his back to me, his scent hanging in the air like forbidden fruit. Ripe and tempting. The man may be my husband, but he's dangerous on so many levels.

"I like that you're jealous," he says. But I don't like it. I don't like it at all.

I'm falling for him, for the man who doesn't love me for anything other than his property. And I should be stronger than this.

I *am* stronger than this.

I close my eyes and breathe in deeply.

"Well good for you," I mutter. "Oh!"

He's kneeling on the bed, both knees on either side of me, his tie in his hand.

"Why are you looking at me like that?" I ask.

"Like what?" He leans down and wraps the tie around my wrists. I'm not sure how to respond. "Like what? Like I want to eat you? That's because I do, little *dratka*."

He did not just say that.

"I want the taste of your pussy on my lips when I talk to my men. I want your lingering scent on my nose when I walk among men. I want the memory of my tongue between your legs following you when we separate."

I don't know exactly how to respond, but I think I say something like *unnnggghhh*, because then he's parting my legs and positioning them just right, while his *fully clothed*, hot as hell body draws closer to me.

"And you always get what you want, right?" I say with a nervous laugh. I'm giggling like a little girl, until I'm moaning. Oh God, oh *God*, his breath is hot and sexy and *right. there.* where I'm throbbing already with need. Lifting my legs up, he places my legs right over his shoulders, the back of my knees resting on the silky fabric.

"Always," he breathes, right into my sex. I feel like I'm at the mercy of a fire-breathing dragon, his mouth at my pussy so hot and seductive I can't breathe. Then he lowers the tip of his tongue to the place I need him most and works his magic.

Slow, steady, seductive swipes of his tongue have me keening with pleasure before I've taken another breath. My wrists are tied fast, somehow heightening the experience. When he suckles my clit, I throw my head back, my breath caught in my throat, then he releases the pressure and teases with the tip of his tongue again.

Over and over he laps and sucks, pausing just long enough to breathe me in so deeply I shiver with delight. It's like I'm meeting a need of his somehow, fueling him like an oxygen mask.

He breathes against my thighs, whispering, "Come for me, sweetheart." But I can't. I'm too pent up, too in my head, that even with his seductive ministrations, I can't go to the place of chasing my release.

"Come, Caroline," he repeats.

"I can't," I moan, squirming under the onslaught of his tongue. "Oh God, I can't."

He plunges his fingers in my core and pumps hard. "You can. *Come.*" He's right. The extra pressure sends me soaring, and I sail into bliss with abandon. Moaning, grinding against his face, I'm milking every second of this ecstasy.

"Fucking beautiful," he says, gently placing my knees back down on the bed. "I love that you granted me that."

I murmur some gibberish about me being the lucky one, or some such fool thing, but I'm not kidding. I'm drunk on pleasure, the feel of his tongue still lingering between my legs, even while my cheeks flush with heat at the thought of how recklessly I came on his mouth.

"Is this part of your plan of seduction?" I ask, as he removes the tie from my wrists and ties it around his neck, slightly crumpled, but doable.

He gives me a wicked grin that makes my rapidly beating pulse spike. He needs to be careful how he wields that grin. It's dangerous.

"I have no plan of seduction, Caroline. You already belong to me."

I give him a curious look, but he only winks at the doorway. "I need to go see my men. You have plenty to occupy your time until I return. I'll be back within an hour." He turns and leaves the room, and I swear he takes a piece of my heart with him. I'm losing myself to him, this powerful man who commands not only an army... but *me*.

Chapter 13

Tomas

THE DIFFERENCE between what I want to do in my head and what I actually do are two very different things. And I need to face that.

I want my wife to behave herself, to fear me. Then before I know what I'm doing, I'm laying her down and eating her out until she comes on my face with reckless abandon, as if carnal indulgence trumps logic and reason. And hell, maybe it does.

I adjust my dick, hard as a fucking rock, while I fix my clothing. Caroline doesn't think she's beautiful, and to most others, she is no model. She isn't what most people would consider beautiful.

But I'm not most people.

The curves she curses make me want to bury myself in her to the hilt, claiming her as all mine. She's like a pin-up model of old, with their creamy, voluptuous thighs, full, taut breasts, soft curves and feminine allure I'd follow like the call of the sirens. When I unleash myself on her, she can withstand me. She doesn't crumple, even when I punish her, dominate her, fuck her.

And I wonder, knowing now what I do, if being dominated helps her let go of negative associations she had with sex. Maybe it empowers her, yielding the way she does.

The woman was made for me.

A man like me likes a sturdy woman with curves and stamina. She's fucking gorgeous.

The way her eyes light up when I bring her to orgasm, the pink coloring of her cheeks. Parted lips and moans of pleasure, her sweet hands clasped about me while she anchors herself for safety. Steady breathing soft sighs. Everything about her is passionate and powerful, and I'm fucking honored how she submits to me.

Submission has many facets, though. She doesn't cave. Not my Caroline. Though she's learning what I like and adapting, she's got a will of iron and a mouth to match it. Witty and sharp, she keeps me on my toes.

Jesus.

Jesus.

I'm falling for her.

Never in my life have I fallen for a woman. I've dated, I've fucked, I've flirted and courted, but never, *never* has a woman wound her way around my heart and mind like Caroline.

It fills me with pride to know that she bears my name, my ring, and some day, I hope she'll come around to being amenable to bearing my children.

So when I leave her in our suite to be dolled up by Elliot, a stack of books by her bedside table and permission to help the kitchen staff prepare lunch, it pleases me to see how she smiles.

"You remembered," she says, her beautiful eyes alight with hope and pleasure.

"Remembered what?" I ask her, sliding my suit jacket on. I know exactly what she's talking about, but I want to hear her say it.

"You remembered that I like to cook."

"Of course," I tell her with mock sternness. "You'd do well to cook me a meal, woman. Wait staff is all well and good, but a good wife knows the way to her man's heart is through his stomach."

I'm teasing her, but I don't think she knows it.

"Does she?" she asks me softly, her head tipped to the side. I can practically see the wheels spinning.

"I like hearty meals," I tell her. "Comfort food. I work hard, and when I eat, I take it seriously. No light fare on my table. Salads are for rabbits."

She gives me an all-out grin, and I swear to God in

that moment I'd give her anything she fucking asked for. "Noted, sir."

Sir. God, she stirs something in me when she calls me that and I know she does it on purpose. I can't fucking wait to take her beyond where she's comfortable and push her to a place of deep, deep submission.

Christ, I'm hard again at the mere thought.

"Do you like sweets?" she asks.

"Far too much," I admit. "I don't keep many around, because they tempt me, but I do have a sweet tooth."

"I'm surprised," she says with a smile, while Eliott styles her hair. "That a man of your physique actually eats carbs."

"Of course he does," Eliott says in his thick French accent, waving his hand as if to dismiss me. "A man with fire like him burns calories by walking. He isn't afraid of pizza or pastries."

She giggles, and it's so damn cute.

I step over to her and brush Eliott away for a moment, before I tuck her hair behind her ear. Leaning in, I whisper, "I like to eat more than carbs, sweetheart. I'll eat you out morning and night. No panties without permission. This evening I'll inspect to see if you've obeyed. And when I tell you, you'll finger yourself to be ready for me. Understood?"

"Tomas!" she says in a heated whisper, flushing bright pink.

"Don't you dare disobey me," I warn, resting my hand on her collarbone and flexing my fingers. "Unless you want to be punished." I grasp her ear lobe between my teeth and bite just enough to make her squirm. Reaching down, I palm her breast. I don't care if anyone sees. Caroline is *mine.*

I leave her panting.

I'll need her ready for me when I get back. The job I have before me now is not an easy one.

I step into the hall and my guards flank my sides. They're ever-present, prepared to protect me at all costs. I nod to them to acknowledge them, but my head is elsewhere. I'm thinking all things Caroline, and how I need to approach the next meeting I'm about to have, so that I don't even notice Nicolai is in the meeting room until he punches my shoulder.

"When'd you get in?" I ask.

"Last night. Jesus, man, you're a mile away," he says. "New wife keep you up all night?"

He shoots me a lascivious wink, then bellows with laughter when my silence confirms his suspicion.

"Well *done,*" he says, but I give him a warning look. My men are entering the room, and we have business to attend to.

"How's married life?" he asks in my ear when he finally gets the point.

"Excellent. And how's life with a pregnant wife?" I ask him pointedly.

He rolls his eyes in response.

I need to get to the point. "Nicolai, I have a proposal I'm going to make this morning, and I'll need your help with what I'm about to do."

He sobers. "Of course, brother. I owe you everything, Tomas. You say the word."

I wonder if he'll be so quick to promise his allegiance when he finds out I'm planning cold-blooded murder and moves that will start war between rival groups. That I am going to murder Aren and Andros and any other man that touched my wife.

The room hushes when I stand up, my hands on my hips, taking in quick attendance.

"Have all arrived?" I ask Lev.

"Yes."

"Where is the guard that went missing last night?"

A young recruit holds up his hand, meeting my gaze but fidgeting nervously.

"Ilya," I say, proclaiming his name for all to hear. He's a new recruit, joining our ranks just last week.

"Explain yourself," I tell him. "Where were you?"

He looks to the side and meets Yakov's eyes. "Tell him," Yakov orders, like a stern older brother.

Ilya looks back my way but stares at the floor. "I was

with my girlfriend," he says. "She'd just flown in from Florida, and I wanted to greet her." He shrugs. "Yakov found me."

Yakov grunts in disapproval, his arms on his chest. New recruits ought to know better than this, that you don't fuck around with important nights like last night.

"Do you have any idea what possibilities went through my mind?" I ask him. I know I'm scolding him like an errant child, but he needs to feel the weight of this.

He hangs his head. "No, sir."

"We have rival Bratva," I tell him. "My men know things that others are not privy to. You being taken means that someone could have been seeking personal revenge, or they were planning to torture you to extract information."

His head shoots up. "I would never reveal confidential information, sir. Never."

"And yet you couldn't even keep your fucking dick in your pants for one night, to attend the reception for your *pakhan's* wedding? It was more important to you that you go see your girlfriend?"

He looks suitably shamed.

"How am I to believe you can be trusted?" I shake my head. "Where is she?"

"Who, sir?"

"The girl."

His eyes widen and he stares at me in disbelief. He doesn't know us yet, and he likely suspects his punishment will be enacted on her.

"Why?" he asks, but Yakov cuffs him.

"You answer your *pakhan* when asked a question," Yakov chides.

Ilya flushes beet red. "She's in a hotel room in the city," he says. "I wanted her safe."

"Safe? A hotel room in downtown Boston is safe, when she's affiliated with one of Boston's underground criminals?" I let the weight of those words settle. "You left her there unattended? Do you have any idea what's at stake?" He doesn't meet my eyes. I take in a breath and let it out again.

Stupid, *stupid*.

"You go get her," I tell him. "Bring her here. You do not have a woman tied in any way to the brotherhood outside the vicinity without heavy protection. Do you understand me? You shouldn't have even brought her here. You'll be punished for that."

"Yes, sir," he says, nodding vigorously. "I'll go now."

"You'll go when I fucking tell you."

He flinches as if struck by a whip. Good. He needs to learn this lesson. It's humiliating to be dressed down by your *pakhan* in the presence of your brothers, but it needs to be done. There's too much at stake to half-ass any of this.

"From now until the weekend, you can be on kitchen duty," I tell him. "Let's see if Lydia finds you as charming as your girlfriend."

"Yes, sir," he says, looking down. I watch his reaction carefully. Anger when being chastened and publicly humiliated by a pakhan means he's someone who can take correction. Humility means he's willing to be corrected and rise to the challenge of brotherhood. Meekness and power go hand, or ought to. A leader who can't learn from his mistakes will let his authority go to his head.

We are old-fashioned men with old-fashioned principles. Assigning Ilya what's traditionally "women's work" will be suitable punishment. I nod to one of my men. "Attend him, please. And perhaps while you're on your way you can explain to him how allegiance to the Bratva works, brother."

"Yes, sir." He nods sternly to Ilya, and the two of them leave. I wait until they're gone before I get the attention of the others in the room.

"There's something we need to discuss," I tell them.

They sit up straighter, focused on me. Nicolai sits at my left and Yakov at my right. I feel their attention on me. These two would fight to the death for me.

Would all of them?

"My new wife," I tell them. "She's revealed information to me that will impact the next few months. Our course of action."

Nicolai gives me a curious look. Yakov sits up

straighter. I don't have a plan of attack, but I need to tell my men what I ultimately plan on doing.

"As many of you know, Caroline came from San Diego." They nod, and everyone's attention is on me. "Her brother Aren is brigadier. Have any of you noticed a scar?"

They nod and none look away. It's nothing to be ashamed of in our line of work, but a telltale sign of someone who's experienced tragedy. Often, our scars unite us.

"The scar was given to her by her brother's best friend." My blood heats, my voice shaking while I try to relay what Caroline told me without losing my fucking mind. "Andros sexually assaulted my wife. And he will pay for this."

"Fuck," Nicolai says. "Was he with her when she arrived?"

I shake my head. "No. Her brother likely knew he'd protest."

"Of course. Jesus."

"They will pay for this," I tell my men. "Both of them."

No one responds at first, and a hush settles in the room. Some no longer meet my eyes, and I'm surprised by their reaction. Do none see how imperative it is that we defend her honor? That we seek retribution for what they've done to her?

Nicolai is the first to speak. "Tomas, what do you

want from us? As *pakhan,* if you start a war with another group…" He looks uncomfortable, looking away from me.

"What do I want from you? Your support. I will not allow their crimes against her to go unpunished."

Yakov clears his throat. "With all due respect, Tomas, my concern is that you've only just met her. It takes months to truly know someone with an arranged marriage. What if—"

"Are you suggesting my wife is a liar?" I'm on my feet, glaring at him. I can't believe none of them see my point of view.

"He's right, Tomas," Nicolai says. As my closest brother, he challenges me when others would back down, but he needs to see my fucking point. "We can't go to war over an accusation someone you've only just met makes."

I glare at him, my anger taking over. "We can fucking go to war whenever I fucking say we do."

Silence.

I hate it as soon as I say it and wish I could take the words back. I've never pulled rank, and I don't like doing it now.

Nicolai holds my gaze, then gives me one firm nod. "Yes, sir."

Yakov nods as well. "Do you feel in your gut that what she speaks is truth?"

They didn't hold her in their arms after making

love, bathed in her tears. They don't know the sincerity in her gaze, or how she speaks of her brother and friend. They didn't see the man I beat who dared come near her; nor did they understand his purpose.

But I did.

I fucking *do*.

"Trust me, brothers," I ask, softening my voice. "I know that what she says is true."

"Every word of it."

I look up to see Caroline standing in the doorway, and my pulse accelerates. She did not have permission to leave the room and she wasn't invited to this conversation. I don't want her knowing they question the veracity of her accusations.

"Come here," I tell her, crooking a finger at her. She bites her lip, and I hope she fucking knows she's in trouble for this. Despite the fact that she's here without permission, when she reaches me, I breathe more easily. I sit and draw her on my lap, facing my men, my arm gently tucked about her waist.

"Tell them, sweetheart," I say, gentling my voice, before I lean in and whisper in her ear, "And we'll discuss why you're here when this meeting is over."

"Andros is my brother's best friend," she says. "One night, before my eighteenth birthday, he came to my room. He'd had too much to drink." Her voice wavers, and I reach my hand to hers. Sweet girl. This can't be easy for her. "He took my virginity that night." She swallows hard. "Against my will."

"Did you tell anyone?" a man to the right asks. It isn't until Caroline places a gentle hand on my shoulder that I realize she's trying to calm *me*.

I'm proud of her as she looks about the room without wavering or backing down, her voice clear and strong. "Not that night, no. He told me if I told anyone he would kill me." She laughs mirthlessly. "I was too young and naïve to realize that he was bluffing. Of course he wouldn't kill me. If he did, who would he rape?"

There's silence in the room. I want to catch the next plane straight to San Diego. I will hunt him. I will hurt him. I will *kill him*.

"I finally told my brother." Her voice grows cold and bitter. "Of course he didn't believe me." She sighs before she takes a deep breath.

The tension in the room is thick, palpable. Nicolai's hands are clenched into fists and Yakov is on his feet, pacing. The traditional men in our order are strong and powerful; they take women who can withstand their dominance and need to assert power. But the deep thread of old-fashioned ideals runs strong. The wife of the *pakhan* was abused at their hands, and my men will not stand down.

"I don't fucking care how long we've known her," Nicolai says, addressing the room. It's almost amusing how quickly he changes his tune when he hears my wife speak sincerely. There's a winsome wholesomeness about her that no one can mistake for anything but authenticity. "From her body language to her story, she speaks truth." He looks to me. "It goes without saying that I'd kill anyone who touched a hair on my wife's head." He faces the room. The men around him nod, some already on their feet, ready for instruction. "And now that Caroline is one of our own, we have a job to do."

"I'm telling you now," she says, and it's the first time her voice shakes. "He'll come to me. He hasn't let me go. Andros still thinks of me as his, and he will seek me out. Everyone knows I'm here now."

"Over my dead fucking body," I say plainly. "If the only way to ensure your safety from that monster is to kill him, my goal is clear."

I don't normally approve of cold-blooded murder. Even among thieves and criminals, we have a code of honor we abide by. Retribution and revenge are suitable reasons for murder. Andros has brought this on himself.

Yakov nods. "We'll form a plan of attack," he says. "You decide what you want, sir." He bows his head to me. "I will hear and obey. Caroline, the brotherhood will avenge you. You are our family now. And no one hurts one of us without suffering the consequences."

They are ready to follow me to battle. I will lay my life down not only for Caroline, but for every goddamn one of them. For my brothers.

My men begin to assemble. They're prepared to follow my lead.

"Will you challenge him?" Nicolai asks. "Demand he show himself? Or do this personally?"

"First, we find him," I say. "Location before action. Then once we do, we make our move."

Caroline turns to face me and rests her head on my chest. Her exhale says what she can't speak. This was hard for her to face, hard to speak.

"My girl is so brave," I say in her ear, then while my men leave the room, I hold her without speaking. I have no idea what will happen when we attack San Diego. When I punish the men who hurt her. But I know that I won't regret a fucking thing I do.

Chapter 14

Caroline

I HAD to see him in action. I wanted to see him as *pakhan*, the leader of these powerful men. I couldn't sit in the room another minute, wondering where he was or what he was doing.

Okay, so *technically*, I wasn't allowed out of the room. He *did* tell me to stay.

Maybe I don't accept my role as captive bride, but willing participant. I may have been forced to marry him, but I'd like to retain *some* autonomy.

Or maybe a part of me wondered what would happen if I left. If he'd make good on his promise to punish me for disobedience.

I don't know why I need him to. I don't know why I need to test his mettle, to be sure he's someone who will follow through on what he says. But I do.

It didn't take long to find him. Though this place is large, it's well structured, and it's clear that social obligations are in one place and business in another. Or maybe it was even some intuition at play, but I found him within minutes.

He doesn't know I heard everything. I sat in the shadows, unseen by any of them, while he reprimanded his new recruit for failing at his duty. He's so stern and powerful when he commands his men, like an older brother, or lieutenant in an army. They defer to him with the utmost respect, and for some reason that makes me feel weirdly proud of him. He's earned this position as leader, and it's hot that others respect my husband.

And then he brought up Andros and Aren.

I'm almost sorry I disobeyed him, because I'd like to thank him for defending me. How, I'm not sure, but now he's looking at me with displeasure.

"You stay right there," he commands, while his men take their leave. He speaks to someone to his right and demands an update this evening. Finally, the last man leaves and it's just the two of us in the room. I worry my lip.

He's going to punish me.

I both fear and crave it.

I swallow hard, clear my throat, and busily begin very carefully inspecting one of my cuticles.

"Caroline."

Tomas stands in front of a desk, still dressed in the formal attire from this morning, his arms crossed on his chest.

"Um. Yes? By the way, thank you for… for starting that," I finish lamely.

He gives me one nod to acknowledge this, then clears his throat. "What did I tell you before I left the room?"

I bite my lip and shrug. "To stay?"

"And what did I tell you about obeying me?" I feel like a child with her hand caught in the cookie jar, but unlike childhood humiliation, this is laced with an understanding that complicates my reaction. My breasts swell, and there's a decided tingle between my thighs. Though I feel young and chastened, his dominance stirs me to arousal.

I laugh nervously. "Oh," I say, trying to make light of this. "You did say something about me earning a spanking?"

His furrowed brow and narrowed eyes only make my heart beat faster. Without a word, he crooks one finger at me.

It suddenly dawns on me that not only does he fully intend on punishing me as I suspected, but he's going to do it *here*.

Ohhhh, no.

But he's sitting there waiting for me, all sexy as sin in his suit, waiting for me.

"*Now,* Caroline."

Gah.

I walk to him on shaking knees, not so sure how I feel about this. When I reach him, he takes me by the chin and holds my gaze with his.

"I don't think you fully understand how vital your obedience is. Do you, little *detka?*"

I shrug. "Maybe not?"

He nods, as if contemplating my demise. "Perhaps I should take you back to the room and show you exactly what happens to little girls who don't know how to obey."

I laugh nervously. "Oh… I don't know if I need a demonstration. I can… imagine."

"You need a demonstration."

Eep.

His nearly playful scolding takes on a suddenly serious edge. "Did you hear me command my men to prepare for battle against your brother?"

I swallow hard. "I did. Yes, sir."

Nodding, still grasping my chin, he continues, his tone razor-sharp.

"Did you hear my men initially question your sincerity?"

I did. I nod, my voice smaller now. "Yes, sir."

"It is vitally important that we unite our forces in

what we face, Caroline. And they will not readily defend a woman who doesn't obviously defer to her husband's authority. We have a hierarchy here, one not even my men will disrupt, for the lives of everyone here are on *my* shoulders. Even yours. Do you understand?"

Now that he puts it that way, I feel ashamed that I left the room.

"To be honest, I *didn't* understand that, Tomas, but now I do."

He nods. "And will you do better next time?"

"Of course. I'm so sorry."

"Good girl," he says. "I will consider that when I punish you."

Oh my God. He's still going to punish me? My heart races in my chest and my palms grow sweaty. There's an inexplicable, expectant pulsing low in my belly.

"Is that still necessary?" I ask, my voice strangely high. I feel I need to at least try to defend myself. "I mean, we've already come to an understanding, and I'm not a child." Now that I'm on a tangent, I can't stop myself. "And frankly, I would like to remind you that I'm not your captive, but your *wife*." I have talked myself into becoming indignant. "And remember, I was the one that convinced them. And to be honest, I don't think you really have the right to punish me."

Weirdly, in my heart of hearts, I don't want him to

let me off the hook. I want to know he's a man of his word. And I'm quite curious about this whole punishment thing.

His brows raised, he releases my chin and reaches for his waist.

"It is absolutely necessary. You're just digging yourself into a deeper hole now, Caroline." I freeze at the sound of his belt being unfastened. "Lift your skirt and bend over the desk."

"Tomas," I whisper. "Here? Anyone could see."

I'm suddenly dizzy with anticipation and fear.

"Good. Let them see what happens to the wife of the *pakhan* when she disobeys. Now, I will not tell you again."

With a tug, he removes his belt from his waist and folds it over, then points to the desk with the looped end.

I don't know how I do it. I'm so in over my head with this. I'm all kinds of scared and turned on and embarrassed, but somehow my body obeys despite my misgivings.

Because I know I need to do this.

I'm like a junkie waiting for her next hit. Chasing the high I get when he punishes me. Testing his resolve.

I obey. I'm aware of how vulnerable I am like this, where literally anyone could see me. Once I'm bared to him, I gingerly place myself over the desk and grasp the edge. I feel like I'm on display for everyone to see, though we're technically alone in here. What if someone walks in?

"Is this part of your kink?" I say over my shoulder. "Do you *like* the idea of anyone seeing me like this?"

"Oh, so now's a good time to mouth off, is it?"

"I just don't know... I mean, really, Tomas... anyone could come in, and I—"

"I like the idea of my wife obeying me," he says sharply. "And knowing that disobedience will bring about swift punishment."

"You remembered my admonition about the panties," he says with approval, making me squirm with arousal and apprehension. "Good girl."

"I am trying, sir," I say, just before the leather lash whistles through the air.

I hiss and make a sound like a little *squeak*, but it doesn't hurt *quite* as badly as I thought it would. It's more like an erotic burn, leaving heat and arousal in its wake.

"As my wife, I'll expect you to obey," he lectures in that deep, growly voice, before another hard stripe of his belt lands across my ass. This hurts worse than the first, and I'm closing my eyes to brace for another spank. "And I don't need a reason to punish you, little *datka*. Give me a reason, and you've made my day."

The leather slices through the air again, and again,

and again, painting my ass with throbbing heat, but it ignites something else within me, molten and simmering just below the surface as he lectures and corrects. He's strong. He's capable. And he's ferociously possessive.

My husband.

I'm panting by the time he's done, vaguely aware of him lacing his belt back through the loops on his pants. His large, calloused palm caresses my scorched ass, and he squeezes. I come up on my toes from the pain and intensity.

"Tomas," I breathe. "Oh, ouch."

"Learned your lesson, then, wife?"

"I have." I part my legs, giving him an open invitation.

"And what is it?"

"If you tell me to stay put, stay put." He doesn't touch me between my legs, and I'm dying for some relief and pleasure. I spread my legs wider.

"Is there something else you need besides a good spanking?" he asks.

I shrug. "Well… you know…" My voice trails off. I'll die if I have to tell him.

"Not every spanking will end with orgasm," he says firmly. "Though it pleases me to know you're aroused with punishment, arousal isn't my only purpose." Grasping my hips from behind, he grinds his crotch against my throbbing backside. I smile to myself when I feel his erection. He likes this as much as I do.

There's a world of possibilities, really.

"Be a good girl for the rest of the afternoon," he says, stepping back. "I have a few things to show you. If you behave, I'll grant you that pleasure you want when we get back to our place. Understood?"

I sigh but do as he says, even though I want to stomp my foot. I know that won't get me anywhere. Plus, I'm curious what he wants to show me.

I pause at his chuckle. "Are you laughing at me?" I ask incredulously.

"Laughing at you? No, sweetheart," he says. "You're just adorable when you pout."

I furrow my brow and let my lower lip stick out, not even bothering to hide my pout. "Am I?" I actually like how it feels to let myself relax like this. To not have to put on a brave face and be all grown up about it. He punished me, and it hurt. I want to come, and he won't let me yet. I just told the men here about what happened to me, and we're all on the cusp of war. My emotions are many and varied.

Turning me to face his chest, he laces his arms about my back and pulls me to him. I didn't expect this tenderness after my punishment. "So adorable it makes me want to punish you all over again just to see that pouty lip."

I make a little *mewl* of protest.

"Sir," I say. "I'm good now." I lay my head on his chest. "I'm your good little girl."

I don't understand why I'm acting this way, all coy and playful, but there's freedom in submission. When I let myself give way to him, despite his stern demeanor and heavy hand, I feel lighter somehow. As if the responsibility of even my thoughts can rest for a while, in the knowledge that he's the one in charge. But I accept this. I grant him this authority.

"Such a good little girl," he says, allowing me to burrow onto his chest. Tipping a finger under my chin, he lifts my gaze to his. There's nothing but tenderness in his look, and kindness in his eyes. "I can't help but want to kiss those pretty lips of yours," he whispers, brushing his thumb over my lower lip.

In response, I let my lips part ever-so-slightly. He's holding me upright, pressed to his chest, my body humming with need so intense I'm damn near dizzy from it, when his lips meet mine. At first, the kiss is tentative. Gentle. But as I sink lower into this, he deepens the kiss. I moan into him when his tongue finds mine, sending tingles of bliss through my body.

Groaning, he pulls away from me. "Beautiful," he tells me.

I love you.

I'm shocked at the intensity of the words that come to me so quickly, so powerfully, I'm mute. I can't possibly love someone I just met. But what is it about knowing that I'm his very special girl? That he's literally just commanded his men to go to war for me, to avenge the wrong done to me? It's somehow accelerated everything I feel, everything I need, right here in this moment.

I have to push it away, and I'm so intent on doing so I literally shake my head.

"What is it?" he asks. "What are you saying 'no' to?"

But how can I tell him I'm denying the feelings he evokes in me? That I'm a silly, wounded girl, who's falling for him like a house of cards. One breath of air, and I'll be completely at his mercy. Levelled.

"Nothing," I lie, and I think it might be the first lie I've actually told him. "It was just a knee-jerk reaction." I smile shyly and look down. "Honestly, sir, I love when you kiss me."

I love him.

I love this fierce, unyielding, jealous man who acts as if I'm his most treasured possession. I love how powerful he is, how stern. Even watching him command his men made me love him that much more.

Oh, God.

I love him.

And then he does the very thing that will seal my devotion to him. My inner voice warns me not to fall so hard, to heed the warning of my vulnerable, wounded heart.

He takes me by the hand, his much larger hand completely engulfing mine. My body's on fire, my mind is at war, and then I quiet a little when he says, "Okay, little *detka*. I've changed my mind for now. Let's take you to the kitchen for just a little while."

Chapter 15

Tomas

I HAVE to meet with Nicolai and Yakov and make our arrangements. I know I do. But there's nothing more I want to do than spend every moment with Caroline. So, I compromise. We'll eat lunch before we part again.

I wish I had time to take her back to our bedroom. But there will be time for that. There has to be.

I never go to the kitchen, I hardly know them, but they know me. I step into the kitchen with Caroline by my side. There's laughter and the sound of voices chattering good-naturedly. But when I enter the kitchen with Caroline, a hush comes over the kitchen staff.

"Mister Dobrynin," says a tall woman wearing an

apron, her hair pinned to the nape of her neck. "To what do we owe this pleasure?"

"I'd like to introduce you to my wife. Her name is Caroline."

She takes Caroline's hand and shakes it vigorously with both of hers. "Mrs. Dobrynin. So pleased to meet you. Welcome. I'm Lydia, head chef here." She introduces her to the rest of the staff. Caroline literally glows with pleasure, grinning.

"So nice to meet you," she says.

She's fucking adorable.

"Caroline loves cooking, and I promised her that I'd allow her to work with you. Shortly I go join my men, and I'd like you to welcome her to work with you."

Lydia blinks. "Work in the kitchen, sir?" she asks. It's unusual for anyone of my position to even step into the kitchen, and it's almost shocking for my wife to join as well. Her staff looks at her expectantly while she processes my request.

"Whatever she wants," I tell them. I want this abundantly clear how vital this is that they give her this, that no one treat her differently because she's the wife of the *pakhan*.

I want everyone to love this woman.

Lydia nods slowly, then smiles at Caroline. "So you'll be helping us prepare tonight's dinner. Good. I can use an extra set of hands." She waves her hand at someone at the back of the kitchen. "Fetch Mrs. Dobrynin an apron," she orders.

Caroline shakes her head. "Please call me Caroline."

I make a sound of disapproval. She's not their equal, and I want her to remember that. She has a place of honor in this home.

But Caroline puts her hand on my arm and smiles at me. "Tomas," she says, those eyes of hers melting whatever wall I've built to damn near nothing. "It's fine. Please. Go, meet with your men and come back when you're ready for me." Holding onto my arms, she goes up on her tiptoes and kisses my cheek and right then, I'd give that sweet girl literally anything she asked for. She whispers in my ear, "We have business to attend to later."

Christ, like I'd forget.

"Behave," I whisper, pulling her to me and kissing her forehead before I leave. And I swear to God when I leave that kitchen, I leave a little part of myself there with her. I don't know how I've earned this woman. What I've done in my life should have earned me damnation, not this sweet woman that calls me husband.

I go about my business, and I don't realize I'm only half paying attention until Nicolai waves a hand in front of my face and snaps his fingers.

"Where the hell are you, brother?" he asks. "Did you hear a word I said?"

"Sorry," I tell him. "Please repeat it."

Yakov snorts and elbows Nicolai. "Someone needs to get back to his wife, I think." He winks and says something filthy in Russian that I only catch the end of, but it's something about my body being here and my cock somewhere else.

"You two want to join Ilya in the kitchen?"

Nicolai laughs and Yakov snorts out loud. "You sure you want Ilya in the kitchen, Tomas? Didn't you send your new wife there? You want her scrubbing potatoes with a new recruit?"

Christ, I didn't think of that. I ignore their laughter as I leave the room and head to the kitchen. No, I'm not sure I want some fucking recruit flirting with my wife. If he gets too close to her, he'll have another kind of punishment to face, much harsher than the one he does now.

I push the doors open to the kitchen and freeze. No one sees me at first, and I unexpectedly get a glimpse of Caroline from another angle.

Large picture windows illuminate the room, and she stands in a pool of sunlight while rolling out dough. She's laughing easily with a young, petite brunette by her side, and a small circle of employees stand around her. She's directing them to add ingredients to a large mixing bowl, and I muse at their rapt attention on her instructions. They love her already. I can see it in the way they talk to her, how easily they laugh and how everyone is eager for her instructions.

It takes me a minute to find Ilya, who's far off in the corner of the room with a massive pot of potatoes and a pile of peelings. He's scowling. I walk over to him before I interrupt Caroline. His reaction to my presence will be telling.

"Good job. What have you done today?"

He looks up at me in surprise, and he immediately bows his head. "Sir. I didn't see you come in." He clears his throat and straightens. "I've done everything Caroline asked of me."

Caroline?

"Oh?"

"She said we needed ten pounds of potatoes peeled, and I'm almost done."

I nod. "Well done. And did you secure your girlfriend?"

"I did, sir. She's in a room on the second floor. I haven't seen her yet, but Yakov assured me she's well taken care of." I like this new recruit. He may have fucked up, but he's making amends for his mistake, and he shows meekness, a necessary trait.

"Well done. And what was your lesson in this?"

"Do the duty assigned me, sir."

"Always. One thing you'll learn about our brotherhood is that your brothers will defend you to the death. Your honor, your integrity, your life. They're your family."

He nods humbly, pausing in his work. "I'm sorry, sir. I promise you; it won't happen again."

I believe him. "Good. After you've finished your job, you may leave for today. Nicolai will assign you your next duty."

"Yes, sir."

I turn to go to Caroline, but he stops me. "Sir?"

"Yes?"

He looks to Caroline, and his eyes darken, the first indication that this man has earned his place in the Bratva. He can be ruthless when necessary. "It would be an honor to punish those who hurt her."

His comment takes me by surprise, but my reaction even more so. My heart squeezes. My beautiful wife, so afraid that others would scorn her for her scars and imperfections. But just by simply being the beautiful woman she is, she's already earned her way into the hearts of my men and my staff.

"When the time comes, I'll have Nicolai give you instructions," I tell him. "Until then, prove your allegiance with obedience."

He nods, and I swear he almost salutes me like a soldier, he's that rigid and serious. "Yes, sir."

I go to Caroline next. During my discussion with Ilya, the staff have realized that I'm here, and Caroline stands just a few paces away, smiling at me. Her hair is a mess, her makeup long gone, she has flour on her nose and her apron's smattered with the telltale signs of cooking, but she's never been more beautiful to me.

I crook a finger and hold my breath when she walks toward me.

I could love this woman. Hell. I may already.

When she reaches me, she unfastens her apron and hangs it on a hook, then brushes her hair off her forehead and sighs.

"You caught me in the middle of some big doings," she says with a smile. "I hope you're hungry tonight." She seems proud, and that pleases me. I haven't known her for long, but I suspect Caroline hasn't had much to be proud of or much to look forward to. I want this for her.

"Starving," I tell her. When she reaches me, I sling an arm around her waist, lean down and inhale her scent. "Do you know how to cook the food of my homeland, little *detka*?"

"Of course, I do. And which name do you mean now?" she asks with a coy little smile. "Baby or brat?"

"That depends. Have you misbehaved?"

Her little smile makes my chest tighten and my breathing hitch. She has no idea how her eyes light up when she's flirting with me, how her cheeks flush with color when she submits to me. And her ignorance of her beauty is part of the appeal.

"Of course not, sir."

"Then you're my baby," I say, pulling her even closer to me and burying my face in her hair. I run my hands through the soft mass, breathing in deeply, before I whisper in her ear. "But I hope you misbehave soon."

"So soon?" she whispers back. "My butt still aches from the punishment you gave me." She swallows hard, resting her head in the crook of my neck. "And honestly, it isn't the only thing that aches."

She needs me to make good on my promise.

"When will dinner be ready?"

"Twenty minutes." Not enough time for what I plan to do.

"How will you cook enough potatoes for an army in twenty minutes?"

Her eyes twinkle and she beckons for me to dip my head low so she can whisper to me. "We don't need those potatoes for this evening. But I overheard you saying that your new recruit needed to be humbled, so I've put him to peeling potatoes. They'll keep in water."

I smile at her. "You'd be a good mother, sweetheart. We would make a good team, you know, you and I."

Her eyes cloud, but I don't push the issue.

She shows me around the kitchen while everyone performs their final preparations. "Now, husband, out to the dinner table. We will serve you momentarily. And I'd like to get ready for dinner."

"I'll go back to our room with you and we'll both get ready."

She gives me a teasing look. "Tomas, if I go with you back to the room, we'll never make it out in time for dinner."

She has a point.

So, I join Nicolai and Yakov at the table and have a cold beer before she comes. It feels good to sit here with my brothers, preparing to eat dinner served by my wife, and I know the plans I have for the evening ahead.

"You let her in the kitchen?" Yakov asks curiously. "Are you sure that's wise?'

"Of course," I tell him. "It's something she's passionate about, and I want her to feel at home. And what harm could befall her there?" We're so heavily guarded, I know she's safe.

Yakov scorns. "It's servant's work."

I nod and take another pull of my beer before I respond. "We've all done our part in hard labor, Yakov. Have we not?" Nicolai was in the military and served as bodyguard for his Atlanta brotherhood for years. Yakov has a history as a bricklayer in Russia before he became Brava.

"But she's a woman."

"It doesn't matter. There's no shame in honest, hard work." I shrug. "And it matters to me that she can pursue her passions."

Yakov's lips thin before he takes another drink.

"What is it?" I press. "What concerns you?"

"You grow too soft with her, too easily," he says. "A spoiled woman will not learn to respect her husband. And as leader of our brotherhood, many look up to you."

"He has a point, brother," Nicolai chimes in.

Unbelievable. These two fell so hard for their women it's become a running joke among the brotherhood.

I snort. "And who was the one who bought a puppy for his woman not a week ago?" I ask Yakov.

"Of course I did," Yakov says. "He's a pitbull. He'll protect her in my absence."

"She bought him a *raincoat*, Yakov."

He shrugs. "That doesn't mean he won't protect her. And it definitely doesn't mean she doesn't obey me when I demand it."

I turn to Nicolai. "And who was the one literally *massaging* his pregnant wife's feet? Hmm? And I'm the one who's grown too soft?"

Nicolai rolls his eyes. "I've known Marissa longer than I've known any of you. And believe me, she knows what I expect of her whether I'm giving her a foot rub or drawing her a bath. In fact, one of the reasons she's so devoted is *because* I take such good care of her."

"Precisely." They quiet when I speak. "And this is no different. In her home, Caroline was not allowed in the kitchen. She was mistreated and abused. She shall not be here. She will do her duty to me as my wife, and I'll expect no less." I harden my voice. Though these two are my brothers and fellow Bratva, I'm still their *pakhan*. "But I'll allow her in the kitchen if she wishes. There will be a time and place to ensure her loyalty and obedience. Just as there's a time and place for *you* to show your loyalty and obedience to me."

They nod and both of them grow sober. "And I won't hear another word about how soft I've grown with my wife."

"You need to take time to get to know her," Yakov says.

I've had enough of their admonition.

"We have the rest of our lives to get to know one another. We're wedded to each other."

"Tomas," Nicolai says warningly. "You're infatuated with her. Don't forget who her brother is. It's in her best interest to earn your approval. She's on her best behavior now, but it won't always be that way."

In the far corner of the room, I see Caroline in the doorway. She's changed into a clean dress, brushed her hair, and waits for me to beckon her to come.

I smile at her and beckon for her to come to me and speak to Yakov and Nicolai in a low whisper she can't hear. "This conversation is over. I don't want to hear another word from you two about how I treat her."

But I can't shake their warnings. Am I infatuated with the newness of us? I can't forget where Caroline came from, and I know that. But sometimes, sincerity and integrity overcome abuse. Sometimes, those who are repressed and hurt rise above the cruelty they've suffered, and beauty rises from the ashes. My gut says she isn't playing me, she hasn't merely put on a show.

I'm tempted to tell them to leave us. I don't want to be reminded of what they've said to me while I dine with my new wife. I want to enjoy her alone. But I decide instead to compromise. They can stay with me for now, but we'll eat dessert alone.

I can't ignore their warnings that play in my mind. I can't ignore my most trusted advisors. Is she really who she appears to be?

Chapter 16

Caroline

I PREPARED for dinner tonight as nervous as a young girl about to go on her first date. But tonight isn't our first time together. My body still hums with need, still remembers the pain of his punishment and pleasure he's granted me. Yet my hands shake when I fix my hair, and I need to have Eliott help me zip my dress.

At first when I came back to the room and found a note from Eliott, I found it a bit over the top.

Ring me to help you prepare for dinner.

Who am I, that I need the assistance of someone for such a silly, daily task? I fumbled with my preparations until I realized I couldn't quite do it alone.

So I called. He came in less than a minute, beaming from ear to ear.

"I'm glad you gave me this opportunity," he said, then in minutes, my dress was zipped, my makeup fixed, my hair done.

"I can't do this every day," I tell him. "I mean, eventually I need to be able to handle my own—beautification or whatever."

He grins and wags a finger at me. "And why can you not do this every day, mmm?"

I shrug. "It seems so shallow and unnecessary."

He shakes his head. "*Mon amie,* you still think like a single girl and not like the wife of the *pakhan.* Your appearance is of vital importance. When you present yourself as haggard or unkempt, it reflects on your respect for your husband."

I laugh out loud. "Eliott, not having a personal assistant fix my hair and makeup hardly makes me unkempt. Need I remind you, the majority of women take care of their own appearances?"

"Hush," he says, dismissing my protests with another wave of his hand. "The majority of women are not wife to the *pakhan.* Eventually, you will learn how to prepare. But don't put me out of a job quite yet, yes?"

So, I let him get me ready. But now that I face my husband, in this massive, impressive dining room, surrounded by those powerful, muscled men he calls brothers, I lose a bit of my resolve. I look to him and wave, then feel heat creep up my neck. I *waved* at him, like we were friends meeting up at a bar. *Gah*. And his reaction doesn't soothe my nerves. He beckons to me sharply, a scowl on his face.

Did I do something wrong? I hate that I fear this, but I do. He's my husband, and I wish to please him.

"You look stunning," he says with pleasure when I reach him. Standing, he places a possessive hand on my lower back and kisses my cheek. My heart does a crazy little skip in my chest at the gentle kiss. I'm pleased with his praise.

"Thank you. I felt silly calling Eliott, but I needed help." He pulls out a chair for me and I sit. I look down at the table and reach for the napkins to steady my shaking hands. "Eventually, I'll know how to do these things myself."

"Then I'd have to fire Eliott," he says. "Are you sure you want that?" Though his eyes twinkle at me, I can't help but take him seriously.

"Would you fire him if I didn't need him?"

"Relax, Caroline," he says, but he looks as if his mind is elsewhere. "Eliott is here to serve you. Allow him."

One of the kitchen staff approaches me before I can respond, and I answer her question about which dish to serve first. When I turn back to Tomas, he's scowling. What have I done?

"I'd prefer to serve you the food I—" I begin, but before I can finish my sentence, he shakes his head sharply.

"I allowed you to cook, but under no condition will you serve me or my brothers. You are not paid staff, Caroline. You are wife to the *pakhan*."

I feel as if he's doused me with cold water, the pleasure I felt just moments ago at his praise dashed that quickly, and now he's scowling again.

Did I imagine any tenderness on his part? Was it merely in my head, thinking he wanted to let me pursue my interests and actually have some semblance of normalcy to married life? And as I mull on this, I feel my own irritation rising. Maybe he only patronized me to placate me, and now he wants me in my place.

How could I have ever thought he could ever love a girl like me?

I look down at my handsome husband, unable to meet his eyes. I'm no longer hungry for the food that I made.

What if he's no better than my brother? What if I haven't escaped to a better place but chained myself to a man who will never love me, who will make me bear his children, and who'll punish me if I step a toe out of line? It's a sobering and fairly nauseating possibility.

"Stop pouting," he snaps, when the server brings us the first course, salad, followed by pierogi.

I swallow the lump in my throat and try to take a bite of the food, but I'm practically choking it down.

I finally put my fork down. My tongue feels too big, my mouth dry.

After a moment of silence, he furrows his brows. "Why aren't you eating?" His tone makes me stiffen my spine and snap my gaze to his.

"I'm not hungry," I say, unable to mask the petulance in my voice.

"I don't care if you're hungry or not. Eating isn't an option. You'll eat a decent meal without question." He dumps food onto my plate with a scowl.

I cross my arms on my chest and glare at him. I'm aware that I'm acting like a toddler, but I don't want to eat anything against my will, and he's being a jerk.

He takes a large forkful of pierogi and makes a low sound of approval.

"Christ, this is good, little *detka*," he says. "You made this?"

The lump in my throat softens a little. "I did," I say. I'm fighting this so hard, but I can't help but still like his praise. "I made it with assistance, but I did teach them. And I'm glad you like it."

I take a little bite myself. He's right. It *is* good.

Maybe he just needs to eat a little, for after half a dozen enormous bites, his plate is empty, and his gaze has softened a bit. I follow suit and eat.

"Good girl," he says with approval. "That's much

better." They bring in the main dish as planned, and now my grumpy bear of a husband actually smiles.

"Is that *befstroganov*? I haven't had that in a decade or more. If you can make befstroganov and well, I may have to reward you. I might even overlook the little attitude you gave me earlier." I had a suspicion a rich meat dish in a creamy sauce over noodles would go over very well with him.

I hide a smile, but when he takes a huge bite and groans out loud with pleasure, I don't bother hiding my smile anymore.

"You like it, then?"

"This is delicious," he says. "It's the best I've ever had." It seems my grumpy husband doles out praise and punishment in equal measure. He's giving me veritable whiplash. I feel like I need to hold on tight to survive the ride.

After he's finished his portion, the final dish comes out and we both eat heartily. He pushes himself away from the table after eating literally three times what I do, and I eat a good amount. Wiping his mouth, he looks at me with approval, nodding slowly to himself.

"That was a meal fit for a king, Caroline," he says. "Thank you."

"Did you save room for dessert?" I'm so pleased he's happy, that he enjoyed this meal that I made, my heart feels light as a feather. I wish I wasn't so sensitive to his approval, so eager for his praise, for my logical mind warns me this places me in danger...in a state of raw vulnerability where I can so easily be hurt.

I wish it didn't matter to me as much as it does, but I can't deny the fact that his approval thrills me. Somehow, I feel winning the heart of the beast makes me victorious, empowered. He's no easy one to love, but I can't help but want to.

"Dessert will be served in our private rooms," he says, standing. Reaching a hand out to me, he lifts me to my feet. "We have much to discuss, and I have no more patience left. I want you alone, *now*."

I get to my feet, suddenly nervous. What will he do to me when we're alone? He's made reference to his tools and the wicked things he wishes to do to me.

Will he make good on that promise?

I get to my feet and take his hand. It's hard leaving the dishes behind, knowing the staff will care for them. I wasn't treated like this in my former home. Though kept apart from waitstaff, I was never waited on. I fixed my own meals and kept my own counsel.

It was a lonely life.

"This food was delicious, Caroline," the man with a shaved head who witnessed my marriage says.

"Thank you."

The redhead sitting next to him, Yvonne's husband, nods with approval. "I agree. I haven't had a meal like that in years." He smiles up at me. "Maybe you can teach Yvonne?"

I look to Tomas on instinct, and I can tell he approves of my silent request for permission when he gives me a small nod.

"I'm sure we can arrange that." But his voice is tight, his eyes hard when he looks at them. "Come here." He offers me his arm. I take it quickly, bow my head and follow him out of the dining room.

Ilya stands in the doorway, frowning.

"We didn't eat potatoes tonight," he says as we pass. "Why did you have me peel so many?"

Tomas stiffens. "Watch your tone, Ilya." He doesn't like that the young recruit is unhappy with me. I hold up a hand to tell him I can handle this.

I give Ilya the truth. "Your *pakhan* thought it suitable to humble you with menial work. Your *pakhan* is my husband, and it is my duty to ensure he's obeyed. But your work didn't go to waste, Ilya. You'll see what delicious meals we'll make tomorrow with the food you've prepared."

H nods his head. "Thank you," he says, then looking at Tomas, he apologizes. "I'm sorry, sir."

Tomas fixes him with such a stern look, I wonder at Ilya's ability to stand in his presence. He's uncompromising, but he seems fair enough. Well, mostly. I'm still not sure why he got all grumpy with me earlier.

"Clean the dishes after tonight's meal, and we'll speak in the morning."

I'm so in my head I don't realize we've made it all the way to our room, and when he opens the door, I start to tremble.

"Are you afraid, little *detka*?"

"Yes."

He unlocks the door, pushes it open, and ushers me in.

"That's good," he tells me. "A little fear can heighten the experience."

My heart beats faster.

"Go to the bedroom," he orders. "And lie down on the bed. The only thing you may take off is your shoes. Understood?"

I nod and walk to the room tentatively. I wonder what he has in store for me. It seemed easier submitting to whatever he asked of me before, but now I'm not so sure.

Do I disappoint him?

Does he intend to use me like Andros did? If he does, he's no better. He might pretend to be kind, and he might be fiercely possessive of me, but it's only because I'm his and he protects what's his.

Is it wrong that I like that?

I flop on the bed, frustrated and annoyed at myself,

but I don't know what to expect from him. He's so damn unpredictable.

I lay on the bed fully clothed, trying to school my features. I don't want my annoyance to show, because I already know that won't go over too well with him. I hear him on the phone.

"Bring the dessert to my room," he says. "Leave it outside the door on a tray. And be sure everyone knows not to disturb me until the morning."

Oh.

Oh.

It's got to be like six o'clock at night, and he doesn't want to be disturbed?

I doubt he's a Monday night football kinda guy.

I'm staring at the ceiling, wondering how things will go when the door to the bedroom creaks open.

"Good to know you've obeyed at least one instruction today," he says.

"Now that's not fair, I've obeyed more than that. In fact, I'm not even sure what else I've done other than leave here, and my ass already took *that* punishment."

"A husband can't tease?"

Is he really teasing? I didn't even know he was capable.

"You're hardly the teasing sort."

He's reaching for his tie, his eyes fixed on me. A moment ago, they twinkled, but he looks a little more serious now. "I'm not? How do you know, Caroline? You don't know me at all."

"And isn't that the problem." It isn't a question but a statement. We don't know each other, and here we are.

We stare at each other and neither says a word. This conversation has gotten way more serious than either of us anticipated. Oh, how I wish I *could* trust him fully.

"And what if I tell you I don't want you to touch me tonight?" I ask. I want to know what he says even though I have no intention of telling him any such thing. Why would I? I'm dying for him to take me to euphoric heights I've never known. He is so capable. God, he is.

Without a word, his dark brown eyes drill into mine, he unfastens his necktie and wraps it around his fist.

"Are you?" he asks. Of course, he puts it right back on me and doesn't play into my trap at all. He won't allow himself to be caught.

I bite my lip, not sure how to respond, when he crosses the room in firm, quick strides. Before I know what's happening, he wraps his silky tie around my mouth and knots it in the back.

"Go ahead. Tell me no."

I open my mouth to speak but all that comes out is a garbled mess.

The *bastard*.

He took away my ability to tell him no. I huff out in anger and glare at him. I have no intention of refusing sex with him. Sex with him is fucking epic. But I hate that he played me like that.

I glare.

"You know what happens to naughty little girls who glare like that at their husbands," he says, wagging a finger at me.

My eyes narrow, but I don't respond because I literally *can't*.

Why don't you tell me, you son of a bitch?

By now he's reached me, and he kneels on one knee beside me, leaning down to whisper in my ear. "They are punished by being denied pleasure, little *detka*. Brats don't come, Caroline."

I'm not a brat, *the jerk*.

He continues to whisper. "Is that what you want? Being on the edge of ecstasy but never reaching completion. Over. And over. And over."

Nooooo.

The bastard.

I'm super grateful he isn't a mind reader.

I don't respond, because I feel myself softening

toward him, and I don't want that, but the idea of him taking me to the edge of bliss and leaving me there... I could literally cry.

I sigh through the tie gag and shake my head.

"Your eyes are begging me," he says, brushing damp hair off my forehead. "Is that what you mean to say, sweetheart?"

Tomas is fierce and powerful, ruthless and possessive. I've seen him nearly kill a man and I have no doubt he's done it before. But he's held me and comforted me and has just commanded his entire brotherhood to take down the men that hurt me.

How could I not love him a little for that?

I hold his gaze and nod my head and don't blink while I silently beg him. He's left my hands free, so I reach for him with both arms. I want to hold him. Touch him. Feel his strength and let it empower me.

To my surprise, he lets me, gathering me in his arms and settling me on his lap. In silence, he holds me in the crook of his arm and begins to undress me.

His large fingers are surprisingly deft with the buttons on my dress, and in no time, he's removed it fully. I lay on his lap with nothing but panties and a bra, which he also makes quick work removing.

It surprises me when he places me on the floor between his legs and unfastens the tie around the back of my mouth.

"Now will you tell me no, sweetheart?" He brushes

his thumb along the apple of my cheek. I hate that he's putting this on me.

"Maybe," I say petulantly, though we both know there's no maybe about it.

"Maybe," he says to himself. "I'm curious, though, Caroline. Why did you get so angry with me at dinner?"

He's positioning me between his legs, in a kneeling position.

"I don't know why you wouldn't let me serve," I tell him. "It's like you're just using me to get what you want, and you don't care at all about what matters to me."

"All of that over one misunderstanding?"

"All of… what?"

"Your anger, your attitude, nearly getting yourself punished again for disrespect."

How can I tell him everything that I fear? That I've convinced myself that he's cold and heartless and incapable of love?

I don't respond, because I don't know how to. I look at the floor. Did I overreact? But he grabs my chin and makes me look at him.

"Do not look away from me," he says, in that stern tone of his that makes my nipples harden and my tummy clench. "No matter what."

I nod. "Yes, sir."

He unfastens his trousers and removes his belt. I swallow hard, and my ass aches in memory of what he did with that belt. Placing it on the bed in a coil, he unzips his pants.

That's when I realize what he's doing.

"Um, so, wait a minute," I say, suddenly nervous. "I... I don't know how to do that."

Reaching over to me, he tangles his fingers in my hair and pulls my head back. Oh, God, I love how that feels. My scalp tingles, my heartbeat racing as he tugs my head back. I didn't know getting my hair pulled was that erotic.

I'm in so much trouble.

"Open."

I do what he says.

He slides his cock between my lips. Tentatively, I close my mouth on him and suck.

It makes him groan, and it's all that I need.

I want to earn his possession and loyalty, to know that when he fights for me it's because of who I am, not *what* I am.

I want to please him so badly I could cry. I'd do anything to hear *good girl*, to see his eyes alight with pleasure, so when he sighs and bobs my head with his hand still fisted in my hair, I suck in earnest.

"Christ, Caroline," he groans. "Just like that. That's it, sweetheart."

I lick and suck and bob my head, watching his cues and doing what it takes to make him groan.

He releases my hair and runs a finger down the side of my face. "There's a submissive inside there, you know," he says. "When you please me, your eyes light up and your whole countenance lightens, like it's Christmas Day."

He closes his eyes while I work my mouth and tongue, my own body humming with need as he gets more and more aroused.

"That's dangerous, Caroline. The heart of a submissive must be guarded." He groans, rolling his hips and pumping into me harder, faster. I can't process what he's saying now. My breasts tingle and swell, and my pussy throbs with need. It's hard to hear him, hard to focus when I'm so overcome with arousal and need, so intent on bringing him pleasure.

He shocks me when he yanks my head away and shoves his cock back in his pants.

"Enough," he says. At first, I worry that I did something wrong, but I soon realize it's only because he doesn't want to climax this way.

"I want in you. On the bed," he groans. "Now."

I scramble on the bed on all fours, looking over my shoulder at him, but when I do, he slams his palm against my bare ass.

"Good girl," he approves, coming up behind me. "I

told you I'd take good care of you. Now on your back."

I flop on my back, stifling a whimper of need. He's on the edge himself, and his gaze is laser focused. If I didn't know he was turned the hell on, I would think he was angry, he's that serious.

"Arms above your head." I obey, leaving my entire body ripe with need and at his mercy. He strips, eyes focused on me, but I quickly look away because I want to look at him.

First, the buttons on his shirt. Sliding out of it, he tosses it in a hamper and stands before me wearing nothing but a t-shirt. I let my eyes roam unabashedly over his body, from his large muscled arms to the breadth of his chest. I swallow hard, a shiver gliding through me.

He's so fucking hot.

Next come his pants. He makes quick work of unbuttoning them and shoving them down. His erection springs free, and I stifle a whimper. He's murmuring things in Russian I can't quite make out, I'm so heady with need and want. He's brought me to the edge of pleasure today and I haven't been the same since.

He lowers his body to mine, and I want to reach for him. I want to touch him, but he's forbidden it.

"Do you have any idea how much I want you?" he whispers in my ear.

"With that erection of yours pushed between my thighs, I have a pretty good idea."

His chuckle in my ear makes me shiver. I bite my lip, unable to stop myself from nearly grinning. It feels like a win, every time. Then the voices in my head come to a stuttering halt and all I can do is *feel*.

"Tomas," I breathe, when he captures my wrists in his warm, firm grasp. He drops a kiss to my forehead, my temple, my cheek, whispers of kisses along my scar that make me shudder.

"Don't," I whisper, but his grip tightens, and he doesn't stop.

"Every inch of you is mine," he says with purpose, his voice tight and controlled. "And I will own you."

Not my heart.

He doesn't hear my internal protest, but he feels it, because his body tenses.

"Do you hear me?" he says in my ear. "*Own* you."

He kisses me again, the roughness of his whiskers belying the softness of his lips. I don't know why I fight this so badly, but I do, as if I can't willingly relinquish a part of me that's still locked away.

When his mouth meets mine, I moan. I try to control it. I try to hold myself back. I don't want to submit to him, but being so near, I'm dazzled with his scent and strength, and my core throbs with need.

Reaching down, he palms one of my breasts, grazing

his thumb over the hardened peak before he takes my mouth. His tongue meets mine, at once possessive. I groan when he fingers my nipple while kissing me. I want so much more. My hips roll beneath him, my wrists pressed firmly in his grasp, and every stroke of his thumb on my nipple makes my pussy throb with need until I think I'm going to come just from his fingers on my breast.

I'm so ready to fly, right on the edge of losing total control.

"Tomas," I moan when he stops kissing me.

"Sir."

I quickly amend. "Sir. Oh, God. Please, sir. I need you inside me."

Being taken by Tomas is so different from what was done to me—I can't speak of it or even think of it—that it's inexplicably healing. Being claimed by him and brought to pleasure makes me feel owned in the best possible way. Yet, I resist it. I fight it. I don't want to be hurt again.

"Christ, woman," he says in my ear. I exhale when he takes the head of his cock and presses it to my clit. "You're so fucking tight and wet. So responsive to me. You're ready, aren't you, little *detka*?"

"Yes, sir. Please."

Without another word, he plunges his thick cock between my legs and thrusts. I groan, melting underneath him as he holds my wrists in one hand and builds a rhythm that's deep, satisfying, bringing me to the cusp of heaven. He brings his mouth to my ear, muttering in guttural, broken Russian. I only hear one word.

"Prekrasnyy."

Beautiful.

Every time he calls me beautiful, he cracks the walls of my heart. My eyes fill with tears and I swallow hard, not wanting to believe he really cares for me. If I fall into this belief, I won't survive it. I've been broken and abused and can't let myself be hurt again.

Then he thrusts into me so hard, I feel like I'm going to split wide open. He groans, burying himself deeper inside me. The grip on my wrists gets so tight it hurts, yet he can't hold me tight enough. And right then, I want him to possess me. I *need* him to.

Right then, I want to be owned by my husband.

So I push. I press my wrists against his, trying to get away, even though I know it's impossible. I arch my back and wrap my legs around him and fight this. I want to be taken. I want him to make me.

"Fuck me," I say, in a voice I barely recognize. I'm angry, and I don't know why. I push harder against Tomas, but he's immovable, and with every thrust of his hips my need to come intensifies.

He thrusts so hard I'm coming apart, and that's when I know this is what I need. I don't want tender ministrations and sweet words.

I want him to fuck me.

"Fuck me."

He lets go of my wrists so he can grab my hair and yank it. I cry out, pain radiating along my scalp and making me crazy with need before he thrusts again, so hard tears fill my eyes.

Over and over he thrusts. My pulse races, my thighs are slick with arousal, and every inch of my skin prickles. Lowering his head to my neck, he sinks his teeth into the tender skin above my collarbone. The erotic pain and pleasure send me over the edge, and I fly into ecstasy.

I'm wracked with pleasure, dimly aware of him grunting his own release. His seed lashes into me and I wrap my legs around him so tightly it hurts. I pulse and clench around him, groaning so loudly I'm hoarse. I ride the waves of pleasure as he comes, my body numb but for the pleasure that wraps me in a cocoon.

I'm fractured but sated when we finally finish, his heavy body atop mine like a security blanket. I weave my arms around the back of his neck and pull him down to me. I kiss him so that he knows I'm his, but he's mine as well. I own him as he owns me.

Heart. Body. Soul.

Chapter 17

Tomas

I don't quite comprehend how someone so submissive can challenge a man like me. She laps up my praise like a kitten with milk, eager to please. She glows under my approval, yet when I take her to bed, the kitten's claws come out.

Perhaps she needs to fight me, so I take her. Maybe she needs to lose control, but on her terms. There are many things about her I don't yet know, but I make it my mission to find out.

After our vicious, blissful lovemaking, I roll onto my back and take her with me. I expect she'll want to lay here like this, but she doesn't. After a few moments, she slides herself atop me, straddling me from above.

"What the hell are you doing?"

Caroline's hair is crazed, giving her the appearance of a wildcat. Her cheeks are flushed pink, her eyes wild and gorgeous.

"I want to ride you," she says. "Teach me to ride you."

I slap her thigh.

"That's enough telling me what to do, little *detka*."

She sticks out her lower lip in a pout, and it's so adorable I'd give her anything she fucking wanted right then. When she places her hand on my chest, she gives me a coy look.

"Please, sir." She cocks her head to the side like a curious puppy. "Or are you too old to get it up again?"

Christ almighty, I'm hard already.

Did she just say what I think she did?

"You call me old one more time, I'll take you over my knee," I tell her.

"Mmmm."

"You'll wear me out spanking your little ass," I say, as I grasp her hips. I can't get my fill of her and Christ, it looks like the feeling's mutual.

"Ride me, then," I tell her. "Like this."

I lift her up and down my shaft, groaning out loud when her tight cunt clenches on me. The way she moans makes me impossibly harder.

"Jesus, woman." I grab her nipples and work them to hard peaks, my cock throbbing in her pussy when her mouth parts open with a moan.

"Sirrrr," she purrs.

"My little kitten." I knead her breasts and lift her up before slamming her on my cock. "Work it."

And hell, she does, and it's fucking glorious. Her head thrown back, shoulders wide open, she rides me like she was meant for this. I'm gonna fucking come again just watching her, and when she groans in ecstasy, I lose all control.

"Fuck me, you're beautiful," I say, my words tapering off to a groan when I chase my climax. Just when she begins to come down from one orgasm, she gasps, a second climax on its heels. I watch her come with utter pleasure. I've staked my claim, and Caroline is mine.

"Come here," I tell her. She's still on me. We're wet, a fucking mess, but I don't care. I grab the back of her head, yank her face to mine, and kiss her sweet, pouty lips, when a knock comes at the door.

She pulls away and looks at me quizzically.

"It's dessert," I tell her. "I told them to leave it outside. Jesus."

I pull out of her, and toss her my t-shirt to clean up, then yell at the door.

"I said leave it!" I yell, loud enough for whoever's on the other side to hear.

But instead of leaving it, the knock comes louder.

Is something wrong? I tug on a pair of boxers and hold my hand up to Caroline, telling her to stay where she is, before I trot to the front door. I look through the peep hole. It's Nicolai. I yank open the door to find him holding a tray and grinning at me.

"You ordered dessert?"

"I ordered dessert left outside this door, douchebag."

He grins at me and barely dodges my fist as he ducks and slides the tray onto the floor and runs. I'll kick his ass, the prick.

I come back in with the tray in hand, muttering to myself. Caroline is sitting up in bed, her hand to her mouth, and her eyes are dancing.

"You guys are so funny."

"You think that was funny?" Christ, maybe I do let her get away with too much.

"Of course it was," she says with a giggle. I crack a smile. I love when she's happy. I slide the tray on the table and lift the lid. I nod approvingly at the *ptichye moloko*. Our traditional bird's milk cake. Mildly sweet, light as a feather, the sponge cake layered with chocolate and custard is one of my favorites.

"It might have been funny to you, but I'll kick his ass for that."

"You won't," she says gently, biting her lip. "You

guys are like brothers, really." I watch as her eyes sober and her brow furrows. "I like it."

"Do you?" She's such a complex little creature.

I nod, beckoning for her to join me at the little table so we can eat dessert.

"My brother isn't like that at all, you know," she says.

I don't know.

"Oh?"

I hold the chair out for her and this time, she actually laughs out loud. "I'm *literally* naked, still hot and panting from being fucked, and you're going to be the gentleman and hold the chair out for me?"

I can't help but smile when she says *fucked*. She rarely swears, and it seems almost out of place. It's cute.

"Of course. A gentleman wears many faces, you know.

"I've gathered that."

"So, tell me what your brother's like, then."

"He rules with an iron fist," she says with a shrug. "He's mean and cold and power-hungry."

I frown. I take the one fork Nicolai gave us and take a large forkful.

"Open." She obeys, her hands in her lap, and eagerly takes the bite of cake.

"Mmm, they did a good job."

I take a bite from the same fork and nod in approval. "They did? Or you did? It's delicious."

She shrugs. "Well, I may have orchestrated it, but I had help."

So humble and meek. I could learn from her.

"Did your brother always treat you the way he does now?"

She swallows the next bite I give her before answering. "No. He was kinder when we were younger, when my parents were alive. But over the years, Bratva life has worn him down. He's become harder. And then he befriended Andros."

"I see."

I despise her brother with a vehement hatred reserved for my enemies. How anyone could be bound by duty to a woman like her and fail her is a mystery to me. I don't realize I'm clenching my fists until she rests her hand on mine.

"Tomas," she says gently, so gently I almost don't hear her at first. I blink and look at her.

"Yes?"

Her eyes are pained. "I lost you there. What is it?"

"I hate that you were anywhere near your brother. I hate that I can't exact vengeance on him now and need to wait until the time is right. I hate that he wasn't good to you." I shake my head. "I have no real-life brothers, only the men who are chosen family. And I'd lay down my life for them."

She runs her thumb over the top of my hand and nods. "I know. You don't have to tell me. I can see it in the way you are with them. I think it's one of the things I love best about you."

I take a deep breath in. It's the sweetest thing she's ever said to me and betrays the fact that she's actually falling for me.

Does she know how I feel about her?

How could she?

But as soon as she speaks, she flushes pink and looks away, even pulling her hand off mine. "I didn't mean to say that," she whispers, shaking her head.

"What?" I ask. "It's wrong to show feelings for the man you're wedded to?"

She shakes her head. "It's wrong to show feelings for a man you *just met*."

"According to whom?"

She shrugs and flushes, shaking her head and opening her mouth to speak, then closing it at once. "I—I'm not sure. Oh, hell."

She gets up out of her chair and comes to me, all curves and grace and beauty, then slides on my lap facing me. I'm so shocked by what she's doing that I let her, my hands falling helplessly to the side as she cups my face in her hands and kisses me. She tastes like the cake we just ate, sweet and rich, and I could kiss her all night long. I wrap my hands around her lower back and pull her closer, letting her kiss me as if she owns me, because she fucking does.

She does.

I intended on owning Caroline, but it goes both ways. I'm her husband, her protector, the one who will defend her to the death.

But we belong to each other.

When she finally pulls her lips off mine, she looks at me in surprise. "I didn't mean to do that," she whispers. "I don't know what came over me. I just—"

I stand with her in my arms in reply and she stops speaking. Her legs encircle me, her naked pussy pressed up against my torso as I walk her to the bed. I lay her down and kneel beside her. Her eyes meet mine, flirtatious and sexy.

She bites her lip before she asks, "Do you have it in you for round three, old—"

"I dare you to say it. Do it. See what happens."

But she shakes her head.

"Smart girl. Don't need another spanking?"

Her eyes twinkle. "Not *yet*."

I join her on the bed and show her that I'm *fully* capable of round three.

Three nights later, my phone rings in the middle of the night.

"Boss?"

I'm half asleep, my eyes still half-closed when I answer. It's Ilya.

"What is it?"

"I'm so sorry to call you this late," he says. "But I was doing watch by the gate, and there's something wrong." I've given Ilya nighttime shift this week, and his explicit directions are to call Yakov if anything is amiss.

I sit up in bed. Caroline wakes, her eyes fluttering open. She holds my gaze in quiet confidence but doesn't speak. It's like balm to my soul when she looks at me like that. I never knew how alone I was until I wasn't anymore. It empowers me to have her by my side, knowing that no matter what happens I come home to her soft voice and gentle touch.

"What is it?"

"My replacement was supposed to check in an hour ago for the shift change. His phone is ringing, and ringing and I can't get him."

I grit my teeth together. "There are many in our brotherhood you could've called before me. Just because one of our men is missing doesn't mean a damn thing." I will ring this boy's neck if he doesn't settle down and learn his place.

"But that's just it, sir. I tried all of them. Yakov. Nicolai. Lev. No one answered."

I scowl into the darkness. Caroline places her arm on mine and gently squeezes. I take in a deep breath.

"*All* of them?"

"Yes, sir. I'm sorry, sir. I didn't know who else to call."

I exhale. "No, you did the right thing. I'll be right there."

I hang up the phone and push Caroline's arm off mine, swinging my legs over the side of the bed. I need to find out what the hell is going on.

"Is everything okay, Tomas?"

I nod. "Go back to sleep," I tell her. "It's fine."

She watches me quietly as I step into a pair of jeans, a t-shirt, and boots. I don't look at her when I open the drawer beside the bed and remove several handguns. Though she knows exactly who I am and what I do, taking my weapons is a stark reminder of what could go wrong at any minute.

"Tomas," she whispers, her voice shaky.

"Go to sleep." My tone is harsher than I mean, but the thought of any of my men being at risk has me on edge. I try to ignore the reproachful look she gives me, and finally turn away. "*Now*."

I open the door to make sure the detail outside

hasn't left their positions. Two of my best men still stand at attention when I go to them.

"Have you noticed anything out of place?"

One frowns. "Not anything that indicates danger," he says.

But in Bratva life, you take nothing for granted. It's worth missing a night's sleep for safety's sake, even if it means leaving the side of the woman I love.

The woman I love.

I've kept her apart from my day to day dealings as much as I can, but our lives are too meshed in it to do so fully. And every time something threatens the lives of my men, I'm reminded of where she came from. Of the danger that lurks outside the safety of the compound walls. I'm ready and willing to protect my woman no matter the cost, and my gut says that day may be sooner than later.

I scrub a hand across my brow as I go down the hallway toward the exit, wracking my brain. It's the middle of the fucking night. Nicolai leaves to go home in a few days and Yakov should be with Yvonne. Or is it Yakov's turn for night shift watch? We don't normally even have night shift, but with recent events I thought it wise. As *pakhan*, I have bodyguards, but I have at least two men on Caroline at all times when she isn't in my presence.

I try to call Nicolai and Yakov in turn, but both times the phone just rings until I get to voicemail.

Shit.

The compound is nearly silent, save for the silent pacing of those on guard, when I reach the first floor. I go to Ilya first, before I do anything else, but his story is the same. Nothing's out of the ordinary, but he still can't get in touch with anyone. The garden wraps around the entrance to our compound, and I see a shadow move. Still beyond the entrance to the compound, but the garden area is clearly marked as private property. No one should be there at this hour.

"Ilya, do you see someone over by the bench?"

"I do, sir. I saw nothing until you came."

There's a full moon tonight, illuminating the garden and front walk that leads to the compound. I squint toward it. Who the hell is in the garden this late at night? I blink in surprise when my vision adjusts to the dim lighting.

It's a woman. *Christ*. What the hell is a woman doing on a bench outside the compound? The only women allowed anywhere near us should be accompanied by their men.

"Tomas—"

I hold up a hand to silence him. I'll investigate myself.

I watch as she rises before I reach her. Standing on ridiculously spikey heels, she wobbles in the grass. Is she drunk? The woman wears a skin-tight black leather dress, her thick, wavy blonde hair framing her face. She's dressed so provocatively; I wonder if she's a hooker one of my men called. I'll kick the ass of anyone who's brought her and left her on our private property. What the *fuck* is this?

"Who are you?" I demand.

She grins in response. My skin prickles with awareness, as if we're being watched. There's something macabre in this night, and foreboding pools in my belly when I approach her.

"The better question is, who are *you*, handsome?" She places her hands on her hips and I swear she sashays a little, as if she's beckoning me to her.

"I'm a happily married man," I say tightly. "And no one's allowed on this property without permission. Tell me who you are before I call the police."

She laughs out loud, the sound ringing through the quiet. "Happily married. Oh, that's rich. As if that *matters*, handsome. I've slept with more married men than single. They're far more eager. And you look like the type that could use it."

"It matters."

When I get within a few paces of her, the garden lights, triggered by motion sensors, turn on. I blink in the sudden blinding light, shielding my eyes from it. It's all she needs. She's close enough that she grabs my shoulder and yanks me to her. I'm so taken aback, I don't react at first, stunned by her bold moves. Grabbing the back of my head she anchors herself on me, pulls my head down, and kisses me with one knee hitched up to my side.

Rage boils up inside me. I could hurt her. Christ, I'm afraid I will. I push her away, and it takes every bit of restraint I have not to slap her. But hell, I don't need a restraining order or assault on my record. Even a man like me would serve time for assaulting a woman, and I don't need that on my record. I have to be careful.

She has the gall to come closer to me.

"Get the hell away from me." I push my hands on her shoulders and shove her away. I don't even feel guilty when she stumbles, barely catching herself on the bench, but she's laughing as if it's the funniest thing in the world. I turn around quickly, thinking I hear someone behind me, but when I turn there's no one there.

"Aw, handsome," she says, rising to her feet on wobbly heels. "No need to get all worked up."

I want to hurt her so badly I'm shaking with rage. I pick up my phone to make a call, but it won't dial out. I bend down, grab her by the arm, and yank her to her feet. It pleases me when her eyes widen in fear and she slaps at my hand.

"Let me go or I'll scream!"

"Scream all you fucking want," I tell her. "You're trespassing, and I don't know who the hell you are, but you do *not* belong here. Get the *fuck out* of my residence."

Ilya's by my side.

"What the hell?" he asks.

"Trespasser," I tell him. "Get her the fuck out of here and make it fucking clear that she's not welcome to ever come back here." I shove her toward him, but the second I release her grip, she kicks off her shoes, eludes his grip, and runs.

Ilya takes off after her, but I stop him. "No. Let her go."

Neither of us needs assault on our records.

He obeys, shaking his head while she runs. "What the hell was she doing here?"

"No idea, but the entire area before the gate is still private property."

Ilya looks at me sheepishly. "She um… she left some red lipstick on you, sir."

I curse under my breath and rub a hand over my cheek.

"You got it," he says, shaking his head.

My phone rings. *Yakov*.

"Hello?"

"Tomas, I heard you were trying to reach me?"

"Yeah," I say with a sigh. "Just making sure all was good. Phone signals weren't working."

"All fine here, brother."

I think about telling him what just happened, but I'm weary and shaken by it.

"Alright. I'm sorry. Get some sleep."

I hang up the phone with him and dial Nicolai as well.

"Tomas? Everything okay?"

I shake my head. "Was just checking on you." I do decide to tell him what happened, nonetheless.

"What the fuck is that about? You haul her ass back into the compound for questioning?"

"No," I tell him. "Can't exactly question a woman the way I can a man. And anyway, she got away."

He's silent for a moment. "I don't like this," he says. "Was anyone else with her?"

"No."

"Ilya saw nothing?"

"Nothing. But what could it mean?"

"I don't know, brother. Let's debrief in the morning."

I hang up the call with him and finally reach Ilya's replacement. When all is settled, I head back to my room. Weary. On edge. Shaken. I haven't been married for long at all, and even though I was attacked by that woman, it feels like I did something wrong. I hate that another woman's lips touched mine. I think about telling Caroline, but don't want to upset her.

"Everything alright, Tomas?"

"Of course, sweetheart." But I bend down to give her a kiss and tuck the blanket back around her. I'm grateful for her simple beauty and gentle spirit after what happened. "Go to sleep now."

I go to use the bathroom and notice red lipstick smeared on my t-shirt.

I yank the shirt of furiously and shove it in the bottom of the laundry basket.

Christ.

I return to Caroline.

I need her. I reach for her face and cradle it in my hands, lowering my mouth to hers and capturing her lips with mine, as if kissing my wife will erase the memory of the other woman from my mind and body.

Can she smell the other? Taste her? I pull away too soon, not wanting even the slightest memory of the other woman to taint what I have with Caroline.

She looks at me in concern, her hand coming to my cheek. "Are you sure everything's okay?"

"Go to sleep, little *detka.*"

Everything is not okay. But if I have anything to do with it, it will be.

Tomorrow, I find Andros.

Chapter 18

Caroline

THE DAYS GO ON, and I gradually take my place in the kitchen staff. Tomas is concerned about their showing respect for me, so though we're friendly and I get along well with them, I have to maintain my distance out of respect for him. I understand that the wife of the *pakhan* has to keep her place. I'm learning.

He's giving me freedom, now. I have my own cell phone, though I have no one to call. And I'm given leave to explore the estate at will. Yvonne sometimes joins me. Our favorite place to go is behind the house to the back, where there's a gazebo, a flower bed, and a little doorway that leads to the cellar. Yvonne told me it's an old root cellar from centuries ago, when new settlers owned this land. It creeps me out a little, though, so I rarely go. But I do love to sit outside by the gazebo and read. It's late fall now, so it's often chilly, and the leaves are falling in droves. Soon, the trees will be barren, and winter will come, but I'm soaking up every last day of autumn I can.

Eliott comes once a day, but I'm learning how to do my hair and my makeup. I like it. Though I still carry a bit of the fear in me that I'll be rejected for how I look, I'm learning to let it go. Tomas helps with that. He worships my body morning and night, bringing me to heights of pleasure I never imagined.

I'm trying out new kitchen recipes, eager to please him. And he eats heartily, commending me on how well I cook.

But something is missing, and I'm not sure what. He's distant and preoccupied. And though he pays attention to me—I mean, he doesn't even take his *eyes* off me—he isn't fully present. Will it always be like this?

Finally, several weeks after he brought me here, while I'm in the middle of preparing a roast for tonight's meal, Tomas comes in the kitchen.

"Caroline, come with me," he says. He hasn't softened a bit. If anything, he's grown sterner lately.

"I need a few minutes," I tell him, as I'm still rubbing herbs and salt and pepper on the roast.

"No," he says, in that tone that must be obeyed. *"Now."*

I sigh, looking to Lydia. She quickly steps in to take my place.

"Go," she whispers. "You do not want to anger your husband."

But I'm the one that's angered. I hate that he just marches in here and tells me to drop what I'm doing as if it doesn't matter.

"I need to wash my hands," I tell him. "You'll have to wait."

His eyes ignite, his body stiffening.

"Do so in our room."

"Tomas, for goodness sakes." How dare he just march in and order me around like this? This is my job. I've earned the respect of this staff, and I'm not going to just cow to him because he demands it. So I ignore him and head to the kitchen sink. "I'm not walking through these floors with germ-infested hands. Honestly!"

A look flashes across his face I haven't seen since we got here. His brows draw together, his lips turn down, and a shadow darkens his features. "You have one minute," he snaps. "And you'll answer for your smart mouth."

I stomp to the kitchen sink, feeling angry and justified,. Yvonne is standing by the sink. She's been coming to help the past few days and is eager to learn. Her pretty eyes are wide and earnest. "Caroline," she whispers. "Don't push him. He got news today he didn't like, and he's in a mood over it."

"Why does that give him license to boss me around?" I whisper back.

"It doesn't," she says. "But he's the *pakhan* and you know what he expects."

I pump soap into my hands and mutter under my breath. She only gives me a look of sympathy.

"Go," she mouths, biting her lip. Grumbling, I dry my hands and leave. He's standing in the doorway, glaring at me, and the entire kitchen staff continues to work in awkward silence.

"For God's sake, lighten up," I mutter, which might have been a stupid thing to say, because he grasps my elbow in response, spins me out in front of him, and slams his palm against my ass. The kitchen doors shut behind us, hiding my flaming hot cheeks.

"Tomas," I say, wanting to absolutely *die*. I can't believe he spanked me in front of all of them like that. "Your kitchen staff are my friends. You just humiliated me in front of all of them! I've worked to earn their respect."

"Let's talk about respect. You do not disrespect me like that in front of my staff," he says, as if that gives him the license to publicly mortify me.

His face is a storm cloud, and he's marching me down the hall so fast I can't keep up.

My heart sinks. Just when I think I'm starting to love

this man, to understand him, to become the wife he needs and he the husband I need, he pulls this domineering alpha bullshit. But my angry thoughts come to a halt when we reach our apartment.

Six armed men stand in front of our door. I recognize them as the strike force for his brotherhood.

Why are they guarding our door?

I'm immediately on guard. Something's happened. What is this? No one ever flanks our door like this. It's unusual. Disturbing, even.

But he isn't surprised to see them. "Clear?" he asks them.

"Yes, sir," the tallest one says. "We're to stay here until you give us further notice, is that right?"

"Precisely."

He opens the door and ushers me in. "Out of your clothes. Go to the bed and hold the post."

I blink in surprise.

"What?"

Without a word, he reaches for my arm and pulls me to him. Grasping my face in his hand, he pinches my cheeks.

"Clothes off. Bed post. Is that clear?"

I'm shaking when he lets me go. Usually his dominance and my submission are a sort of dance. He leads and I follow. It's hot as hell, and our lovemaking recently has explored the depths of where this could take us.

But this night is different. He's serious, not at all playful, and ready to punish me.

Do I have a choice?

I go to the room and strip out of my clothes, leaving them in a basket in the bathroom, before I go to the post and grip it. What will he do?

Honestly? He could do anything.

I'm nervous as hell, waiting in here, and he takes his sweet time about it. I hear him on the phone, then he walks through the room opening windows and doors. What on earth is he looking for? My arms begin to ache, my shoulders burning from holding this position, when he finally comes in the room.

"Good girl," he says. "Still feel like mouthing off?"

I frown and shake my head. I don't understand why I'm here. Did I push it too far? But I hardly did a thing.

"Good," he says. "I'm not in the mood to fight you tonight."

Walking around to the bedside table, which I've since learned houses a *variety* of kinky things, he takes out various items in black and red. He has so many things in his hands, I can't differentiate any. He tosses them onto the bed and comes to my side.

"Close your eyes, little *detka*," he says. I obey. He

pulls something scratchy but soft over the top of my head, and it takes effort not to pop my eyes open. "This is a lace hood," he says. "It will keep you quiet and humble, and it's very pretty."

I try to open my mouth, but the fabric presses up against my lips. "I should've known you'd want to cover my face," I mutter petulantly. I don't think he'll actually hear me, because he's playing with the other toys on the bed, but to my surprise he responds.

"On the contrary, Caroline," he says. "There is no one whose face I'd rather see. But tonight, I want you deprived or your senses so you can focus." I gasp when cold nips at my breasts, but I can't see what he's doing since I'm still wearing the hood.

"I'll tell you everything I use before I use it," he promises. "This is a lace sensory deprivation hood. Next up, a pair of cuffs."

My wrists are quickly secured.

"And a pair of nipple clamps."

I freeze, but there's nowhere to go. He's putting… what? On my *what*?

Standing in front of me, he holds something in his hands that between the pattern of lace on the mask, looks like a metal chain with little clips at the end.

Over the past few weeks, he's been almost gentle with me. Our lovemaking is intense, and he occasionally slaps my ass, but he's been gentler.

I wonder if it's odd that I miss his dominating me.

But it looks like that's about to change. Now, for some reason, it looks like he might've pulled out all the stops. I stop breathing for a moment when the cold, painful metal anchors on the most delicate part of my body. "Oh God," I moan. "Ohhhh."

But he quickly replaces the pain with pleasure when he gently tugs the chain between the two clamps. It hurts, but my pussy pulses with need, aching for release and pressure, just from the heaviness of the clamps.

"How does that feel?" he asks.

"Painful." I'm gasping, writhing, the hood blocking my vision but letting me breathe, and it's all a little much.

"Good."

Good? He thinks it's good that I'm in pain?

"Tomas..." but my words fade when something wet and slick glides along my ass. Oh my *God*. I gasp when he pushes a plug through the tight ring of muscle. I'm instantly full, and it's as if someone's pushed a button that makes me submit. I couldn't defy him right now if I tried.

My hands grasp the wooden edge of the bed post, my grip tightening when he moves behind me. He's clamped and plugged me. The hood allows me to breathe, but I can't do much more than that. My vision's blurred, my ability to speak muted.

I can see him pacing around me. He's shrugged out of his suit coat and stands in front of me with his shirt sleeves rolled up to the elbow. He holds something in his hand obscured by the lacy hood. Running it along his palm, he paces around me.

"Beautiful," he says. "You're simply gorgeous trussed up like this."

I wonder what's happened that's pushed him to control me. Does he gain something by acting out his sadistic impulses? He must. He already looks calmer, even through the limited vision the hood affords. I know without him having to tell me, that he needs to master me. Dominate me. That whatever's happened today has pushed him to this.

Fortunately for me, I love when he does just that, even if I fight it.

"You'll be punished for disrespecting me in front of the kitchen staff," he says.

"You disrespected *me*!"

He brings back his hand and the implement he's holding flies. I hear the sound of the falls before I feel them, a whistling sound that warns me this is going to hurt. I gasp when the leather falls of the flogger lick my skin. He's used this on me before, but it was for foreplay, not punishment.

"I expect you to obey me," he says tightly, before lashing me again, this time the falls landing across my breasts and shoulders. It stings and burns, and I can't stop him. Walking around to my back, he flogs me with the leather, my ass lighting up underneath the stings of the falls. "Did it ever occur to you that it was imperative you come right away? Hmm?"

Several more lashes of the flogger fall, and I'm whimpering now, my body pulsing with need but still desperate to stop the pain. It isn't the worst spanking I've gotten by far, but it hurts like hell.

"You could've just said that," I say through gritted teeth.

"No," he snaps, whipping the flogger across my ass harder than he has yet. "I shouldn't need to give you an explanation. When I give you a command, you obey me, no questions asked."

I'm so angry and this hurts so badly I throw my head back, an animalistic growl escaping my lips. "Yes, master," I toss out sarcastically. "Whatever you say, sir." My voice drips with sarcasm. I hate this. I like it so much better when I've earned his approval rather than his anger.

I hate this.

In silence, he continues the lashing, with steady flicks of the falls to my skin, until my whole body is on fire, laced with cuts of the flogger. The flogger is far from a harsh implement, but the pain builds in intensity with every cut of leather.

"Need to mouth off to me again?" he asks. I watch through the hood as he places the flogger down and lifts something else into his hand. I inwardly cringe, even as somehow, against all reason and rational logic, I want him to continue this. To bring me to the point of submission I don't readily grant, the relinquishment that has to be wrestled from my grasp bit by agonizing bit.

Because I *like* when he's in charge. It fills me with pleasure to earn his approval.

And why haven't I lately?

"Say you're sorry, Caroline," His stern voice is laced with warning. I bite my tongue and say nothing.

Thwack. I yell out loud when something solid and painful whacks against my ass. I try to look to see what he's using, but I can't see anything but black in his hand.

"Say it." Still, I refuse.

He spanks me again, harder this time. I whimper and try to move but I'm in this position, and there's literally no escape. The cuffs hold my wrists in place, and every movement of my body's inhibited by something. A plug in my ass and clamps on my nipples, and behind me, that awful thing he's using to punish me. It's got to be some type of wooden paddle or something. I've been through enough with him to recognize the feel of wood when it's being used on me.

"Say you're sorry," he commands a third time, and when I don't, he smacks me again. I choke on a dry sob. It hurts so badly, and yet somehow this is what I need. I brace for another stroke, but it doesn't come. Instead, I feel him at my back, working the plug with one hand while he tugs the chain between the clamps with his other.

"Ahhhhh!" I'm half-screaming, half-moaning, not knowing what to do with myself. Then his fingers are between my legs and he's working me hard and fast, until I'm rocking on his hand, dying for more. The spanking's heightened my senses, the clamps and plug putting me at his total mercy. He's stroking, circling, tugging, working me to the point of utter bliss, and when my body tenses just before I collapse into total ecstasy, he stops.

"Say it."

I am *dying* to come, but I clamp my mouth shut and whimper to myself. I'm not ready. I breathe in deeply through the lace. Unable to see clearly, my senses are intensified by his unapologetic mastery over my body. I'm so close to coming, I'm trembling when he slides his fingers inside my core while he palms my ass, stroking the plug. I'm on the brink of coming, on the very cusp of pleasure when he stops.

He doesn't need to command me this time.

"I'm sorry, sir. Tomas, I'm sorry. Please, sir." I don't recognize my tight, needy voice, begging him to grant me pleasure.

"That's a good girl," he says. But he doesn't make me come. First, he takes the hood off. I breathe in deeply, the room suddenly bright. I squint in the sudden light, when his mouth captures mine. He kisses me, and my body ignites. His lips are the softest part of him, so tender and gentle I sigh into him. But as he kisses me, both of his hands find my breasts, each one palming and weighing the fullness, but there's no more tugging the chain. Instead, he removes it. Blood rushes to the abused flesh, and my breasts swell, tingling with the relief it brings. The best part about the clamps are their removal, the way the flow of blood makes my breasts ache and my body teem with pleasure.

The cuffs come next and my wrists swing free. I reach for him, but he pushes my hands away, bending to lift me in his arms, so close to his chest I'm drowning in his scent. He lays me on the bed, spreads my legs, then drops to the floor. I'm still plugged, now aching with need and throbbing with the pain of the brief, brutal session, when he buries his face between my legs.

One, two, three strokes of his tongue, and I spasm with pleasure. He probes my channel with the very tip, while working my clit with his thumb, and at the third stroke, I fly into ecstasy. I come so hard against his face I whimper and shake, my body tense with contracting muscles chasing utter ecstasy. And just when I'm coming down from the first earth-shattering orgasm, so intense I've lost my voice with screaming, a second builds on the first. Sweeter. Harder. Impossibly more intense.

"Oh, God, Tomas," I groan, as a second orgasm wracks my body. I'm still wrapped in ecstasy when he pulls his cock out and lines himself up at my core. I grasp his shoulders, needing to anchor myself, just before he impales me with his full, hard cock.

I swear and writhe and hold onto him as he slams into me before pulling his hard cock all the way out. All the way out, then slamming into me again, over and over. "Tomas," I moan. "I'm sorry."

He thrusts in me one more time, bringing his mouth to my ear. "My love, I am, too."

I soar into climax when he does. We're gripping each other like we're the only two survivors in a world of destruction, desperate and aching for oneness.

He's never called me *love* before. Not once. And he sure as hell has never apologized.

He lowers his body, his forehead touching mine.

"I needed that," I tell him. "God, Tomas. I may regret saying this later, but I need that intensity sometimes. I don't even know I do until you deliver, but I can't enjoy sweet sex like that. Am I crazy?"

His forehead still on mine, he breathes in, like he's inhaling my very scent and essence.

"No more crazy than I am," he says. "I was pissed and needed to regain control. So I went to you."

"I know."

He lifts his forehead off mine and looks into my eyes. "Do you, love?"

"Yes. I could sense it, that you needed to control me. Are you ready to tell me what happened?"

His eyes cloud over again, and for a brief moment I regret asking him. I like the sincere conversations with him, when we're just two lovers, and neither of us shields ourselves from the other in an effort to self-protect. "Let's get cleaned up."

He pulls out of me and we're messy and sticky. I'm aching, throbbing from what he just did, but blissfully satisfied.

"Bath," he whispers. He's stripped to his boxers when he holds a finger up to me. "Stay here until I call you."

He walks to the bathroom, then seconds later I hear the sound of a bath being drawn. Right now, I couldn't disobey him if I wanted to. When he strips me down like that, fucking me and spanking me and dominating every inch of my body, I surrender fully. Eventually we'll play the game again—him needing to control me and me fighting until he breaks me down in surrender. But for now, I'm his little *detka*.

"Come, Caroline."

I walk to him, every step making my body ache. My ass throbs, my breasts tingle. But God, that bath sounds good.

I take his hand and let him help me into the tub. The warm, fragrant water envelopes me, the scent of vanilla calming me. To my surprise, he follows, sitting at one end of the tub and drawing me onto his lap.

He washes my hair and lathers me up but doesn't say a thing. I don't push him. He'll tell me when the time is right.

When my body's clean and my hair wrung out, he turns me to look at him.

"I've had a man on Andros since I married you," he says. "Every fucking day. We were tailing him, with the intent of acting when the time was right. We were ready to strike. Ready to punish him for what he did to you." He takes in a deep breath and lets it out slowly. "But as of this morning, he's gone."

Even though I'm fully submerged in warm water, I shiver.

"He's gone?"

If he's gone, he could be literally anywhere.

"We'll find him," Tomas says.

A loud knock sounds at the door. "I swear to God, if that's Nicolai again…" but his voice trails off when the knock becomes more insistent.

"I'll be right there!" he shouts. He helps me out of the tub and towels me off, but I can tell he's doing this quickly. He wants to know who's at the door. Still draped in a towel, he grabs a gun from the bedside table and heads to the door. "Do not move, Caroline."

I obey. I still couldn't disobey if I wanted to. I'm still

spinning in my head about everything that he said. If Andros is missing… and I know he wanted me for himself… where has he gone to?

Where the hell has he gone?

Tomas opens the door. "What is it?"

"Ilya, sir. He's been taken."

Chapter 19

Tomas

I HATE THIS. I fucking hate this. I take Caroline with me to the meeting, because I don't trust even my most dedicated men to protect her now.

My men eye Caroline when she sits beside me. Though she's changed, her hair is a little wild, her cheeks flushed. Women rarely attend our meetings. But in our line of work, you learn to trust your instincts, and my instincts are telling me that something's foul here.

"Ilya's missing," I tell them. "What do we know?"

"Could it have anything to do with the arms trade with the Brazilian cartel, sir?" Yakov speaks up from the back. "They've been less than honest in our dealings with them, and it seems their fearless leader isn't as fearless as we thought."

I shake my head. "No. He ran like a pussy when he knew I found him out. I confronted him myself yesterday."

That confrontation involved a beat-down, a loss of teeth, and a bloody confession he wrote out in his own hand, but I'm pretty confident we won't be dealing with his bullshit again. "It wasn't him. I suspect San Diego." Caroline sits up straighter.

"On what grounds?" Yakov asks, not challenging me, but suddenly hyper alert. He knows my feelings for Caroline run deep, and it's his job to be sure my allegiance to her doesn't cloud my judgment. But he's also learned to trust my instincts.

Still, how can I tell him I have no grounds? That literally the only evidence I have is that Andros has eluded the detail I had on him, and no one knows where he is?

But Lev speaks up from the back.

"Not five minutes ago, we found footage showing how Ilya was taken."

My skin feels cold and prickly, while at the same time my stomach clenches with anger. I hate that someone put a hand on one of my men. They will answer to me for this.

I pull out my phone and dial the head of security.

Caroline's eyes meet mine, wide but trusting, and it brings solace to me. I swallow hard. I love this woman. She's feisty as fuck and we've only just begun, but her quiet acceptance and trust empower me.

"Sir?"

"We're in lock down," I tell him. "Shut and lock the gates and windows and call the guards."

Caroline swallows hard and reaches for my hand when metal bars descend on the windows, and the snapping of locks fills the room. Outside the window from where we sit, the massive iron gates that lead to our estate slowly pull shut. Though everyone stirs, all await my command in silence.

"We have footage?" I ask Lev.

"Yes, sir, and we're in the process of retrieving it now."

"Show us."

Lev hits a button on a remote, and three wide screen TVs spring to life. The footage is right outside our gate. It's dark out, and the time stamp shows it was late last night. Ilya stands guard at the gate. A hooded man approaches, and Ilya pulls his gun. The anticipation and silence are deafening. It's hard to get a profile on someone wearing a hood.

I'm on my feet, Yakov to my left, Lev in front of me, and Nicolai on my right.

"*Christ,*" Nicolai mutters. "*Shit.*"

The hooded man draws a weapon. Ilya attacks. He doesn't last long, though, before his assailant has him cuffed and immobilized. Christ, I have to train that boy better. I will find him, kick his ass for not taking down his assailant, and teach him better self-defense. Four more men surround Ilya.

In the skirmish, the hooded man's hood falls to the side.

I recognize him.

"I know that man," I say. "Zoom in."

Lev obeys.

"I know him, too," Caroline whispers.

"He's the one that tried to touch my wife in Atlanta," I say.

Nicolai nods. "I was there. It is indeed the same man."

"Where did they take Ilya?"

Lev shakes his head. "No idea. They left by the front gates, and our footages soon cuts off."

"Why would they want him?" I ask.

"They want him to get to me," Caroline says. "I told you Andros wouldn't let me go. He's coming for me. He will use Ilya to get to me."

I pace the room. No one speaks.

She's right. She's fucking *right*.

My men are at risk, and so is Caroline.

I turn to Nicolai. I can't leave this room, as I have an army awaiting my commands.

We go through footage but find literally nothing else that could lead us to Ilya's abduction. I'm leery, though. I'm waiting for the other shoe to drop. This is only a warning. The prologue, if you will.

I stand and take Caroline by the hand. "Look through all our footage until you find something. You will *find him*," I say to my men. I turn to Lev. "Get Aren on the phone. And *no one* fucking leaves here without permission."

They scatter, and Lev pulls up Aren's information on his phone. He dials, and on the third ring, Aren picks up.

"Hello?"

"It's Tomas," I tell him. "Your brother-in-law. It seems we have a bit of a situation."

"Oh, there's no situation," he says tightly. "You got my sister, now you get off my ass. I don't owe you a fucking thing."

My grip tightens on the phone and I take a deep, steadying breath. "I think you're sadly mistaken. Your men have come after mine."

"They haven't. Christ, are you that bored with my bitch of a sister that you need to make up stories?"

Caroline's wide eyes meet mine. She heard him through the speaker.

I turn away from her, reigning in the fury that pounds at my chest like wild stallions. "I told you to speak of her with respect," I warn him.

"Oh, right. Sorry."

The fucking prick.

"Find Andros," I tell him. "One of my men was abducted last night, and our footage shows at least one of *your* men was here."

Aren doesn't respond at first, then after a moment, he mutters, "Impossible."

"Not impossible. I have evidence." What he doesn't know is that we were fully prepared to go to war with his brotherhood. He's merely given us an excuse. "You have until tomorrow morning to find Andros and report back to me, or I'm coming to find you."

I hang up the phone. Caroline closes her eyes and rests her head on my shoulder.

"Is it wrong that a part of me hopes he gives you reason to hurt him?"

The question actually makes me smile. "No, sweetheart. Is it wrong that I'm not actually giving him a chance? Your brother has already earned what he has coming to him, whether he calls me back or not."

She nods quietly, then closes her eyes and grips my arm tighter.

"He's here, Tomas," she whispers, her voice shaky and scared. The certainty in her voice chills the blood in my veins.

"Who, sweetheart?"

I hate hearing the terror in her voice. I will do whatever it takes to put her fears to rest, so she knows she need never fear any of them again. "Andros. I know he's here. I don't want to tell you how I know."

"Tell me."

"I… it's like a sixth sense," she says. "Whenever he was coming after me, I knew it before he came, and I feel it now. I haven't felt this since I came here."

I fucking hate that for her. *Hate it.*

I pull her so hard to my chest she gasps, wrapping my arms tightly around her. "He isn't going to find you, Caroline. Not now. Not ever." I'm not letting her out of my sight.

But I'm not going to run. I won't hide. He can take me head on if he wishes because that's the only fucking way he'll get me.

I pace the room with her, the sky darkening out the window. I gave Aren until tomorrow morning to find Andros, but I'm torn between wanting to keep her safe and wanting to kill the bastards who dared come here.

"Get away from the window," I tell her. I don't trust that the men after her won't scale the fucking sides of our compound. If I were the one after her, I'd stop at nothing.

But she's staring at her phone and doesn't respond.

"Caroline?"

The eyes that meet mine are wide with hurt and betrayal.

"Tomas," she whispers. "How could you?"

I have no idea what she's talking about. "How could I what?"

But she backs away from me toward the window.

"Get away from there."

She stands as if frozen, staring at me then back to her phone.

"I thought our vows meant something to you," she says. "I can't believe I've been such a fool." Her eyes fill with tears. I look to the phone in her hand. What is she looking at?

"Give me the fucking phone." I'm walking toward her, but she's backing further away.

"I found your shirt," she whispers. I shake my head, still confused. What the hell is she talking about?

"The one with the lipstick on it," she whispers, her lips quivering. "I thought it was something else. Blood, maybe, but my gut said otherwise. I couldn't imagine you'd be with another woman."

Christ.

"It isn't what you think it is," I tell her.

"Isn't that what they always say?" She's crying freely now, tears running down her cheeks.

"I can explain—"

"Also, what they always say." She shakes her head and closes her eyes, her back pressed up against the large window. "I knew you couldn't love me. I knew you never would."

My pulse races, and I want to shake her. "If you don't get the hell over here—"

She races past me and shoves me out of the way. I reach for her arm, but she slips out of my grip. Yanking open the door before I reach her, she bolts, her phone falling to the ground.

"Get her!" I bellow at the men standing by the door, who stare at her in bewilderment a second before they spring into action. But she's too fast, too smart for them. She yanks an end table over behind her, sending a vase with flowers and water toppling over and blocking their exit.

"Caroline!" She can't run, not now, not when there are predators who want to take her from me. Not when I fucking need her. I whip out my phone and call the guards at the gate while I chase after her, stepping through the cracked glass and leaping over the upturned table. But she's thinner and quicker than I am, and I can't get to her.

"Caroline, stop!"

Why is she running from me? And where will she go?

She opens the door and bounds down the steps away from me, and when I reach the door, I yank it open and look for her.

Fuck.

She's gone. That quickly, she's gone. Panic sweeps across my chest as I look wildly from left to right. Was someone waiting to ambush her? Where the hell is she? How could she have left so quickly?

My pulse races as I scream her name. "Caroline!"

When I get my hands on her, she's in so much goddamn trouble for running from me. But it's a useless, crazed thought. *Christ,* I need her safe, *now*.

Where is she? Where the *fuck* is she?

My men stand at attention, having followed me out. They're waiting for orders.

But for the first time since I've held this position, I have no idea what orders to give.

Chapter 20

Caroline

I JUST NEED to get away. I need space to think, to breathe, to be away from my husband.

My traitorous, cheating asshole of a husband.

I knew our marriage was just a fabrication. I know it didn't hold the weight of love or devotion or anything like that, but as I've gotten to know him, I've fooled myself. Tricked myself into thinking that I actually mattered to him, that I wasn't just the little fuck toy I feared I was.

But now…

I don't know who sent me the pictures. It could be anyone.

But I'll never erase them from my mind. Tomas,

with his lips wrapped around some whore's. Her knee tucked up to his side, her hands wrapped round his neck, and she's kissing him with passion I could only dream of. And she's gorgeous. So beautiful.

And he's wearing the shirt I saw in the laundry basket from the night he supposedly went to help Ilya.

I hardly see where I'm going, but I don't need to. I know this path to the gazebo like the back of my hand. I don't want him to touch me or to speak to me. I need some time alone.

How could he?

I sit at the little table and draw my knees to my chest, rocking back and forth. I let the tears fall freely.

It is better to have loved and lost than never to have loved at all is a lie.

Such a lie.

I never would have hurt this badly if I'd never loved him. How could I have let my guard down? I close my eyes and weep for what I've lost.

I actually believed for a while that he'd grown to care for me, and eventually he'd maybe even love me.

How stupid of me.

No one could ever love a girl like me.

I'm deep in the throes of self-misery when I hear a high-pitched scream. I jump to my feet, my sorrows forgotten.

Where did that come from?

I stand still and listen when I hear another scream.

I stare at the cellar door. It's coming from the cellar.

"Help!"

Oh, God. It's Yvonne. Someone has her in the cellar, and she saw me come from below. Her screams become muffled and I hear the sound of scuffles.

Without thinking, I yank open the door, and race down the stairs. I should get Tomas. I should get Yakov, or Nicolai, or someone to come with me. I have no weapons. I don't even have my cell phone. But when I hear her screams, I can't help but run to her.

She's cuffed to a post, rope lashed about her body. Her dress is torn from her, and blood streaks her arms and legs. Nausea clenches my belly.

"Oh my God! Yvonne!" A sob catches in my throat when I see her.

"I'm so sorry," she cries. "So sorry."

"You're sorry? Why? Who did this to you?"

"I did."

I know the voice before I turn to him.

Andros.

"He made me," she weeps. "He said if I didn't call you, he'd kill Yakov. I'm so sorry."

I was afraid that Ilya would be used as bait. Instead, he used Yvonne.

I turn, terrified of what I'll see. But when I look, he's merely sitting in a chair with his ankle crossed on his knee. Ilya sits beside him, cuffed and gagged, but his eyes are furious, his face red, and I notice with sickening realization that a clumsy, blood-soaked bandage covers one hand.

They use thumbprint recognition to gain access to the compound.

Bile rises in my stomach.

Andros used Ilya to get in here. Literally.

"This is your fault, you know," he says, shaking his head. "All these innocent people hurt because you left me."

"You're sick," I say, looking around the cellar for something to use as a weapon, but what do I possibly have? "I was never yours and I never will be."

"Ilya's maimed now because of you and will likely be struck from service to his Bratva for betrayal." He shakes his head. "This poor girl put up a good fight before she caved and agreed to call you. She was the one who told me you'd run here, and you did. Just like a little rabbit to a trap." He grins and it sickens me. "And the man you call husband? He will pay for touching *my woman*."

"He will kill you," I say, my voice wavering.

"Why would they do that? They'll never even know I was here, because you're coming with me."

"Never!"

He smiles. "You'll stay with a worthless man who cheated on you?"

"How do you—"

Then I know. He orchestrated this. I don't know the truth behind what I saw, but I know he set me up. He set us all up. I don't know how or why, but I know now that I shouldn't have run from Tomas.

Andros stands. I forgot how tall and menacing he is, and I hate that my body responds instinctively in fear. I recoil, wanting to draw my hands up over my head to hide from him.

"My husband didn't cheat on me," I say through gritted teeth. "You set him up, didn't you? How far did you go to do it, Andros?"

He grins. "You're so pathetically attached to the asshole, I had to take drastic measures to get you apart," he says with a shrug. "It was an easy matter to pay the whore to do it." He suddenly grows furious, the smile fading from his face and his eyes wide with anger. "But you know what that's like, don't you?" He steps closer to me and reaches for me. I smack his hand away, and he backhands me so quickly my head snaps back and I lose my balance. Gripping the back of my head by the hair, he yanks me to him. "You know what it's like to be a fucking whore."

I kick at him, but he's too big, too strong, and I can't get away. I don't say a word, biding my time until an opportunity comes to defend myself. I can't call to Tomas in the cellar. He might not hear me, and he wouldn't be able to get to me in time. I have to wait until we're on level ground again.

I change my tact.

Andros is a psychopath. I need to play this differently. And the one good thing I have going is that Andros is on our battlefield. Tomas has been hunting him. Now he's here. Andros is sick enough that his anger could cloud his judgment.

"I'm sorry, Andros," I say. "I never should have left you."

"That's right, you fucking whore," he says, yanking me by the hair again. "I thought anyone would see that you weren't worth it. I guess I was fucking wrong. But now that I have you back, you'll never leave again."

"You're right," I say, giving him exactly what he wants. "I belong with you." I'm physically sick playing this part. But I have to play this safely.

"We'll keep these two down here," he says. "Useless pawns. Come."

He drags me up the stairs, and I scream when he yanks my hair. "Scream again and I'll cut out your fucking tongue," he says. I shake. He would.

We get to the area just outside the compound. I can see a car approaching us and realize suddenly that it's his car. But Tomas leads an army, and there's no way Andros has silenced all of them.

I look wildly around for a weapon, and finally see a large gardening hoe leaning against the cellar door. My heart skips a crazy beat. Maybe I can use it. I pretend to stumble, taking him closer to it, and when we get near enough, I brace myself for the pain that will come when I yank my head away from him. With a deep breath, I fall to my knees.

My hair rips from my scalp and Andros screams in rage, but I'm louder.

"Tomas!" I shout as loudly as I can. *"Tomas! Someone help me!"*

Andros knees me, but I deflect it, elbow him in the ribs, and in the split second he's winded, I grab the hoe and swing it with all I've got. It hits his stomach with a sickening thud.

"You bitch!" he spits out, releasing his grip on me, and I swing the heavy tool again before he can touch me again. I hit him again in the belly.

"Tomas!"

It all happens in a blur. Andros is on the ground, raising his hands to protect himself. I lift the hoe again and bring it down with all my strength. Blood spurts from his nose and I hear the snap of broken bone, but I raise it again when strong arms grab me from behind. I kick out and scream, trying to shake them off me, when a familiar voice comes in my ear.

"Leave this for Tomas." I stop flailing. "You don't want his blood on your hands. Leave it for him." Nicolai holds me back, and Yakov stands on his other side. And then I see him. Tomas stands over Andros, his gun at his head.

I've never seen such cold, calculated rage on his face before. His hand shakes.

"Believe me, Caroline," Nicolai says. "He wants to kill him."

"Cuff him," Tomas orders, his gun still trained on Andros' face.

"You son of a bitch, you took my woman," Andros says.

"I'll remember you called her your woman before I kill you," Tomas says evenly, surprisingly calm. Yakov cuffs Andros and Tomas yanks him to his feet, then he looks to me. "Nicolai, let her go." Nicolai releases me. "Caroline, come with me."

I do so gladly. I want to throw my arms around him and weep, but it isn't time. Not now. I turn to Yakov and Nicolai.

"Yvonne and Ilya are in the cellar," I say. "He hurt her, Yakov."

Yakov and Nicolai race to the door, while Tomas drags Andros along with him. Tomas' men have come in droves, literally dozens of them. The car that would take me is surrounded by men. There are shouts and cries and the sounds of gunshots, fists, and screams, but I can't listen. I can't focus.

Tomas will exact his revenge, and he wants me with him.

I'm shaking so badly I can hardly walk. I nearly killed a man tonight. I came so close to being taken from the only safe home I've ever known.

My husband didn't cheat on me.

"He set you up, Tomas," I say, as Tomas drags Andros through the front door and down the hall that leads to the interrogation room.

"Of course he did," Tomas says. "We'll discuss that later." Tomas' men follow him on instinct, but he shakes them off. "No one but me and Caroline," he says. "Get rid of every trespasser we have here but bring her brother to me."

My brother?

"He's here?"

"Yes," Tomas says tightly. "When we spoke earlier, I knew I recognized where he was, but it took me a minute to piece it together. He's here."

I look around me, as if my brother will leap out and grab me at any minute, when Tomas shakes his head.

"No, baby," he says. Andros roars with fury but Tomas just shakes him to silence him. "He won't touch you."

This place scares the hell out of me. I know what it is, as we had one in San Diego as well. The interrogation room. It's stark, and outfitted for torture, with cuffs and chains and tables laid out. The walls are thick, the room windowless, the floors concrete. Designed for easy clean up and muting screams. My stomach rolls.

"You will not see this," Tomas says. "You don't need to see this. But he does owe you an apology before he dies."

Tomas' men stand by the door, awaiting his commands, as Tomas drags Andros into the room. I follow, and he shuts the door behind him.

He forces Andros to his knees and puts the gun at his head. "You will apologize for harming my wife. For touching her. For assaulting her, calling her names, and threatening her safety. All of it. *Now.*"

Andros glares at me furiously and says nothing. Tomas places his gun down, turns to Andros, and punches him so hard his head snaps back and blood pours from his nose.

"Apologize."

"Why?" Andros snaps out. "You're still going to kill me. Then do it."

Tomas laughs mirthlessly. "And grant you the satisfaction of an early death? I'll send you to hell, but not until you've paid the price for what you've done."

I can hardly watch as Tomas hits him, again and again. Andros screams and Tomas doesn't waver, until Andros' eyes are swollen shut and his face is barely recognizable.

"Apologize."

"I'm sorry," Andros finally moans. "I'm sorry."

Tomas gives one short nod. "Caroline, wait for me outside the door."

Shaking, I stand to obey. He's going to kill him and wants to save me from having to see it. I'm not sure that matters, though. I want to know he's dead. I want to know he'll never touch me again.

"Let me stay, please?" I ask. I don't recognize my voice. It's hollow steel, detached and merciless.

The door behind me opens. "We found him."

One of Tomas' men drags Aren in the room.

"You fucking bitch," Aren growls at me, his face splotchy red in anger. "You betrayed our family."

I shake my head. "I did no such thing. You were the one who used me to pay off your debt. And you're the one who didn't believe me when I told you about Andros."

"I'll kill you for what you've done."

I shake my head. "I'm afraid you're mistaken, brother."

Aren's eyes widen when he finally notices Andros' beaten body, lying at Tomas' feet. He pales. Tomas crooks a finger, and Aren pales.

"Bring him here."

Aren is brought to Tomas. Tomas grasps him by the shoulders. He looks to me. "The choice is yours, my love."

Despite the sickening situation before us, it warms me that he calls me *love*. I watch my brother's eyes widen in shock at Tomas' words. Tomas loves me, and he wants my brother and Andros to know that before they die.

A lump rises in my throat. It's an end to an era of terror.

"I want to stay," I whisper. "I want to know beyond a shadow of a doubt that these two will never threaten me again."

Tomas nods once but says nothing. There are too many things to be said, but I know the unspoken implications. He doesn't want me to see him kill them, but he leaves the choice to me. He will not shield me fully from Bratva life.

I am wife to the *pakhan,* and I will face my new life beside him.

Because he loves me, and I love him.

"I love you, Tomas."

He stands taller.

"And I love you."

I sit, unblinking, and watch my husband avenge me.

Chapter 21

Tomas

I'M STILL WEARING the blood-soaked clothes I wore earlier. Hers are tattered and torn, stained in red. Neither of us has changed or showered. We're back in the privacy of our bedroom. Once we were certain that every one of the infiltrators had been dealt with, that our compound was clear and the bodies disposed of, when my cleaning staff had restored pristine cleanliness to every inch of our home, I brought her back with me.

We sit on our couch, and she's tucked up against my chest. At first, she shook, but when I draped my arms around her and held her, she eventually settled. I didn't want her to witness what she did tonight, but when she asked me, I saw how much she needed it. How she needed to see the proof that the tormenters of her past were gone so she could put it behind her.

I shielded her from nothing. I let her watch me beat the men that harmed her, to punish them for their sins against her. I extracted apologies. She accepted them. And she watched when I pulled the trigger. Twice.

When they lay lifeless on the floor, she crawled over on her hands and knees and took Andros' wrist between her fingers, feeling for the pulse. Satisfied that he was dead, she did the same to her brother. Then she got to her feet, trembling but certain.

"Thank you."

I left my men to clean up the mess, lifted her in my arms, and carried her straight here. We've been here ever since.

"You are brave," I tell her, running my fingers through her hair over and over, until she sighs a little.

"I was terrified," she whispers.

"Fear doesn't mitigate courage, my love. Courageous people face their fears instead of running from them." I hold her to me. "I've never known anyone braver than you."

I realize she's quietly crying. "I can't believe they're gone forever," she says. "Even when I was here with you, in the back of my mind I knew they could come for me. And hell, they did. The *bastards*."

I rock her gently, letting her process this. Giving her space to exorcise those demons.

"I know, love," I whisper. "But yes, they're gone."

A few moments of silence pass before she speaks again. "I'm sorry I thought you cheated on me. I should have known better."

"He set this up well. He was conniving, orchestrating this from the very top. He hired her and hired someone to take those pictures. I have no doubt. He admitted as much. But I want you to know something, Caroline."

I take her chin in my hand and lift her tearful eyes to mine.

"I would *never* betray you. You are my wife, and I will follow you to the ends of the earth." I run my thumb along her scar, and gently brush my lips to hers before I continue. "I love you, Caroline. I thank my lucky stars to have a woman like you by my side."

"And I love you," she says, placing her hand atop mine. "Thank you." She blinks, and a tear rolls down her cheek. "I thought I was worthless. That no one would ever want me."

"And here you are, all mine," I say. "Sweetheart, your worth is beyond measure."

I pull her to my chest and kiss the top of her head fiercely.

"Now it's time to put this behind us." I stand and

hold her to my chest, walking toward the bathroom. When I reach the tiled floor, I gently slide her down my body and begin to strip off her clothing. She allows me, lifting her arms so I can take them off. When she's stripped, I take my clothes off as well. I lift the pile of dirty, ruined clothing, and shove them in the trash bin.

Holding her naked body to mine, I turn the shower on. When steam billows around us, I take her by the hand and guide her into the hot water before I join her.

It feels good, the hot liquid scalding our skin like this. I turn her to face me. She lifts her chin and lets the hot water cascade over her head and face. I lift the bottle of shampoo, tip some into my hands, and lather her hair. She holds onto my shoulders as I clean her hair, then soap her body, cleaning every drop of blood, sweat, and tears from her. And when I'm done, she takes the soap from my hands. We don't speak. There's no need.

First, she washes my hair, standing on the very tips of her toes to reach me. I bow so she can do the job. Then she washes my shoulders, her hands massaging the taut muscles until I relax under her touch. Next my chest, my back, and my legs, until she's washed me clean as well. I hold her to me when we're done, under the steam and heat.

She whispers to me. "I want your babies, Tomas."

I blink in surprise. I can't believe this is where her mind goes after a night like tonight. And what changed her mind? I hold her tighter. I know she has more to say. After a moment, she does.

"The only way to fully put this era behind us and begin again is to start a family of our own," she says. "To truly unite us. And the idea of bringing new life into this world pleases me now."

It amazes me how quickly circumstances can change. Months ago, I didn't even know who Caroline was, and now I'm here with her, we've washed away the memory of the two men I killed tonight for her, and now we're planning our future.

She lays her head on my chest, and wraps her arms around me, as the hot water continues to pound down. "And you've wanted that from the start, haven't you?"

I hold her to me. "I want to see my children with your eyes, your laugh, your radiance and beauty," I tell her.

She doesn't protest. Maybe now she actually believes me. If she doesn't, I'll whisper it in her ear when she wakes and sing it to her as she goes to sleep at night. I'll tell her every single day until she knows to her core how much she means to me. Though she's beautiful to me, her beauty transcends the physical. Her heart and soul are precious. I don't deserve a woman like her, but I'll be the best husband I can possibly be.

I don't speak this to her. Not tonight. But I will.

We have a lifetime together for me to prove to her how much I love her.

I reach behind her and shut off the shower. Still, she clings to me. I hold her to me with one arm and reach for a towel with the other. In silence, I towel her off, then wrap her up, sling a towel over my waist, and carry her to bed.

I toss the towels to the floor. We don't dress but climb under the covers exhausted. I lie on my back, pull her up to my chest, then drape the blanket around her. She'll sleep fitfully tonight, but every time she wakes, I want her to feel me around her.

Protecting her.

Shielding her.

Loving her.

Chapter 22

Caroline

"May I serve you tonight?" I ask. It's one week since the ambush on our compound, and Tomas has allowed me to return to the kitchen. At first, he wouldn't let me out of his sight, and I had to follow him literally everywhere. From meetings, to trips he made, meals and the like, I was his shadow through it all.

Ok. I still am.

But the past day or so he's lightened up a bit. For Tomas, that means he smiles a bit more. The crease in his forehead has softened, and he speaks in gentler tones.

Sometimes.

Today, he seems preoccupied again, and he doesn't look up when I speak to him.

"Tomas?"

He looks to me and blinks as if just seeing me. "Yes?"

"May I serve you today?" I've made one of his favorite meals, a baked fish with vegetables and bread I've baked with my own two hands.

He pushes back from the table and reaches his arms out to me. I go to him without question. He needs me.

Lacing an arm around my lower waist, he slides me onto his lap, closes his eyes, and nestles his nose in my hair. He inhales, then sighs deeply.

"Not today, baby. I don't want you even that far away from me."

I sigh. Something is troubling him again.

I signal the waitstaff.

"Yes, ma'am?"

"Tonight, I'd like you to bring our food to us in the privacy of our room, please."

"Yes, of course."

Tomas tightens his grip around me and nods but doesn't speak. He likes this idea.

"Come, husband," I say, rising from his lap and taking his hand. "Join me?"

I can tell when he needs me. As leader of the Boston Bratva, he bears the weight of responsibility no one else does. And though he never crumples, sometimes he bows under the weight of it before rising again. When he's disturbed or riled, it's my job to quiet him.

Though I don't like when he's upset, it fills me with joy to see the worry lines around his eyes soften. To know that though I have no power or responsibility within the brotherhood, I minister to the man who leads them all. I sit on his lap and massage his shoulders or rub his back. Sometimes I kiss him. Sometimes I get on my knees and worship his cock or bow to him and let him have his way with me. He's a dominant man with strong sadistic tendencies, but it's a privilege to submit to him. I love letting him work out his aggression with his flogger or his belt. Every time he takes me to the erotic edge where pleasure and pain meet, I trust him a little bit more.

But we're only halfway down the hall when his phone rings. I wait as patiently as I can while he answers it.

"Yes."

He grunts into the phone and scowls at me as he listens but says nothing at first. "Fine," he finally says. "Meet me in my office."

I sigh when he hangs up the phone. "What about your dinner, Tomas?"

"Dinner can wait," he says tightly, taking my hand and turning around toward the hall that leads to his office. "Stefan has paid us a visit."

"Stefan?" I've only met Nicolai's father once, when he officiated at our wedding. "What's he doing here?"

He huffs out an aggravated breath. "I have no fucking idea."

But he's told me how he views Stefan as a father-like figure, so if Stefan is here to visit, Tomas will drop everything to see him. We walk in silence to the office. It's quiet here tonight. After the showdown with my brother, Andros, and their men who ambushed us, we had to deal with the aftermath. Because Tomas has had me go with him to every meeting, I know that Stefan played a hand in mediating when San Diego wanted to war against us. Stefan and Tomas had a secret meeting with my brother's superior, *the pakhan*. And the end result was not only peace between the two brotherhoods, but an ample payout in retribution for the pain San Diego inflicted on us.

Ilya is recovering. He lost a finger thanks to Andros, but I daresay the boy is stronger than he was before. And having been through what he has, he now follows Tomas' instructions with utter precision. And he's so very good to me, Tomas has hinted about assigning him as my primary bodyguard in his absence.

We reach the office, and Stefan is already waiting outside.

"Tomas," he says, nodding to my husband and shaking his hand. "Caroline." He embraces me and kisses first one cheek, then the other. He takes both my hands in his and beams at me. "You look lovely tonight."

"Careful," Tomas grunts, though his lips quirk up at the edges. I know he's only joking good-naturedly, though.

"Relax," Stefan says. "You two look perfect together."

"You're getting soft in your old age," Tomas says. "Where is Nicolai?"

"Nicolai's back home," Stefan says, but offers nothing else at first. "Let's go sit down."

Tomas opens his office door, ushers Stefan in, and takes me with him. Instead of sitting by his desk, he has me sit on the little loveseat. Stefan sits in an armchair directly across from me, Tomas goes to pour everyone a drink. I decline, but Stefan and Tomas both take shots of vodka.

Tomas settles down next to me, tugs me so that I'm flush against his side, and wraps his arm around my shoulders.

"Marriage looks good on you, brother." Stefan smiles at him.

"Thank you," Tomas says. He squeezes my hand. "Caroline makes it easy."

"That pleases me."

They sit silently for a moment. "What brings you here, Stefan?"

"I wanted to talk to you about the San Diego brotherhood," he says. "How have things gone? Have they upheld their end of the agreement?"

"Absolutely," Tomas says. "They've been nothing but compliant."

"Good," Stefan says.

Tomas grows serious. "Now to the real purpose of your visit?"

Stefan smirks. "There's no pulling anything over on your husband. You know that, Caroline?"

I smile. "Oh, I do."

Stefan nods, bringing his fingertips together. "I came for a reason you likely won't suspect, Tomas."

"Oh?"

Stefan nods. "You're right. I have grown softer in my old age, yet harder in others. More stubborn, as it were."

Tomas waits.

"I left Nicolai in charge in Atlanta," he says. "Because I'd like to step in as temporary *pakhan* for the next two weeks."

"What?" Tomas looks perplexed, but Stefan carries on.

"You two need a proper honeymoon," he says. "In the past few decades, as I've been in this position of leadership, I've witnessed countless unions. Those that go on with business as usual often struggle over time. But those that make their relationship of paramount importance? They thrive." He pauses, giving the words time to settle, before he continues. "And I want to see you two thrive. No one deserves it more."

"You came here to tell me to take a vacation?"

"No, Tomas. Not a vacation. A honeymoon. In fact, your brothers have already made the arrangements."

My heart is lighter than it's been in weeks. Time alone with my new husband?

Oh, *hell yes*.

"Do it," I whisper. "Tomas, we must."

"Must we?" he says tightly.

"Of course. You don't want your brothers' gift to be in vain, do you?"

"Caroline," he says warningly, but Stefan nods.

"She's right. They've given up their own time and money for you. Step away, Tomas. Let others take control for a little while."

I place my hand on his shoulder. "Please?"

Leaning over, he kisses my cheek, then shakes his head. "I don't know if there's anything you can ask while giving me that look that I could refuse. Alright, little *detka*. We shall go."

I'm elated with this turn of events, so excited I can barely contain myself.

I'm going away. With my husband. Alone, just the two of us.

He leans over and whispers in my ear. "You are in so much trouble."

My pulse races with excitement. I lean over and whisper back. "I can't wait."

EPILOGUE

One week later

I SIT IN THE DARKNESS, by a crackling fire, nestling a cup of hot spiced cider in my hand. Tomas pokes the logs then rests his stick on the ground and sits in the fold-out camp chair next to me. I lay my head on his knee and close my eyes. The warmth of the flames and sounds of the flickering fire make me sigh with contentment.

I never knew I could have anything like this. My love for him is endless, my joy complete. What I have here with him, this love between us, is so vast, it's unfathomable.

Beyond measure.

"You know, poking it doesn't actually change anything," I say teasingly. "I know it's probably some innate part of the male species to continually ram sticks into fires. I bet the Neanderthals did it. It doesn't mean you need to."

"Did Neanderthals even know how to use fire?" he asks. "I thought they were alive before fire."

I smile. He would ask something like that.

"You ought to know. You're a direct descendent."

That earns me a hard whack to the ass I feel straight through my fleece-lined leggings. "Hey!"

"Hey yourself," he says, but his tone is teasing. I've never seen him so relaxed. We're staying at a cabin deep in the woods in northern New Hampshire during peak foliage, surrounded by a canopy of burnt orange, deep red, and golden yellow. It's as far away from civilization as I've ever been, and I love it. The cabin itself is immaculate, with an enormous king-sized bed covered in a handsewn quilt, large stone fireplace, rustic kitchen, and running water—my one request.

In the morning I make pancakes and fry bacon on a cast iron griddle, while he brews coffee on the stove. We eat until we're sated, hike deep into the woods, roast marshmallows by the fire at night, and make brutal, savage love whenever we feel like it.

In short, it's heaven. And we're here another week.

"You know," I muse, while I watch a log snap and fall in the fire before me. "I like that the money San Diego paid covered our honeymoon. It seems fitting, somehow. Like it's a dowry or something."

"Or something," he mutters. The money they were forced to relinquish more than paid for our honeymoon. I'm glad that it did, though I don't know if he cares much. He wants as little to do with San Diego as possible.

"You know what else?" I wonder out loud.

"You're wondering a lot, Caroline. Why don't you rest that mind of yours a bit?"

I yawn widely. "I don't want to."

I could fall asleep just like this. By the fire, with the warmth of the flames surrounding me and my husband's fierce protection beside me. I can't even remember what I was going to ask him. It doesn't matter. I have everything I need, right here. Well...there could be *one* more thing...

Minutes or hours later I wake when Tomas stands with me in his arms. I blink and yawn. "Why are you carrying me?"

"You fell asleep," he explains. "And it's time I get you to bed."

I'm so sleepy now.

My head hits the pillow, and he tucks me into bed.

But there's something I need to tell him.

As I'm drifting off to sleep, I can't keep it in any longer. "Tomas?" I end on a yawn.

"Yes, love?"

I roll over with my back to him. "My period is late.

His arm slung around me tightens. "Your what?"

I yawn again. "My *period*."

He sits straight up in bed. "My God," he says. "Are you serious?"

I can't help but giggle. "Totally."

He's walking around the cabin, pacing. "Are you ever late?"

"Not at all."

"*My God,*" he repeats. "Where can we get a test?"

I laugh and smile to myself, half asleep. "Nowhere near around here. But that's okay. We can take one when we get home."

Maybe it would've been smarter to tell him when we were closer to a pharmacy. He reaches a hand to my belly. "Any kicking yet? Are you ill?"

I snort. "God, no. We have to test. And even if I am pregnant, it's way too early."

"We have to test," he mutters. I fall into a deep sleep.

Two months later

"Twins," the doctor pronounces. Tomas beams,

stands, and paces the room, running his hands through his hair.

"Twins?" he asks.

"Twins," the doctor repeats.

I only swallow hard and watch my husband absorb this information. Two babies instead of one? I bite my lip. I'm overwhelmed and a little awed.

"Don't you worry, baby," Tomas says. "I'll hire a nanny. You already have a cook and cleaners. You'll see how easy this is."

Is he crazy? But still, it's cute how excited he is.

"If you say so, handsome," I say with a smile. "Can you tell the genders?" I ask the doctor.

"Looks like a boy and a girl."

I grin at Tomas and he grins back, beaming at me with so much pride, my heart squeezes.

"I love you," I tell him.

"And I love you."

Seven years later

"Be careful," Tomas says. "That's hot!"

"Honey, she's been using a skillet for a while now." I grin. "She learned from the best."

"From the best?" he says with a teasing scowl. "How many times have we seen the doctor for a burnt hand or a cut with a kitchen knife?"

I wave a hand to brush him off. "Oh, don't be silly. A chef must learn to use real tools."

"Real tools my ass," he mutters.

"Or real tools *on* my ass," I mutter back in his ear, so only he hears.

"Darling, not in front of the children," he says with mock reproach.

"Afraid you'll get me pregnant again?" I whisper back. "Hard to get a pregnant woman pregnant."

I rest my hand atop my swollen belly and smile at him. I never dreamed I'd have any children, much less *two* sets of twins.

"And anyway, I wasn't talking about me, but Camila."

Shortly after we came back from our honeymoon, I asked Tomas to hunt down the chef my brother fired. It seems so long ago now. It took some time, but he found her, and to my delight, he hired her for our own kitchen. It makes my heart squeeze to see Camila working alongside my own children.

We've long since outgrown the lavish apartment in the compound and have settled down in suburbia just north of Boston. The Boston Bratva is alive and well, though the San Diego brotherhood collapsed after failed leadership about five years ago. The men

I knew have scattered to different brotherhoods. I'm grateful. Knowing they're no longer banded together somehow makes it easier to live my new life. To accept that I have a new family, and I'm the mom in this one.

"This looks delicious," Tomas says approvingly at the simple meal of grilled cheese and homemade tomato soup. Our daughter, the spitting image of me, shoots him a toothless grin.

"Thank you, daddy," she says.

"Let's hope it's edible," her brother says.

"Edible?" Tomas repeats. "Behave yourself and be kind to your sister." But he shoots me a wink. "That's a pretty big word for a little boy. Must come from all those books your mother reads you."

"Must be." We eat while the kids chatter about their friends at school, the playdate at the park, and how they can't wait for the leaves to change.

"Mom, today I learned about California," my daughter says. "The teacher showed us pictures. I want to go some day." I freeze, but Tomas takes it in stride.

"San Diego is a beautiful place to visit," he says. "What is it that you want to see there."

"The zoo!"

He lapses into great details about a zoo in Maine, and my daughter claps her hands, San Diego forgotten.

But I'll never forget it.

And I'm glad that I won't.

Remembering where I came from, and the pain of my past, gives me reasons to be grateful for the simple blessings of my life.

Though still bound to the Bratva, Tomas works hard to make sure his family is distanced and protected, and I do the same. We maintain as much normalcy as we can, and most days are perfect, simple perfection.

"Will you tell us about your family someday, mama?" My daughter looks up at me with her large, curious eyes.

I smile at her. "Sure thing, baby. My family is made up of my fearless, fierce husband. Two precocious six-year-olds. And soon, another set of babies that will grow into mischievous children."

She smiles. "You're talking about us."

"I am. And Uncle Nicolai and Aunt Marissa, Uncle Yakov and Aunt Yvonne."

My daughter takes a big gulp of milk and swipes her hand across her mouth. "We have the best family."

Sometimes family isn't bound by blood but loyalty. Sometimes family is found, not born.

I reach for Tomas' hand across the table and squeeze.

"The absolute best."

. . .

AUTHOR NOTE:

Thank you so much for reading *Beyond Measure: A Dark Bratva Romance*, a stand-alone entry in the Ruthless Doms series. The Ruthless Doms series is a spin-off of the Wicked Doms, so if you're looking for more dark romance, take a peek at a few previews that follow. And thank you so much for your support!

~Jane

PREVIEWS

Priceless: A Dark Bratva Romance (Ruthless Doms)

PREVIEWS

I look at the sea of faces in the cramped, humid high-school auditorium.

Cheerful. Youthful. Full of hope and promise and pride.

But I see past every one of them.

I'm not here to observe the masses getting their rolled-up diplomas and marching off to college, holding flowers from grandparents and parents and boyfriends, posting goddamned selfies all over social media. I've ignored every word the politicians and speakers said, more intent on the conversation around me than anything. I see every eye that looks at her. Everybody within arm's reach.

I know each exit in this school, and every few minutes run my thumb along the cold metal I have tucked into my pants and the knife in my boot.

Ever vigilant. Ever watchful. Because this is my job.

I don't give a shit about anyone else in this place.

The rest are faceless, nameless, my focus on the one girl who stands out from the crowd because of her sheer, vibrant beauty. The belle of the goddamned ball. She's reckless and impulsive and brilliant.

My charge. My ward. The girl I've been commissioned to protect for four years.

The longest fucking years of my life.

Marissa Rykov.

Seventeen years old, just two days away from her eighteenth birthday. On the cusp of legal adulthood.

And the daughter of my father's best friend.

Off limits, *in every fucking sense of the word*.

I've been Marissa's bodyguard since she was thirteen years old. I've stayed in the background, attempting to give her the freedom a burgeoning teen needs, but honest to fucking God, screw that. I failed on that end. I could count every hair on her head. I could tell you the name, date of birth, location, and history of every single damn person she's interacted with, and every boyfriend knew *exactly* who I was. I got to know them, too, and each has a folder on file with detailed background checks. Slightly over the top for teen-aged kids, and the files were admittedly slim, but I have no regrets.

She was just a child when we met, innocent to the

ways of The Bratva. Ignorant of the work her father did.

And now, as she prepares to go off to college, it's my job to keep protecting her.

I've kept myself aloof. Detached.

She's a *child.*

But as I watch her walk across that stage, her brilliant smile lighting up the whole fucking Northern Hemisphere, my heart squeezes, and I swallow hard. Jesus, I'm proud of that girl. And I'd give fucking anything to keep that smile on her face.

I look away and school my features. I shouldn't have allowed my admiration to show even for a second. If anyone... *anyone* suspected how I feel about her...

My phone buzzes, and I ignore it at first, watching as Marissa walks down the stage on death-defying heels she should never have been allowed to wear. I swallow hard as her father embraces her and hands her flowers. She scans the auditorium, as if looking for someone, when her eyes meet mine.

I give her a small nod before I turn away and answer the phone.

"What is it?"

Laina, my younger sister, is on the line.

"Do not take your eyes off of her, Nicolai."

I'm instantly on guard. I swivel around to look back at Marissa, my pulse racing when I see her father at first, but I don't see her. She was here a second ago.

"What the fuck are you talking about?" I hiss into the phone as I push my way through the crowd to get to her.

"I overheard something I shouldn't have," Liana says, her voice shaking.

"Tell me." My voice comes out in a choked whisper.

Where the fuck is she?

I knock a lady's bag off her shoulder in my haste to get to her. "Hey!" she says, but I plow on, ignoring the angry crowd I shove aside, making my way toward the front of the auditorium.

"I can't speak freely right now," she says. "I'll call you as soon as I can, but listen to me, *do not* let her out of your sight."

And then I see Marissa. Bending down to pick something up, then laughing as she adjusts the ridiculous square graduation cap on her head.

I exhale a breath I didn't know I held.

"You fucking tell me what's going on, Laina."

"I'll call you right back."

The phone goes dead. Cursing, I shove it in my pocket, keep my head down, and take my place beside Myron, her father. He shoots me a curious look.

I turn my focused gaze on Marissa. She's walking

hand in hand with her motherfucking boyfriend now, and I clench my fist. I hate when he touches her and have had to endure night after night watching her sneak away to be with him. I give her a semblance of privacy. His background's clean, but Jesus what I wouldn't give to break his pretty boy nose for coming near her.

He has the fucking balls to shoot me an audacious glare. I glare back, narrowing my eyes on him. He knows I'm watching his every fucking move. The prick swallows hard and visibly pales.

Good.

My phone rings again. I answer on the first ring.

"Yeah."

"Listen to me." It's Laina. "I had to go where no one would hear me. I'm alone but I don't want anyone to overhear. Do you see Myron?"

"Yes," I say, my eyes reluctantly moving from Marissa to Myron.

"I went on a walk just now and overheard a talk between two of his men." Her voice is hushed, shaking. We deal with high stakes in the Bratva, and I know intuitively anything that would send Laina into a panic matters. "He made a deal, Nicolai."

The blood rushes in my ears so hard and fast it's hard to hear her. I know the kinds of deals she could be talking about.

"He's sold her," she says, her voice breaking. "He's put her up for auction. *One week*."

"Who did?" I want utter clarity.

"Myron," she breathes into the phone. My hands clench into fists of rage so tightly my knuckles turn white. I could kill him, right here, I could beat his motherfucking body to within an inch of his life before I slit his fucking throat.

This can't be. Our brotherhood does not deal with human trafficking rings. There are no auctions with us.

What can she possibly be talking about?

"How do you know this?" I demand. This is no small task she's given me, no small accusation she makes.

"I heard it with my own ears," she says on a shaky whisper. "You have to take her. There's no other way."

Take her? What the fuck is she talking about?

"No," I whisper into the phone. "I can't do that. I'll come home and we—"

"Everything okay, Nicolai?" Myron stands a few feet away, his dark black eyes suddenly looking more menacing than I remember.

Is it my imagination? Or is he really guilty?

Laina would not lie.

"Fine," I tell him. It takes effort to keep my voice steady. "Are we off to the party?"

He's rented a large hall. Food will be catered and he's even hired a live band.

"Yes," he says, and then he reaches for Marissa. He strokes his hand along her hair with a wistful expression and kisses the top of her head. A fatherly gesture, but in light of what Laina's told me, his gesture makes my skin crawl.

"Nicolai," Laina pleads into the phone. "You have to believe me. She's being taken. Groomed. And put up for auction."

"Where?" I ask, rage boiling inside me at the very thought of anyone touching Marissa.

"I don't know," she whispers. "I have to go. *Get her out of there.*"

The phone goes dead.

I look wildly around the auditorium.

If Laina is wrong, my father will lose his mind, and I'll be punished as a Bratva traitor, facing painful, brutal torture and death.

If she's right...

I curse under my breath and follow them to the party.

READ MORE

The Bratva's Baby (Wicked Doms)

Kazimir

. . .

THE WROUGHT IRON park bench I sit on is ice cold, but I hardly feel it. I'm too intent on waiting for the girl to arrive. The Americans think this weather is freezing, but I grew up in the bitter cold of northern Russia. The cold doesn't touch me. The ill-prepared people around me pull their coats tighter around their bodies and tighten their scarves around their necks. For a minute, I wonder if they're shielding themselves from me, and not the icy wind.

If they knew what I've done... what I'm capable of... what I'm planning to do... they'd do more than cover their necks with scarves.

I scowl into the wind. I hate cowardice.

But this girl... this girl I've been commissioned to take as mine. Despite outward appearances, she's no coward. And that intrigues me.

Sadie Ann Warren. Twenty-one years old. Fine brown hair, plain and mousy but fetching in the way it hangs in haphazard waves around her round face. Light brown eyes, pink cheeks, and full lips.

I wonder what she looks like when she cries. When she smiles. I've never seen her smile.

She's five-foot-one and curvy, though you wouldn't know it from the way she dresses in thick, bulky, black and gray muted clothing. I know her dress size, her shoe size, her bra size, and I've already ordered the type of clothing she'll wear for me. I smile to myself, and a woman passing by catches the smile. It must look predatory, for her step quickens.

Sadie's nondescript appearance makes her easily meld into the masses as a nobody, which is perhaps exactly what she wants.

She has no friends. No relatives. And she has no idea that she's worth millions.

Her boss, the ancient and somewhat senile head librarian of the small-town library where she works won't even realize she hasn't shown up for work for several days. My men will make sure her boss is well distracted yet unharmed. Sadie's abduction, unlike the ones I've orchestrated in the past, will be an easy one. If trouble arises eventually, we'll fake her death.

It's almost as if it was meant to be. No one will know she's gone. No one will miss her. She's the perfect target.

I sip my bitter, steaming black coffee and watch as she makes her way up to the entrance of the library. It's eight-thirty a.m. precisely, as it is every other day she goes to work. She arrives half an hour early, prepares for the day, then opens the doors at nine. Sadie is predictable and routinized, and I like that. The trademark of a woman who responds well to structure and expectations. She'll easily conform to my standards… eventually.

To my left, a small cluster of girls giggles but quiets when they draw closer to me. They're college-aged, or so. I normally like women much younger than I am. They're more easily influenced, less jaded to the ways of men. These women, though, are barely women. Compared to Sadie's maturity, they're barely more than girls. I look away, but can feel their eyes taking me in, as if they think I'm stupid enough to not know they're staring. I'm wearing a tan work jacket, worn jeans, and boots, the ones I let stay scuffed and marked as if I'm a construction worker taking a break. With my large stature, I attract attention of the female variety wherever I go. It's better I look like a worker, an easy role to assume. No one would ever suspect what my real work entails.

The girls pass me and it grates on my nerves how they resume their giggling. Brats. Their fathers shouldn't let them out of the house dressed the way they are, especially with the likes of me and my brothers prowling the streets. It's freezing cold and yet they're dressed in thin skirts, their legs bare, open jackets revealing cleavage and tight little nipples showing straight through the thin fabric of their slutty tops. My palm itches to spank some sense into their little asses. I flex my hand.

It's been way, way too long since I've had a woman to punish.

Control.

Master.

These girls are too young and silly for a man like me.

Sadie is perfect.

My cock hardens with anticipation, and I shift on my seat.

I know everything about her. She pays her meager bills on time, and despite her paltry wage, contributes to the local food pantry with items bought with coupons she clips and sale items she purchases. Money will never be a concern for her again, but I like that she's fastidious. She reads books during every free moment of time she has, some non-fiction, but most historical romance books. That amuses me about her. She dresses like an amateur nun, but her heroines dress in swaths of silk and jewels. She carries a hard-covered book with her in the bag she holds by her side, and guards it with her life. During her break time, before bed, and when she first wakes up in the morning, she writes in it. I don't know yet what she writes, but I will. She does something with needles and yarn, knitting or something. I enjoy watching her weave fabric with the vibrant threads.

She fidgets when she's near a man, especially attractive, powerful men. Men like me.

I've never seen her pick up a cell phone or talk to a friend. She's a loner in every sense of the word.

I went over the plan again this morning with Dimitri.

Capture the girl.

Marry her.

Take her inheritance.

Get rid of her.

I swallow another sip of coffee and watch Sadie through the sliding glass doors of the library. Today she's wearing an ankle-length navy skirt that hits the tops of her shoes, and she's wrapped in a bulky gray cardigan the color of dirty dishwater. I imagine stripping the clothes off of her and revealing her creamy, bare, unblemished skin. My dick gets hard when I imagine marking her pretty pale skin. Teeth marks. Rope marks. Reddened skin and puckered flesh, christened with hot wax and my palm. I'll punish her for the sin of hiding a body like hers. She won't be allowed to with me.

She's so little. So virginal. An unsullied canvas.

"Enjoy your last taste of freedom, little girl," I whisper to myself before I finish my coffee. I push myself to my feet and cross the street.

It's time she met her future master.

READ MORE

Preview *The Bratva's Bride (Wicked Doms)*

Demyan

THUMP.

Thump.

Thump.

I slam my fist against the thick punching bag, dust sparkling in the single stream of sunlight like diamonds. My vision blurs, sweat dripping in my eyes from the exertion. I take a second to wipe my arm across my brow, before I'm back at it again.

Pain wraps across my back with every swivel and spin of my torso. Perspiration drips down my body in rivulets, my breathing fast and ragged in the humid room, and yet I'm nowhere near satisfied. I won't stop until I've exhausted myself. Until the storm within me calms. Until I've exorcised my demons.

For now.

I pound the bag, the only sound in the room my grunts and the soft *thumps* when my fists connect. Sometimes, I imagine the bag holds the face of my enemies. Sometimes, my father. But in those moments, I don't come away sated with revenge but thirsty for more. I'm left dissatisfied and empty, because you cannot beat a man who lies in a grave. When I pummel the bag, it leaves me unfulfilled and restless, but mercifully fatigued. It's a weariness I welcome, as if somehow, I can beat the anger away with my fists if I try hard enough.

So when Maksym pushes the door to the basement open, he does so tentatively, my only indication he's arrived the creak of the door between swings of my fist. He doesn't interrupt me at first, out of respect. The man is like a brother to me.

"What is it?" I snap. I lift the bottle of water on the floor, tip my head back, and douse my mouth with the cool liquid before drenching my face with it.

"Filip found more details, Dem."

That gets my attention. I grab the towel beside my water bottle and swipe it across my face to clear my vision before I look at him. His ankles are crossed, one shoulder leaning against the door frame. Large and broad, with a thick beard and black eyes that shine, he easily looks the most formidable of our lot, though he has a soft spot, and she lives in a remote cabin in Istra.

"Tell me."

In the past two weeks, large sums of money have disappeared. Filip, our bookkeeper, is brilliant and impeccable, and until now, we've seen no loss in revenue since I've been head of our brotherhood. In fact, quite the opposite. Our income has soared, padding our pockets and investments, and Filip's masterful manipulation of our funds makes illicit transactions fly under the radar. His careful calculations and technological finesse make it possible to have funds allocated in multiple countries that no one can touch. Theft is not uncommon in our line of business, but the severe penalty for stealing from us has kept us safe from extortion since I've run this brotherhood. Until now.

Maksym clears his throat. "It's a woman, for one."

I curse and kick the concrete wall. I have no qualms about exacting retribution and meting out punishment, but typically the thieves we've dealt with were men. Men, I can handle with fists, a knife, or worse. Women, though...

Damn. I can be vicious and cruel, but prefer the more fragile creatures punished in other ways.

I turn to face him.

"What else?"

"She's left her location wide open as of last weekend."

"What do you mean?" I frown at him and cross my arms over my chest.

"It seems almost intentional, Dem. She's as easy to track as a performer in the public square."

I shake my head. Why would someone willingly steal money from us and then not bother to cover her tracks?

"Where is she?"

"Kazak."

An hour from here, near one of our brother groups. I feel my brows rise in surprise. So bold.

He leans against the wall and steps into the room. "If you want, I'll go."

I can see it in his eyes, though. He doesn't want to go. Maksym is no wilting violet, but he has a code he lives by, and as he's the most faithful to our brotherhood, I want to honor that code. He will take down our most violent opposition, and in recent months has risen to the top as our most accurate assassin, but when it comes to women...

When our brother Kazimir abducted a woman named Sadie last year, Maksym cursed out Dimitri and almost resigned. There is typically no real resignation from the Bratva but death. To Maksym, retribution was one thing but abducting innocents was another. He insisted she did nothing to earn how we treated her. And now that Kazimir and Sadie have settled back in the U.S., he keeps regular contact with them like a sort of doting uncle.

But this woman... what she's done... she's earned whatever happens and he knows it.

Hell, if this were a year ago and Dimitri still ran our organization, he'd murder her with one rapid command, not even bothering to punish her before death. And for a moment I fear being in this position of power has weakened me.

"Show me her picture." I drain the bottle of water and drag the towel over my face again. He takes a picture out of a slim folder, and holds it up to me.

I swear under my breath, shaking my head.

It's a grainy picture, but I can tell she's fucking beautiful. Black hair. High cheekbones, pointed chin, thick, dark eyebrows and lashes over light brown eyes. With her softly rounded, oval face, full lips, and pale complexion, she looks like a little pixie. She could be a model for a high-end fashion company, instead of the ruthless hacker who's undermined our efforts and taken what doesn't belong to her.

"Is she as small as she looks?"

"As tiny as a child," he says, frowning. "Just under five feet tall, one hundred pounds."

I stare at her picture in silence.

"Do we know why she's done what she has? Are there any ties in any way?"

He shrugs. "Her father and sister were killed in a car accident three years ago, but the papers report it purely accidental." That means nothing.

I curse again and throw the empty water bottle toward the trash barrel. It nicks the edge and falls to the ground, bouncing along the floor.

"And still, she needs to be stopped." I'm thinking out loud. I could sit back and let others enact our revenge, or I could use this to my advantage. If I take her myself…

Suddenly, the right course of action seems vividly clear.

I nod, making up my mind. "I'll go," I tell him. "I want to extract her myself, and it's time I paid our brothers in Kazak a visit." I haven't seen them since I've taken this position of power. I was only a brother in a line of many before. Now, I'm the *pakhan*, voted in by my brothers.

I snort. "Hell, it's a write-off."

He huffs out a laugh in reply.

"Show me her most recent infractions."

Maksym nods, and takes out several printouts. "Her recent history," he tells me. "There's been half a million dollars in blocked transfers in the past month but done from multiple accounts and in small batches. Normally, it would be hard to track someone like her, but as I said she left it wide open this time. It would seem either she wants us to come for her, or it's a fatal mistake."

I curse looking over the evidence. If we hadn't caught on, she could have destroyed one of the most lucrative transactions in decades.

"And that mistake was?"

"She made every transaction from the same location. The same room. The same computer."

"Someone so brilliant yet so stupid?"

He shakes his head. "At first we even thought it was a trap. But after further investigation, we found out more about her... It has to be intentional, and there's no indication she's affiliated with any of our rivals."

I shake my head. "She'll pay for this, Maksym. Her name?"

"Calina," he says. "Calina Brague. And of course she will pay," he says, but then he looks away, as if he wants to hide what he has to say next. "But there's something else you need to know."

I look at him questioningly. I've already decided to go to Kazak and abduct her myself. What else could there be?

"Tell me," I order, taking the papers from his hand and reading them over again.

"Her location, Dem..."

I'm losing my patience. I raise a brow at him and nod, waiting for him to continue.

"She's a resident at Saint Andrews Hospital," he says. "It's a... mental institution."

I swear under my breath and mask the cold sweep of anger that sweeps over me.

"Does she work there?" I ask, already knowing the answer to my question.

"No, Dem." He shakes his head and doesn't meet my eyes. "She's a patient."

Christ.

READ more

ABOUT THE AUTHOR

USA Today bestselling author Jane Henry pens stern but loving alpha heroes, feisty heroines, and emotion-driven happily-ever-afters. She writes what she loves to read: kink with a tender touch. Jane is a hopeless romantic who lives on the East Coast with a houseful of children and her very own Prince Charming.

What to read next? Here are some other titles by Jane you may enjoy. And don't forget to sign-up for my newsletter!

CONTEMPORARY ROMANCE

Dark romance

Island Captive: A Dark Romance

Undercover Doms standalones

Criminal by Jane Henry and Loki Renard

Hard Time by Jane Henry and Loki Renard

Ruthless Doms

Priceless

Wicked Doms

The Bratva's Baby

The Bratva's Bride

The Bratva's Captive

NYC Doms standalones

Deliverance

Safeguard

Conviction

Salvation

Schooled

Opposition

Hustler

The Billionaire Daddies

Beauty's Daddy: A Beauty and the Beast Adult Fairy Tale

Mafia Daddy: A Cinderella Adult Fairy Tale

Dungeon Daddy: A Rapunzel Adult Fairy Tale

The Billionaire Daddies boxset

The Boston Doms

My Dom (Boston Doms Book 1)

His Submissive (Boston Doms Book 2)

Her Protector (Boston Doms Book 3)

His Babygirl (Boston Doms Book 4)

His Lady (Boston Doms Book 5)

Her Hero (Boston Doms Book 6)

My Redemption (Boston Doms Book 7)

And more! Check out my Amazon author page.

You can find Jane here!

The Club (Facebook reader group)

Website

Manufactured by Amazon.ca
Bolton, ON